LITTLE
HOODLUM

HOOD RIVER HOODLUMS
BOOK TWO

There are few people in this world I thought I could count on.
My brother. My two best friends. And him.
Jordy Martinez.

Problem is, Jordy thought protecting me was his sole mission
in life.
He gave up everything for me and my brother, including his
freedom.

Losing him left me hollow and empty.
But after three long years, I've learned to live without him.

Until I get mixed up with a guy who has dangerous
connections in Hood River and everything begins to crash
down around me just in time for my senior year of high
school.

Possessive boyfriend with a penchant for violence.
Best friend turned enemy.
Fights with my big brother.

Everything's a mess and I'm not sure there's any fixing it.
I might just need that bully ex-convict who'll do anything—
again—to keep me safe.

All I want is peace, happiness, and love.
And I won't go down without a fight in order to get it.
I'm a Hoodlum after all.

They call me Little Hoodlum, but I'm not so little anymore...

To my husband, the original Hoodlum.

LITTLE
HOODLUM

CHAPTER ONE

Jordy
March—Twenty-One Years Old

Eyes on the wall. Straight ahead. Ignore the fuck out of this guy. If I blink or wince or even drop my gaze, Hauser and his gang will be all over my ass like stink on shit.

"Yo, pussy kid," Hauser barks out. "I'm talking to you. Your sugar daddy's not around to protect you."

Don't look at him. Don't look at him. Don't look at him.

Fuck it.

I crack my neck on my shoulders and drag my stare to Eddie Hauser, a big fucker with a penchant for violence. He's been taunting me ever since he transferred in here eight months ago.

"I don't need protecting," I growl. "Especially not from you."

He pops his knuckles and glowers at me. "The fuck you say?"

"You know what I said, motherfucker." I puff my chest out and take a threatening step toward him. "Back the fuck off me or I'm going to make you."

His two goons crowd him from behind. Sure, they're all three big, and together they'll easily kick my ass.

But I'm bigger.

Meaner.

Pissed at the world.

They can fucking try me. I'll go down swinging.

"The three stooges here giving you a problem?" a guard named Dave asks. "Solitary missed them. Just say the words, Martinez."

Hauser's nostrils flare. "Nah, man," he says to Dave while staring me down. "We were just talking to the kid. No problems here."

I smirk in triumph, knowing I thwarted another ass whipping. It pays to know people. Dave may be a guard, but he's a cool guy if you don't give him shit. He has looked out for me since the day I walked my broody ass into Oregon State Penitentiary.

"Remember what I said," I call out to Hauser as they start to walk off.

"What's that, kid?" Hauser hisses.

"I'll tell ya later." I wink at him, loving how his face turns purple with fury. So much for trying to lie low. It's goddamn difficult in this place when everyone fucks with you.

Dave chuckles, patting my back as the guys walk off down the corridor. "I told you to stay out of trouble."

"I try, man, but those assholes make it impossible." I shrug him off.

"You have to try because you're looking at an early release. Don't fuck it up because you can't keep your goddamn mouth shut." He shakes his head in frustration. "Come on. You have a visitor."

My heart thunders in my chest. I don't take visitors. Not my parents. Not my brother Juno. Not Roan. Especially not Roux. It kills me for them to see me like this.

Today is different, though.

I sent a letter requesting this visit.

A mixture of excitement and dread claw at my insides. I don't want to have this conversation, but it's absolutely necessary.

For her.

Always her.

Dave guides me through a series of halls I've long since memorized. Prison isn't so bad aside from the men who are always trying to assert their dominance over you. If you keep your head down, you can get your shit together. I managed to get my GED right away and have been plucking away at some college courses through the prison's college partner program. School sucks, but when you have nothing better to do, it's amazing how much you appreciate it.

"I'm surprised you're taking a visitor," Dave says. "Have you ever?"

"Nope."

"What's the special occasion?"

"A girl."

Dave snorts. "Of course. You know this isn't a conjugal visit. If you start wanking it in there—"

"It's *about* a girl," I interrupt. "She's in trouble."

He frowns as he unlocks a door. "Same girl you got yourself in here over?"

"Yep."

"Must be pretty special to deserve such stupid loyalty."

"Lay off," I grunt out. "You don't know shit."

I follow him into another hallway. He glances over his shoulder at me. "I read your file, Martinez. I know enough. I'm well aware that you don't make good decisions where she's concerned. At the detriment of yourself."

We reach a door and are buzzed in. I'm glad I don't have to respond to his dumbass comments. He doesn't know Roux or Roan. No one understands. No one but me. I walk along a bank of plexiglass cubicles with phones attached and small stools bolted to the floor. Most of the criminals are cuffed to the table as they visit, but others like me have the freedom to move our hands.

"Stall nine," Dave grunts out. "I'll be nearby when you're ready to go."

I give him a nod of thanks before throwing myself down onto the stool, making sure not to look at *him*. My best friend. Roan Hirsch.

Tap. Tap. Tap.

I'm drawn to the sound and lift my gaze. Familiar amber eyes sear into me with the intensity of a fiery volcano. He's pissed. Understandably so. I refused to speak to him for three goddamn years.

He picks up the phone and nods with his head at mine. I note that his skin is tanned as though he's spent too much time recently in the sun. His hair is the same, but he's broader. Based on the way his biceps strain in his Henley, I note that he's been lifting a lot.

With a heavy sigh, I pick up the receiver. "Hey."

"Hey?" A loud huff. "After three years, all I get is a demanding letter to come see you and then a hey. Fuck you, Jordy." The anger in his tone barely hides the hurt. It guts me. Everything I did was for them. To keep them safe. And yet he's still hurting.

"Sorry," I mutter. "But… Can we not talk about that right now?"

He flashes me a murderous expression. Flared nostrils. Blazing copper eyes. Mouth twisted into a snarl. Rather than chewing my ass out, he gives me a clipped nod. "Speak, brother."

I hate that emotion clogs my throat, making my eyes prickle. I'll be goddamned if I cry and that shit gets back to Hauser.

"Roux's in trouble."

Concern chases away his angry expression. "What? I just saw her this morning. Seemed fine."

"She still hanging around that douchebag?"

"Kayden?"

"That's him."

His mouth parts and his eyes flash with confusion. "He's her best friend."

"Is that the lie she's telling you?"

"Jordy," he growls in warning. "Get to the fucking point because you're pissing me off."

"The point, *brother*, is Kayden's brother is Renaldo. Word around here is he's got a big fucking handle on Hood River."

Roan stiffens, his lips pressing into a thin line.

"You remember how Renaldo was with me and I wasn't his blood. He will have Kayden pulling all sorts of shit if he doesn't already." I give him a pointed glare. "You really want Roux around that?"

"Fuck no," he snaps. "I just…" He sighs. "Hollis and I will talk to her."

A snort escapes me. "Still with the rat?"

"Yeah, man, and it really sucked having Cal up there as

best man when it was supposed to be you." He waves his hand at me, showing a wedding band on his finger.

"You got fucking married?" I ask in astonishment.

"And the moment I got back from my honeymoon, I had word from your dumb ass that I needed to come see you for the first time since you'd been locked up. Way to kill the mood."

I'm still shocked he got married. Roan of all people never seemed like the type to settle down ever. Worse than Cal or Terrence.

"Congrats," I mutter.

"Jordy…"

I lift a brow. "What?"

"Kayden has been good to Roux. This… She's going to be so fucking upset over this."

"I already sent her a letter warning her to stay away," I tell him with a shrug. "It won't come out of left field. Trust me."

He scrubs his palm over his face, dragging his flesh, eyeing me with a look of utter frustration. "You're sure about this? I can't undo this once I lay down the law. Roux is going to hate me. If I'm doing this because you're just being your typical overbearing ass, I'm going to be pissed."

I lean forward, pinning him with a serious glare. "These fuckers are in a whole other league than Alejandro was. Vicious, Roan. So fucking vicious. Some of his gang buddies are here with me and they won't shut the fuck up about the shit they pulled. If she gets mixed up in that world, she'll get her ass raped or killed or worse."

He gapes at me, disgust flashing in his eyes. "What could be worse than rape or murder?"

"I don't fucking know and we're not going to find out either. Just end things with Kayden and her."

"Fine," he concedes. "I'll do it, but I don't want you shoving me back out of your life after this. I want you to let me visit any time I want. I miss you, man."

My gut clenches with guilt. "You could visit your dad instead."

"Don't be an asshole."

"I'm just saying since you're here and—"

"I said fucking don't," Roan snaps. "Don't."

"Fine. I'll talk to you, but you better fix this shit with Roux. Otherwise, everything I've done is a big waste."

It's his turn to look guilty. His brows scrunch together, and he rubs at his neck with his palm. "I'll take care of it. And when she turns eighteen, I'm saying whatever the fuck I have to say to get you out of here. She won't be taken from us. Worst they'll do is lock me up for eighteen months or so."

Roan would die in this place.

He wears his heart on his motherfucking sleeve. Always has. I'll be damned if I let that happen.

"Stay out of it," I grunt. "I'll work on shit on my end."

His amber eyes flare with happiness. "You'll try and appeal?"

"I'll figure something out. Let me worry about that. You worry about our girl."

I start to hang up, but he places a palm on the glass. "Wait."

We stare at one another for a long beat before he continues.

"Thank you for what you did for me. For us. We love you. Always have. That will never change no matter how stupid you can be sometimes. When you get out—and you fucking will—you have a place with us."

7

The emotions threatening to pull me under and drown me are too overwhelming. I give him a clipped nod, unable to formulate words, and hang up the receiver.

We'll keep Roux safe.

We have to.

I'll move heaven and hell making sure that happens.

CHAPTER TWO

Roux

KAYDEN GROANS AGAINST MY MOUTH AS HIS HAND teases my flesh beneath my shirt on my stomach. A small whimper escapes me, making him smile against my lips. We've only been officially dating for a week and I love kissing him, but sometimes it feels like things are moving way too fast. When his fingertips brush along my bra, I push at his shoulders.

He lets out a heavy sigh before pulling away, a frown marring his face. "What?"

"I'm not ready...for that." I chew on my bottom lip and straighten my glasses. "I'm sorry."

"What is *that*, Roux?" he challenges with a smirk.

"You know what *that* is," I grumble. "We can kiss, though."

He rolls his eyes and checks his phone. "It's fine. I know you're my little prude. I'll wear you down eventually." His tone is playful, but I don't miss the glint of irritation in his gaze.

"Just give me more time to warm up to all of this." I take his hand in mine. "Don't be mad."

"I'm not mad. I've just waited a long time for us to happen."

"We *are* happening," I assure him. "All those things will come with time."

He flashes me a smile that doesn't reach his eyes. "Sure thing, babe. I gotta go. Renaldo wants me to drop by the shop. I'll pick you up in the morning for school."

Disappointment floods through me. We were supposed to study together tonight. Since Roan isn't here and Hollis is at school, I thought we'd have all that time to ourselves. But, apparently since I'm not putting out, Kayden's ready to bail on me.

Kayden rises from the sofa and stretches. He's probably the hottest guy at Hood River High and I somehow landed him. Me. Roux Hirsch. Big, awkward nerd. But it's not exactly how I imagined it.

Something's missing.

Guilt niggles at me. Of all the girls he could have ended up with, he's chosen me, and all I can think about is maybe he chose wrong. Maybe he'd be better off with someone like my best friend Charlotte or one of the other popular cheerleaders. He certainly deserves more than a girl who questions it every time he wants to touch her.

Because you think of him.

Jordy Martinez.

My brother's best friend who's serving ten years at OSP for killing four men.

"Hey," Kayden says, cupping my cheeks. "I'm not mad. I know how you are. I've known you for a long time. We're good. I really do have to go."

He coaxes a smile out of me when he kisses my forehead.

"Call me later." I stand on my toes and meet his lips for another kiss. "Okay?"

"As soon as I deal with my asshole brother, I'm all yours." His hands find my hips, drawing me to his obvious erection. "I really don't want to go. I'd rather study naked with you."

I laugh against his lips. "You're crazy."

He opens his mouth, no doubt ready for a smartass retort, when the front door flings open. We jerk apart as though we've been burned. I turn to see who interrupted our kiss.

Lovely.

"Hey, Roan," I squeak out, my cheeks flaming with embarrassment. "Didn't expect to see you here."

Roan's amber eyes that match mine exactly narrow as he regards Kayden. "What's going on here?"

I glower at my brother, crossing my arms over my chest. "We're studying."

Since when does Roan have a problem with Kayden coming over? He's one of my best friends. It's always been that way.

"Studying?" Roan cracks his neck and then glares at Kayden. "Probably time to go, kid."

Kayden, who once used to be intimidated as hell by my brother, lets out a derisive snort. "I'm not a kid."

Oh, great.

"Ignore him," I tell Kayden, clutching his arm through his hoodie. "He's just grumpy because his honeymoon's over. I'll talk to you later."

I can tell Kayden really wants to kiss me by the way his eyes dart to my lips, but I give him a warning glare. Now is not the time to admit to Roan I'm seeing Kayden romantically. And certainly not by kissing in front of him. I need to ease into telling my brother because I know he'll be overprotective about it. If Kayden kisses me, Roan will lose his shit and probably tackle him.

Ugh.

I wish Hollis were here.

He diffuses every situation that involves my brother.

"Later," Kayden grunts out as he walks away and slams the door.

I flinch. "Hey. I thought you had work."

Roan studies me for a long couple of beats. "I told you I had something to take care of. I don't go back to work yet."

"Oh," I utter. "That's right. So what's up?"

He walks into the kitchen of our garage apartment and rummages around in the fridge. I follow him, leaning against the counter. Once he finds a container of leftover meatloaf Kelsey sent over with Charlotte yesterday, he pulls it out to nuke it.

"You and Kayden looked awfully cozy," he says, his back to me. "What's up with that?"

I let out a heavy sigh and decide to come out with it. "We're seeing each other now."

Roan whirls around, his eyes flaring with fury. "What?"

"He's my boyfriend," I state, lifting my chin. "You know I've always liked him."

"Liked," he growls. "It was a crush. I didn't think you'd actually go out with him."

I cross my arms over my chest and shrug. "It's not a big deal."

The microwave beeps, indicating it's done cooking, but Roan makes no move to pull it out. His eyes flare with an unfamiliar anger. Truth is, we don't argue or fight. This feels foreign and I don't exactly love the feeling.

"You're seventeen." His voice is low and furious.

"So?" I bite out, throwing my arms in the air. "You were fucking Sidney and half of the other girls in this town long before that."

"It's different," he snaps. "I don't want you seeing him."

"Well, you don't get a choice!" I shriek. "I like him and he's my boyfriend."

"No."

"You can't no me on this, Roan!"

"I will because I'm responsible for you. He's bad news."

It all clicks into place.

"This is because of Jordy, isn't it?" I demand, seething with anger. "He sent you a stupid letter too? Come on, Roan, you know Kayden. He's been a permanent fixture around here for years. Where the fuck was Jordy? Oh, that's right, he bailed on us." Hot tears blur my vision, but I'm not done blowing up. "He left us and refused to see us. Screw him and his letters."

Roan's features soften. He hates when I cry. "I went to see him."

"What?"

"That's where I went today."

I gape at him. "You went and saw Jordy and didn't take me with you?"

"It's complicated."

"It is not complicated," I cry out. "I should have gone with you!"

Guilt shines in my brother's eyes. He stalks over to me and pulls me to him for a hug. I clutch his hoodie, inhaling his familiar scent. Roan has been my rock—my stand-in parent—for as long as I can remember.

"Kayden's brother is Renaldo. He's a shithead who's into a lot of illegal stuff. Jordy is worried. I'm worried. It's for the best."

Anger bursts up inside of me again. I push away from his hug, shaking my head.

"Kayden is different and you know it. He's a good friend, and so far, a great boyfriend," I state with a huff. "He doesn't even pressure me to have sex." White lie.

The look of horror on Roan's face is priceless.

"You better not be fucking him. Or anyone, Roux. You're too young."

"I can fuck whoever I want," I volley back. "You're not my dad."

He flinches at my words. Okay, so that was a low blow. Ugh.

"You're right," he growls. "But I'm your big brother and if I feel like someone could potentially hurt you, I'll do everything in my power to prevent that from happening. Don't make me turn into an asshole over this. I will. For you, I will. Even if that pisses you right the fuck off."

All guilt I felt dissipates.

"Maybe I should move into Mike's," I hiss. "He's my legal guardian. At least he won't bully me away from dating someone I like."

Roan sneers at me. "Your threats won't work with me. We both know Mike will be stricter on you than I could ever be. Accept that you and Kayden are over. If you want to date someone else, then you can let me meet them. Kayden is a hard no."

"I hate you," I whisper, storming out of the kitchen before I do something stupid like punch him.

He calls after me, but I ignore him. I grab a hoodie and throw it on before shoving my feet into some shoes.

"Where are you going?"

"To Char's," I grind out. "Unless I'm restricted from seeing my other best friend too?" I glower at him. "What do you say, Dad? Am I allowed?"

"You're being unfair," he mutters.

"That makes two of us."

I push out the front door and stomp down the steps, furious at my brother. I'm so focused on how much he pisses me off, I nearly tackle Hollis in the process. He grabs my shoulders, steadying me.

"Hey, squirt. What's wrong?"

I angrily yank off my glasses and swipe at my tears. "Roan is in a mood. Can you run me to Charlotte's?"

He looks up the stairs, probably having a silent conversation with his new husband about me, and then nods. "Sure. Let's go."

We climb into his purple Mustang. I refuse to check if Roan is watching us. I'm being an emotional bitch, I know, but I can't help it. Between Kayden getting pissy with me for not wanting to go to second base and Roan throwing out ultimatums, I need a break from boys altogether. Hollis is the only boy not on my shit list, but since he's madly in love with my brother, I know where he'll stand on the issue, and it won't be with me.

"You want to talk about it?" he asks when we arrive at his sister's house.

"I want you to talk sense into my brother. Tell him he's overreacting. I'll see whoever I want to see." I challenge my brother-in-law with a glare. "Can you do that?"

15

He lets out a heavy sigh. "I'll talk to him."

"Good luck." I fling open the door and charge up to the house. Charlotte's home has been a second home to me ever since she moved here in the middle of eighth grade a little over three years ago with her family. They left Vermont after Hollis came out as gay. His dad freaked and his mom, Kelsey, went into protective momma bear mode. She brought her family to stay with her sister, Karen, and they've been close to us ever since.

Hollis waits until I'm inside before he drives off. I wave to Karen and Penny, who are watching television, before heading upstairs to Charlotte's room. I nearly run over Kelsey in the process.

"Hi, sweetie," she says in her usual motherly voice that makes me love her a little more each day. "Everything okay?"

"Boy problems," I grumble.

"Kayden?" she asks with a knowing smile.

"Yeah. And Roan."

Her smile falls. "He's not taking it well?"

"Nope."

"He loves you and worries about you," she tries, forcing a smile. "He'll come around."

I can't tell her he won't because this involves Jordy and the fact they think my boyfriend is a crime lord like his brother Renaldo. Instead, I nod.

"I hope so."

Kelsey hugs me and kisses the top of my head. "Love you, little Roux. I'm always here to talk."

"Love you too."

We pull apart and I slip into Charlotte's room. Where my room is painted navy blue, is filled with black and white pictures and poetry and random items to reflect my personality, Charlotte's is perfect and showroom ready. Teals and golds and white. She's the neat to my messy. Light to my dark. We're total opposites who somehow work.

"Hey, hootch," she says when I enter, not looking up from her textbook.

She's also the smart to my dumb ass.

Even now, I still have to be tutored. Luckily, her brother does most of my tutoring these days rather than Ms. Frazier.

"Hey," I mutter as I kick off my shoes and crawl into bed with her.

She closes the book, turning her intense blue eyes on me. "What's wrong? You've been crying?"

"You don't look so good yourself," I grumble. And it's the truth. Dark circles under her eyes color her golden skin. Her normally smiling lips seem chapped and downturned.

"Boys," she grumbles.

I snort out a laugh. "Same."

"What? Not my boo Kay. He's a good boy." Her eyes narrow. "He better be. Bestie or not, I'll castrate him if he hurt you."

I roll my eyes. "He'd probably rather be castrated."

Her perfectly sculpted eyebrows hike up her forehead. "Why do you say that?"

"Because, unlike me, he's not happy with just making out."

"He can get over it," she huffs. "You've been dating a week."

"I think he'll be fine," I mutter, "but it's more than that. It's Roan. He doesn't want me seeing Kayden. Says he's bad news."

Her brows deepen. "Because of Renaldo."

"Yup."

"You're my best friend, so I'll always side with you," she

17

says slowly, "but Kayden has been spending more and more time with Renaldo. I know you're smart and you know what you're doing. Just be careful."

Her words hit me right in the gut. Logically, I know Roan and even dumb Jordy have a point. Kayden was born into a dangerous family. But they don't know Kayden like I do. He's a good person who likes me. I like him. It'll be fine. Everyone is overreacting.

"I'll be careful," I assure her. "If I don't sleep with him, he'll probably break up with me anyway."

Her lip curls up. "Then the asshole doesn't deserve you!"

I grin at her. "This is why I love you."

"I'm your favorite," she says with a smirk.

"So why are you down? What are your boy problems?"

"Ryan."

Ryan Cunningham is her newest flavor, but he's lasted longer than I expected. Charlotte dates around. A lot. And it's rumored at school that she sleeps around a lot too. But Charlotte and I spend a lot of time together. She says she's not sleeping with all these guys and I believe her. The other girls spreading the rumors are just jealous because she's beautiful and smart and athletic. People can't handle when someone is the full package. They live to tear them down, even if it's just their reputation.

"Why? What did he do?"

"He gets jealous easily." She huffs. "Like Kayden, for instance. Ryan thinks I have a thing for Kayden."

Uneasiness settles in my gut. "But you don't."

"I know that. Ryan just sees me with you and him all the time. Jumps to ridiculous conclusions."

"So break up with him."

She frowns. "It just feels different with him. More intense or something. I don't know. I can see us becoming more."

"At least we have one thing in common about our boy problems," I say, shaking my head. "Roan apparently hates both our boyfriends."

"Oh, God," she groans. "If he calls Ryan or his brother 'Cuntingham' one more time, I'm going to punch him in his stupid fireman abs."

A laugh escapes me. "He really hates the Cunninghams. It's almost comical. I think it's because he thinks Tyler is going to try and steal Hollis. We ran into him and his boyfriend at the movies last month. Roan was so pissy after that."

"As if Hollis would ever leave Roan. They're so obsessed with each other." She shakes her head, rolling her eyes. "I guess Roan is just going to have to get over himself. Kayden is your boyfriend and Ryan is mine."

"Maybe we should double date so Ryan can see Kayden's not going to put the moves on you or something," I suggest.

Her eyes darken. "He won't go for it."

"Why not?"

"He really, really doesn't like Kayden. Bad idea."

"Why do you like him again?" I blurt out.

Her features pinch in obvious hurt. "I just do. Same reason you like Kayden even though he's a pushy, spoiled bastard who is used to getting his way. They're just brats and we're somehow attracted to them."

"Yeah," I mutter, leaning my head on her shoulder. "Maybe we should ditch the boys and date men."

Like Jordy?

My flesh heats in embarrassment. He's in prison. Just because I used to crush on him when I was younger doesn't mean I want to date him, even if that were a possibility. He's Jordy. Like a brother to me.

"Or we could just save ourselves a lot of trouble and date each other," she teases, nudging me.

"You're too high-maintenance for me," I joke back.

"Plus, I love the D," she says with a laugh.

Okay, so maybe she's not as virginal as I once thought.

"Have you and Ryan..." I trail off and look up at her.

"Yes." She bites on her bottom lip. "When we're alone... he's really good to me."

Something about her statement irks me. "What about the rest of the time?"

"Then too," she says, huffing. "I'm just saying he's so sweet when we're together."

"Why didn't you tell me you were sleeping with him?"

"Because I didn't want twenty questions about it," she mutters in a defensive tone. "He uses protection. He's gentle. Mom doesn't know. Does that answer all your questions?"

I let out a heavy sigh as I turn to give her a side hug. "Be safe and don't be afraid to talk to me, Char."

She toys with a strand of my hair. "I will. I'm sorry."

"It's fine," I assure her. "Now can we turn on some Lizzo while you do homework so I can pretend I don't have to go back home in a little bit to deal with my overbearing brother?"

"It's a date."

CHAPTER THREE

Jordy
Three weeks later...

"**G**IVE ME ANOTHER WEEK," SAMANTHA SAYS, smiling at me. "We have this in the bag."

I nod at my new attorney. "Thanks."

She stacks her papers in a neat pile and looks over at me beneath her dark lashes. "You don't belong here, Jordy, and I'm doing everything in my power to get you out of here." She tosses her blond hair off her shoulder and leans forward, giving me a prime view of her cleavage in her low-cut blouse. "And when you do get out, come see me so we can properly celebrate."

Samantha is hot—tall, blond, big tits—but not my type.

"Sure," I grunt out, knowing full well that's not going to happen. "Are we done?"

"For now. I'll keep you posted."

As soon as she's gone and I'm led out of the office, I find my way to the kitchen where I'm on duty. Cooking for convicts isn't as fun as cooking at home, but it's better than cleaning toilets.

"Look at you, One-Up. Is that fuckin' hope I see in those eyes?" a deep voice growls.

I sweep my stare over one of the biggest assholes in the pen. Thank fuck he's my friend.

"Samantha thinks she can get me off soon."

He lets out a low rumble of a laugh that reminds me all too much of my best friend. "I bet she can get you off. That bitch is thirsty as fuck. You don't want a piece, tell her to represent me. I'll let her get me off all damn day." He makes a crude gesture of jerking himself off.

"Fuckin' loser," I toss out at him. "The game's changed since you went in, old man."

"You're a goddamn fetus, boy," he grunts. "What the fuck do you know about dating?"

"More than you." I shrug.

"That lawyer bitch of yours would eat out of my hand," he boasts, squaring his shoulders at me. "Send her my way."

He's probably not wrong. Jace Hirsch is taller than me and could beat my ass in a second if he wanted to because he's beefed to the max from all the lifting he does. With the whole tatted up, mean convict vibe he has going on, I'm sure Samantha would love to fuck the fire right out of him.

"Keep dreaming, old man. The only action you're gonna get is with your hand."

"Disrespectful little shit," he grumbles. "Well, if you do bang the blond bitch, write me and let me know how it was."

"I'm not writing you a porn letter."

He laughs. "Why the fuck not?"

"Because it's fucking weird, man."

"Did you see my boy?" he asks, sobering up.

Fuck.

I always hate broaching the subject of his kids. Roan won't let Roux see her dad, and Roan refuses to visit him. Since Roan and I've reopened communication, he's visited weekly, and each time brushed off my suggestions for him to see Jace.

"Yeah, I saw him earlier."

He straightens. "How's he doing? Still a fireman?"

"Same as last week."

"I always knew he'd do something fuckin' heroic. That's my boy." He grins and slaps me in the arm hard. "How's Roux?" I bristle in irritation at his question. "Still friends with baby Ramirez?"

"She told Roan she's not, but they're still always together. It's a touchy subject between them." I crack my neck. "He needs to man up and force her to cut ties."

This is something Jace and I agree on wholeheartedly. Renaldo Ramirez's shit crew keeps popping up at OSP. The newest one, Deke, was a wealth of information. Information Jace had to beat the fuck out of him in the showers in order to get.

Renaldo still chops cars and my brother Juno is practically his business partner where that's concerned. But it's not just the cars. Renaldo runs drugs all over Hood River. His hands dip into all sorts of dirty pots.

Roux needs to stay far the fuck away from him.

"She sent me a card," Jace says. "Wrote me a poem."

The big, mean ass motherfucker's jaw clenches like he's holding back emotion. "She's just a little girl, but her words are big, man. They fuck with my head." He scrubs at his face in frustration. "I did wrong by those kids."

I nod because we both know it's true. But I don't have much room to talk. I fucked them over too. We've got that in common.

"Roux's a good kid. I miss them."

"You're gonna get out of here real soon, Jordy, and then it's up to you to keep looking after them." His words are part plea, part threat. "I'm counting on you."

He slaps me on the shoulder and then saunters off to his crew. I head for the kitchen to check in before José hands me my ass. Before I make it there, Deke and two other guys appear in the doorway. Deke's face is bruised and swollen thanks to Jace.

Fuck.

"You're Juno's brother?" Deke asks, his fat lip curled up, eyeing me up like I'm a piece of shit.

"Yep."

He cracks his neck. "Lucky asshole."

I shrug, waiting for him to get to the fucking point.

"Word is you're getting outta here." His brow lifts in question. "That true?"

"Not that it's any of your goddamn business, but yeah."

He runs his tongue over his teeth, his dark eyes glinting. "Juno asked me to give you a message."

I brace myself. My brother is a sadistic fucker. I have the scars to prove it. If Deke thinks he's going to kick my ass, he's wildly mistaken. Cracking my knuckles, I never take my eyes off this dickhead.

"My boy said for you to come see him. He's gonna take care of you."

Fuck that.

"Is that all?" I grunt out.

His grin turns wolfish. "He said you'd probably give me shit about it and if you did, to tell you that you don't have a fuckin' choice."

"Yeah, man. Got your message loud and clear."

"I told her to suck my dick," Terrence says, laughing. "And this bitch squats down in front of my desk like she's gonna fucking do it."

"Did she suck it?" Roan asks.

"Fuck no because Miss Sanchez is a cockblocker. Eleanor lied and told her she dropped her pencil when Miss Sanchez asked her what she was doing." He shakes his head. "I would've let her too. Who the hell turns down getting their dick sucked?"

Roan laughs because that fucker never says no to head. I've walked in on Sidney blowing him more times than I care to. For only being sixteen, he gets more head than most grown-ass men. The dude has game, that's for sure.

"You know who I want to suck my dick?" Cal asks from his lawn chair, sprawled out on it like he's the king of the damn public pool.

"Ms. Frazier?" I laugh when he throws his flip-flop at me.

"No, but not gonna lie," Cal says with a wicked smirk, "I'd be into it."

We all groan because just thinking about our principal on her knees sucking dick is enough to give me nightmares.

"Nah, I was thinking that girl in art class with the big fuckin' attitude," Cal says. "Moaning Lisa."

We all chuckle.

"No one wants to see you get a boner over this shit, man," Terrence gripes and dumps his Coke into Cal's lap, snorting with laughter.

Cal jumps to his feet and sways, drunk from whatever liquor he managed to smuggle into the pool. He's pissed, fisting his hands like he's going to level Terrence's ass.

"She doesn't want your pencil dick," Terrence says, backing away.

"I don't have a pencil dick and you know it."

"No one wants to hear about your threesomes," I groan.

"Do you do each other?" Roan asks, taunting them. "Who tops? I think Terrence looks like he tops."

Cal starts bitching out Roan now, but my eyes are on the gate. Roan's twelve-year-old sister, Roux, has just been dropped off by Ms. Frazier and is walking toward us, her backpack slung over her shoulder. Roux's a cool kid. Her home life is shit, but she has us and we look after her. Sometimes, she looks so fucking sad, though. It kills me. I know it kills Roan too.

Today, she's frowning and her shoulders are hunched. Something's wrong. If her idiot brother wasn't in a shoving match with Cal's drunk ass, he'd notice. I rise, ready to yank apart these idiots, when Cal storms past Roan right toward Roux.

She looks up, realizes his intent, and darts her amber eyes my way. It happens in slow motion. Cal grabbing her arm and dragging her toward the deep end of the pool. I fucking leap over several loungers, dead set on killing his ass for touching her. I'm almost there when he shoves her into the water.

"What the hell?" I snarl as Roan whizzes past me to jump into the water.

Cal flashes me his stupid, arrogant smile and I lose it. My fist flies out before I can stop it. The second my hand hits his face, I know I've fucked up. The sickening pop brings clarity to the situation.

"Jordy!" Roux squeaks out as she climbs out of the pool, drenched as fuck. "You punched Cal!"

Terrence is gaping at us and Roan is frowning as he follows her out of the pool. Cal's bleeding all over the fucking place.

"You bwoke my nose," Cal whines in a nasally voice, still swaying. "We were just horsing awound."

While Roan and Terrence tend to our drunk-ass friend, I swivel around to face Roux, who looks like a drowned rat.

"You okay, Little Hoodlum?" I take her glasses from her hand and set them back on her nose. "Did he hurt you?"

Her smile is sweet. "No, but you hurt him."

"Nobody fucks with you, Roux. I've got your back."

"Thanks," she murmurs. She stares at the pool, frowning hard.

"What's wrong?"

"Now we don't get to swim."

Guilt kicks me in the goddamn balls.

"Oh shit," I grunt out. "I can stay with you. They don't need me." I glance over my shoulder to look at Roan. "I can watch Roux while you deal with that fuckface."

Relief flashes in his eyes. "We'll be back."

Once they're gone, Roux sits down to pull off a worn, soaked tennis shoe. "I'm not a baby."

I stare down the little girl with the big coppery eyes. "Yeah, you are."

"I can swim and I can handle Cal. He's always like that."

"I don't like him or anyone putting their hands on you," I bite out, anger bleeding into my tone. "I gotta protect you, Little Hoodlum."

She gives me a sassy look. "I guess you can be my bodyguard."

"Mouthy like your brother," I tease. "Go get changed so we can swim."

Her grin makes all the dark, aching parts of myself light up with happiness. As she bounds off toward the restrooms, I can't help but take her joke seriously. I'll be her bodyguard and protect her. God only knows everyone besides Roan seems out to get her.

I'll be damned if I let anyone hurt her if I can help it.

Even if it means breaking one of my best friends' noses.

I will protect her from everyone.

CHAPTER FOUR

Roux

"**S**TAY STILL," CHARLOTTE CHIDES, BLOWING IN MY FACE. I laugh but obey my makeup artist. "Don't make me look like a ho."

"The only ho that'll be at the party is Tarrin." She curls her lip up. "I swear she makes it her goal in life to fuck everyone she knows."

"I heard she fucked Mr. Banner."

"Ew, he's married."

"She fucked Lucy's boyfriend of three years. I don't think she cares."

Charlotte brushes on some mascara, frowning hard. "If she even thinks about fucking Ryan, I'll rip her ugly black extensions out of her hair."

"You think they're extensions?"

"I follow her on Insta. She hashtags some place that does hair extensions like they're going to notice her and somehow make her a famous influencer." She starts swiping mascara on my other eyelashes. "Just because you call yourself an Instagram model, it doesn't mean you're actually a model."

"She's pretty," I say, playing devil's advocate.

"Until she opens her bitchy mouth."

"Instagram doesn't have to hear her."

"Lucky them."

We both giggle.

Tarrin Hopper is on the cheerleading squad with Charlotte. They pretend to like each other when they're face to face, but they're really arch nemeses. Tarrin, no matter how much makeup she cakes on or how many guys she sleeps with, will never be as popular as Charlotte. No one is. It comes naturally to her. Everyone loves Charlotte.

"Who is this woman and what did you do with my kid sister?" Roan asks from the doorway.

Charlotte recaps the mascara and hands me my glasses. "She looks hot, huh?"

"I'm not allowed to weigh in on that statement," Roan grumbles. But his worried gaze skims over my appearance, which means I do look hot enough that he thinks boys might try and steal my virginity.

"Well, she is," Charlotte sasses. "You and Hollis going to dinner?"

It's been almost a month since Roan forbade me to see Kayden. At first I was pissed, but then I decided what Roan doesn't know won't hurt him. I know he and Jordy won't budge on the matter. So, rather than make waves, I just see Kayden in secret. Roan and Hollis are gone enough that they don't know that Kayden still picks me up for school every day or that he's still very much my boyfriend.

"Nah," Roan says. "Cal and Terrence are in town for the weekend. Thought we'd hit up Campfire Chaos."

Charlotte and I exchange an annoyed look. The guys may

have started Campfire Chaos years ago, but once Roan, Cal, and Terrence all graduated, they stopped going. The school, however, did not. It's a Hood River tradition now.

It's also where I planned to make out with Kayden all night.

He's going to be so pissed our plans are foiled.

"Oh yeah?" I say lightly. "You're not going to be bothered hanging out with a bunch of underage teens drinking beer?"

"I gotta make sure those dumbasses like Cuntingham haven't ruined our spot," Roan says with a shoulder shrug.

Right.

I know my brother.

His attempt to seem nonchalant doesn't work on me. I know all his tells. He's hiding something.

"Ryan doesn't like it when you call him Cuntingham," Char says primly. "Don't say that to him."

Roan snorts. "I've been calling them Cuntinghams for as long as I can remember. Sorry, kid, but I can't change that."

He saunters out of my bedroom, leaving us alone. Charlotte huffs, sitting down on the bed beside me and making it bounce.

"This isn't good." She bites on her bottom lip, shooting me a panicked look.

"It'll be fine. Roan and the guys are snotty brats anyway. They stick to themselves and don't pay anyone else any mind. They're not going to mess with us."

"It's Ryan…" She sighs. "He hates Roan."

"Roan brings it on himself," I joke.

Her lips press firmly together. "Not for being an asshole. Because of me."

"What?"

She stands and walks over to my mirror on the wall. Tonight she's extra hot in a tight pair of dark jeans and an off-the-shoulder black sweater. Her golden-blond locks are wavy, hanging nearly to her butt. Char is perfect in every way.

"Ryan thinks Roan wants me."

I scoff and shake my head. "You're joking."

"I'm not." She glances over her shoulder, her brows furrowing.

"Why? Roan is gay. And married to your brother. That's the most ridiculous thing I've ever heard."

"You know how irrational Ryan can be."

"He's possessive to a fault," I grumble.

She shoots me a hurt look. "Thanks for choosing my side on this."

"I'm not choosing Roan over you," I mutter. "I just think Ryan is being a jealous dick. Roan has eyes only for Hollis. Besides, if Ryan trusted you, it shouldn't matter if other guys think you're pretty or flirt with you."

She scowls. "Let's not go. We can just have a sleepover here."

All this makeup going to waste kind of sucks, but something in the worried glint in her eyes tells me it'll be worth it.

"Sure," I say, standing and walking over to her. "We'll rent movies and make popcorn. Just the two of us."

Her smile lights up the room. "Thank you. I need to call Ryan, though, and break the bad news." She tugs her phone out of her pocket and dials. He answers on the first ring. "Hey, babe," she chirps in her high-pitched cheerleader voice. "Say hey to Roux."

"Hey, Roux," Ryan says.

"Hi."

"Listen," Charlotte says, a slight tremble in her voice. "Bad news. We can't go out tonight."

Silence.

I frown, wondering if they got disconnected. She waits patiently, her lips pursed together and her body tense.

"No."

He finally speaks and the one word out of his mouth confuses me. Char swallows, dropping her eyes to the carpet.

"I wish I could go, but I can't," she whispers. "I'm sorry, Ry."

"Take me off speakerphone," he orders, his voice gruff with authority. "Now."

My hackles rise at the way he's speaking to her. She won't look at me as she mashes the button and brings the phone to her ear.

"Yeah, okay, hold on." She lifts her blue eyes that have dulled to look at me. "Roux, can you give us a moment?"

I don't want to leave, but she's putting out anxious vibes that I don't like. She definitely wants me to go. I rush out of the room, leaving her alone. The television is playing in Roan's room and I can hear Hollis laughing. They could be watching television or doing gross married couple stuff that I don't care to overhear. I make my way into the living room and sift through the mail. When I find a card from my dad, I smile. I rip it open and laugh at his sad attempt at a poem.

Don't boo hoo, little Roux.
Daddy'll watch over you.
Every day. Every night. Even when you sleep.
Daddy is always near.
Love you, baby girl.

I'll write him back and tell him it was equal parts creepy

and sweet. It's been strange getting to know my father through letters. I revealed my poetry to him and he wrote me a ten-page letter praising me. It was nice to feel the love of a parent considering Mom never showered us with one ounce of it. Dad is making up for it, even from prison.

I'm about to hang it on the fridge when I see the other letter.

Also from the prison.

Addressed to me.

My blood runs cold as I pick it up. Jordy's neat handwriting slices through the white paper, black and unforgiving. By the indentions in the envelope, I can tell he was angry when he wrote it.

Crap.

I know he talks to Roan, but how could he possibly know I'm still seeing Kayden? I've kept it on the down-low, playing it off to Kayden that my brother is just overprotective and doesn't want me to date at all. If he knew the real reason, he'd be upset.

With a defeated sigh, I open the letter. My heart stops in my chest.

Little Hoodlum,

I wasn't fucking kidding. People talk. His people talk. And most of his people are locked up here with me. When I get out of here, I'll follow you all over that fucking town if it means you'll stay away from that piece of shit. Don't test me. I'm a monster and you know it. I'll show you how big of an asshole I can be.

J

I'm so infuriated, my hand shakes, making the paper crackle. Tears threaten, but I refuse to let them fall and ruin

Charlotte's hard work. Instead, I pull some paper out of the drawer and pen him a letter back while I'm still angry. A tear leaks out, smearing the ink, but I swipe it away and scribble more furious words.

Screw him.

He lost his chance to be my other big brother when he gave us up.

This is my life.

I fold up the letter and carry it with me back to my bedroom. When I push inside, Charlotte is rummaging in her purse.

"Everything okay?"

She nods absently at me as she tosses a pill in her mouth. I hand her a bottle of water on my nightstand. After she swallows it down, she glances over at me. Her blue eyes are empty. Not sad or angry. Vacant.

"Char," I murmur, taking her hand. "What did he say?"

"Oh, the usual," she says in a flippant tone. "You messed up your makeup."

I groan when she motions for me to sit down. While she works me over, adding more makeup to fix the smudges I made, I stare at my best friend. With each passing second, her eyes grow glassy and she relaxes.

"What did you take earlier?" I ask, my voice small.

Guilt shines in her eyes. "What?"

"The pill. Wasn't for a headache, was it?"

Her sculpted brows furrow. "One of Hollis's anxiety pills. Is that okay with you, Dr. Hirsch?"

I flinch at her tone. "Yeah. I was just making sure you're okay."

"I'm fine," she says in a cheery tone. "Now let's find you something hot to wear. And since our brothers are going to be there, let's make them wish they weren't."

The party is in full swing. Campfire Chaos is always the same. A bunch of horny drunk teenagers all trying to show off by how much they can drink and not die. It's where Kayden likes to act like he's the entertainment of the party, making everyone laugh with his stories. It's where Ryan gets in a fight with at least someone every time, just so he can prove to everyone he's the most badass person here. It's where girls like Tarrin dress like skanks and openly give blowjobs to any guy with a working dick, no matter who's watching.

And, tonight, it's where three of the original Hoodlums sit on the cabin porch like kings. Hollis sits at Roan's side like Jordy once did. The four of them are like gods. Arrogant. Bossy. Rude. Not to me. I'm a Hoodlum too, though a little one. But to everyone else, they're such assholes.

"It's killing me not to drag you to my tent," Kayden says, sidling up behind me. "Roan's not watching. We could run off."

My skin prickles with anxiety. The last thing I want is for Kayden to piss off Roan. And speaking of… Roan's eyes lock on Kayden. Hollis is happily sipping his beer, unaware of his husband's glowering, but Terrence and Cal have also joined in on the tense staring contest.

"Fuck," Kayden grumbles. "I need to go see Zac anyway. Come by my tent later when those assholes don't look like they're ready to beat my ass."

"See ya," I murmur.

He gives my ass a squeeze before sauntering off toward his buddy Zac. They slap hands, something passing from Kayden's to Zac's.

Crap.

Of course now all the Hoodlums are watching him. It was so obvious he just passed Zac drugs, too. He does it all the time at school. Though he doesn't come out and tell me he deals, I'm not stupid. It's just something we don't talk about.

But doing it in front of the Hoodlums is a bad idea.

It only gives my brother and Jordy more ammunition.

"Oops," Charlotte says, bumping into me when she stumbles my way. "Tripped over something."

How about nothing?

I grip her arm to steady her. "You're wasted, Char. What the hell?"

"I'm not," she hisses. "I tripped!"

"We should go home," I murmur. "I'll get Roan—"

"No," she snipes, yanking her arm from my grip. "Ryan will get pissed. We can ask Cal or Terrence, but not Roan."

I grit my teeth together. "He's my brother." In case she forgot.

"I know, but—"

"Hey, babe," Ryan says, stepping up behind Char and wrapping his arms around her. "What are you two up to?"

"She's drunk and needs to go home." I narrow my eyes at him. "Unless she needs permission?"

His jaw clenches. "Catching all kinds of attitude, Roux. What the fuck?"

"I'm fine," Charlotte murmurs.

He roams his palms over her breasts. "See? She's fine." He nuzzles her hair. "Right, babe? We're fine. Want to go to the tent?"

I grab her wrist. "No. She's going home with me."

Fire flashes in his gaze. "Nope."

Before I can yell at him, a flash skates past me, tackling

Ryan to the ground. Charlotte gets knocked out of the way, but Hollis is there, steadying her. I stare in horror as Roan pins Ryan to the dirt by his throat.

"Roan!" I cry out, yanking on his hoodie. "Stop it."

"The girls are going home. Walk away, Cuntingham." Roan stands up, shaking me off him, and spits on the ground beside Ryan. "Bye, asshole."

Ryan bounces to his feet, his nostrils flaring. "She's *my* girlfriend."

Hollis steps up beside Roan. "She's *my* sister. My under-age sister whom you got drunk and are luring to your tent. Best you walk the fuck away, man."

"It's not like that," Ryan growls.

"I'll be fine with him," Charlotte whines. "Please don't do this, guys."

Kayden joins the fray with Zac, coming to stand behind Ryan. I shoot him a glare. Wrong side, buddy.

"Everything okay here?" Kayden asks, cracking his neck in a threatening way.

What the hell?

Roan's shoulders tense as he shifts his anger toward Kayden. "Actually, things are not fucking okay around here," my brother snarls. "Not with you dealing drugs right in front of my face."

Kayden doesn't back down. "Don't know what you're talking about."

"I'm not fucking blind," Roan growls.

"While you claw each other's eyes out like little bitches, Char and I are going to the car," I snap. "Come on."

Cal snorts and Terrence smirks at me. I shove past them, dragging my drunk friend behind me. Hollis pulls up the rear, wisely not saying a word. When we reach his Mustang, I fling open the door and help Charlotte into the back seat. Once we're settled in the back, I hug her to me and stroke her hair. She starts to cry, clinging to my sweater.

"I fucked up," she whimpers.

"Everyone gets wasted sometimes," I murmur. "Even perfect Charlotte English. It's okay."

"Ryan will be so mad at me."

"Maybe it's time you break up with his broody ass," I suggest.

She sniffles. "Maybe."

"I guess we don't have to worry about our boyfriends much longer," I tease. "Roan probably already killed him and Kayden both. Terrence and Cal might be helping to bury the bodies as we speak."

We both giggle.

"Boys are so annoying," Char says.

"Sooo annoying."

She hugs me tight. "Love you, Roux."

"Love you too."

CHAPTER FIVE

Jordy
Two Months Later…

STARE AT THE ONLY LETTER I EVER RECEIVED FROM Roux. Guilt claws up inside of me. She was so pissed when she finally wrote me. My thumb rubs the tear smudge. I hate that I can't be there right now with Roan and her. It doesn't feel right. Never has. I did all this to keep them together, but who's there to protect them now? Hollis the rat sure as fuck can't. If anything, Roan has his hands even fuller taking care of him too.

Samantha says I'll be out of here soon.

Not soon enough.

My eyes skim over her letter, grazing over the furious words to her name at the bottom.

Love, Roux

I don't think she meant to put that, but she did. Or maybe she meant to. Who the fuck knows? It gives me hope that she'll still see me as another big brother when this all blows over. I want to be back in their lives. I want to cart Roux all over the damn place, taking her from school to tutoring or wherever. Always keeping my eye on her. I want things to go back to normal.

Then she can date someone normal. Someone I can personally shake the shit out of and threaten within an inch of their life. I just want her to be safe. Kayden is anything but safe. Roan told me all about his cocky ass dealing fucking drugs in front of the Hoodlums at Campfire Chaos. He nearly beat his ass, but Cal and Terrence ended up dragging him away.

If I were there...

The truth is, I'm not.

I can't do shit here.

I make a mental note to contact Samantha for an update. Until then, I watch the clock, waiting for my visitation with Roan. He's supposed to update me on everything. Now that we've gone to regularly seeing one another, I miss the fuck out of him. I look forward to our meeting all damn month.

"Martinez," Dave says. "Let's go."

I fold the letter up and tuck it in my front pocket before standing from my cot. Dave ushers me out of my cell and down the hallways. My mind is on a million other things, so when I'm seated in the visiting stall, I'm confused at first as I take in the woman in front of me.

The only woman I've been up close with in years is Samantha. So when I see the full, dark pink lips on the brunette, my cock thickens.

"Wrong stall..." I trail off, dropping my gaze to her perky tits and then back up to her lips. "Yo, Dave. Wrong stall."

The woman bites on her juicy lip. I dart my gaze up to her eyes. Amber eyes filled with fire and fury.

Wait.

"Little Hoodlum?"

She swallows and nods at the phone. I'm too transfixed by how she looks now. Her dark brown hair lies just past her shoulders, silky smooth, accentuating the fact she has tits now. I reluctantly tear my gaze from them.

I pick up the phone receiver and clear my throat. "Where's Roan?"

"Don't be a dick," she snaps, her voice a throaty purr that goes right to my cock. What the fuck. I need to get a hold of myself.

"I thought I was seeing Roan."

"He decided to visit Dad instead. To see if it was safe for me to visit him next time." She gives me a bitchy smile that does nothing to calm the state of my dick. "Guess you're stuck with me."

"Roux..."

She shakes her head. "Don't. I've had three years to think about what I wanted to say to you. Then..." Her bottom lip wobbles. "Then you pull all this shit with your letters and making my brother do your dirty work. I have a lot to say to you now, Jordy, and you're going to hear every bit of it."

Since when did she get a mouth on her?

She licks her lips, drawing my gaze there. "You broke our hearts."

The breath is sucked straight from my chest. Images of that night flash inside my mind. The way those motherfuckers tried to rape her. She was just a young teen. That shit still gives me nightmares. I'd kill them all over again if I had to. I'd take pleasure in that shit.

"You were family," she whispers, a tear racing down her cheek. "Family doesn't abandon family."

I shouldn't have refused to see them, but it felt like the safest for all of our hearts.

I was wrong.

My throat is hoarse with emotion. I want to look away so I don't have to see her pain, but it's fucking impossible. "Roux."

"I was devastated. We were so lonely without you." She sobs, breaking what's left of my heart. "You cut us off like we were a limb that was diseased. Like you didn't need us anymore."

"I n-needed you," I choke out. "I still do."

More tears roll down her pretty apple cheeks. I fist my hand, wishing I could swipe them away for her. "Why?"

I scrub my palm down my face. "Because I had to. You know I had to."

"You didn't have to shut us out, though," she snaps. "You didn't have to deny us visitation. It was cruel." A pained whimper escapes her, obliterating the last bits of my soul.

I'd only recently reinstated visitation for everyone, only expecting Roan to ever show.

"Roux, honey, listen," I utter, my voice tight with emotion. "I'm sorry."

Her lip wobbles wildly. "I missed you." She presses her fingertips to the glass. "We both did."

My hand mimics hers, and I wish like hell I could touch her. "I missed you too."

"When are you coming home?"

"Soon."

She smiles. Small. Sweet. So fucking innocent. It's in this moment I'm reminded this is Little Hoodlum. Roan's little sister. His seventeen-year-old sister. I pull my hand from the glass. As much as she looks like a woman, she's not. I've been locked up in here too long without female interaction. It's natural I'd be attracted to one of the first ones I see.

"Stay away from Kayden."

All progress is lost and her smile fades.

"Fuck you, Jordy."

She slams the phone into the receiver and stands. My eyes rake down her body, drinking in all of her new curves. Her hips have flared out and she has an ass now. Fuck, she has an ass. As she walks away, she looks over her shoulder at me. All sadness is gone as she glowers at me. She flips me the bird before stalking off.

I watch her ass the whole way.

Oh, Little Hoodlum. Everything's so fucked up now. You've turned into this beautiful woman and if you don't think I'll move heaven and earth to keep you safe from every motherfucker in this world, you're sadly mistaken.

"Martinez."

I yawn, rising from my cot, and nod at Dave. "Hey, man."

"Act a little excited," he grumbles. "You could be leaving this shithole."

"Trying not to get my hopes up."

He smirks. "I'm pretty sure that attorney of yours has blown her way through the entire parole board. I think you're safe to get those hopes up."

I follow him through the halls. Jace sees me and whistles.

"Get the fuck outta here, One-Up!" He grins and then flips me off. "Take care of my baby girl and son."

With newfound purpose, I straighten my spine and nod at him. "We'll see. I might get laughed at."

Jace shakes his head. "Naw, kid. They're gonna let you out. I know how this shit works. They know you don't belong here. Come visit your ol' buddy, though. Don't forget about me."

Dave snorts. "Keep moving, Martinez. Don't let Hirsch distract you from getting the hell out of here."

I give Jace a two-finger salute before turning down another hall with Dave. He takes us to a room and ushers me inside. Four people sit at a table, all wearing stern expressions. Samantha sits nearby, her pencil skirt riding up her creamy thighs, a shit-eating grin on her face.

"Please sit," an older man with a white mustache says.

I take a seat and straighten my back, bracing myself for whatever it is they're going to say to me.

"Miss Livingston has been working hard on your behalf," the man says. "Gathering all sorts of testimony, even going as far as securing you a job on the outside." He nods at Dave. "And the people who see you every day here have also provided us insight into the kind of man you are."

I give him a solemn bow of my head.

"But this file?" He thumps it with his finger. "Says otherwise."

"I understand that, sir."

He frowns. "Mr. Williams." He sighs. "I see what you were convicted for, and it's one helluva crime. But I also had a chat with the judge who presided over your case. You know what I've come to determine?"

"No, sir."

"That you're a scared little boy."

I bristle and clench my jaw. "Why's that, sir?"

"Because you did what you had to do to protect the ones you loved and then shut down for fear of what came after. Just took the punishment rather than letting people in to help you. Assumed the worst of the system. Let it swallow you whole."

"I don't know what you mean, sir."

Mr. Williams scoffs. "That line of bullshit is what got you in here in the first place. If you have any hope to get out of here, I need to know that you've grown up, son. That you're ready to face real life like a man. You're not a boy anymore."

I meet his stare. "What do you want from me?"

"The truth."

"It doesn't affect my sentencing. Why does it matter?" I ask. Then, I glance over at Samantha. "This doesn't reopen the case, does it?"

She shakes her head. "They just want to know what happened. To understand you. They're trying to determine if you're even able to merge back into society. It's okay to be honest," she says gently. "Let them understand you."

I frown, letting my mind go back to that night. The words flow from my mouth as I explain the absolute terror I felt when I learned Roux was in trouble. How all I could think about was getting to her. I recount how I walked in on them brutalizing my best friend and stripping the clothes off his little sister. The rest was a blur. My overwhelming need to protect my family at all costs. There were threats and I was to stand before them. When I finish, my cheeks are wet and my hands are trembling.

"I see," Mr. Williams says, his voice hoarse. "Where's your family now?"

I smile. "Roux's being a typical teenager giving her brother hell." Everyone chuckles. "Roan is a firefighter." I swipe at my wet lashes. "They turned out okay."

"They must miss you," Mr. Williams says.

"Yeah," I reply. "They're probably both gonna kick my ass when they see me next. Neither one of them was exactly happy with me over how all this went down."

"You were scared," Mr. Williams tells me, his voice gentle. "We all do things out of the norm when we're scared. It sounds like they're tough kids, though. Maybe you don't have to be the one always taking care of them. Maybe they can take care of you too."

I smile at that thought. "Nah, they both kinda suck at it."

The parole board chuckles.

"We'll be in touch, Mr. Martinez. There are some parameters I'd like to discuss with the board, but you'll be notified once we've sorted it all out."

He's smiling at me.

Smiling is good.

"Thank you, sir."

"Don't make me regret this."

"I absolutely won't, sir."

CHAPTER SIX

Roux
August 7th

THE SUN BAKES DOWN ON ME, HEATING MY FLESH and warming me to my soul. Lying out on the banks of Hood River with my best friend is my favorite place to be. It's peaceful and quiet aside from Spotify playing "NFWMB" by Hozier. Penny is on the other side of me, chomping loudly on her gum.

"You sound pissed," I say, shielding my eyes from the sun and craning my neck to look at her.

"Not pissed," she clips out. "Hot."

"The river's over there," I say with a laugh. "Go cool off."

"Pass."

"Penny's just mad that Mom made her come with us," Charlotte sasses from my other side. "Apparently we're not cool enough for her."

"Oh please," Penny groans. "Like I give two shits about cool."

Testy.

"You *could* be cool if you'd smile and stop being a bitch

to everyone," Charlotte grumbles. "I mean, I've practically handed popularity to you on a platter. You're willingly starving yourself of it."

"I don't want minions," Penny snipes, waving in my direction.

"Hey now," I chime in. "I'm not a minion."

"No, but everyone else worships the ground Charlotte walks on. It's nauseating."

"It's better to be cool than to be a nobody." Charlotte sits up and sprays more suntan lotion on.

These two can go on for hours like this.

"I miss Dad." Penny clears her throat and then huffs. "I guess I'm the only one." With those words, she stands up and stomps off toward the river.

Charlotte sighs. "Ugh. I guess I need to go console her and remind her that I miss Daddy too."

"Big sister duties," I agree. "Just don't try to hug her. She might bite."

We both giggle as Charlotte runs off after her sister. I close my eyes, singing along to "Trouble" by Halsey. A shadow blocks the sun over me.

"Did you survive?" I ask Charlotte.

"Barely," a gruff, masculine voice mutters.

My entire body comes alive with a mixture of heat and emotion. A voice I've heard only once since he was locked away.

"Jordy?" I croak out.

I peek out from under my arm to see his tall, muscular form standing over me. He's here. Oh my God. With a squeal, I scramble to my feet, throwing myself at him. His strong arms haul me to him, hugging me tight.

"Missed you, Little Hoodlum." His warm breath tickles my neck where his mouth is only inches from. "So goddamn much."

I burst into tears, overcome by the fact he's out. Here with me. I don't understand how, but I'm so happy. He kisses my neck. Just a soft, sweet peck that makes my nerve endings come alive. I note that he doesn't remove his lips. And I don't let him go.

"You smell like coconut," he says with a chuckle.

"You smell like Jordy."

"Yeah? What's that smell like?"

"Home."

He strokes his fingers through my ponytail. "Your pussy-ass brother cried when I saw him earlier."

"So did I," I toss back at him.

"But you're little Roux, so it's okay. I'm used to you crying."

I pull away to give him a sour look. "I kind of grew up while you were gone. Not so little anymore."

As though he's just now realizing this fact, his dark brown eyes drop to my lips, then to my throat, and finally to my cleavage in my bikini top.

"I can see that," he grumbles in irritation.

Flutters of excitement dance in my stomach as I wonder if he likes what he sees.

"Did you come to swim with us?" I ask, inhaling his masculine scent and memorizing every detail of his face all over again.

He's broader than the last time I hugged him. Clearly been spending every waking minute of his life lifting weights. His hair that was once buzzed short has grown long on top and flops into his eyes, giving him a younger, softer look than I remember. I also never noticed how long his dark lashes were or how flecks of gold are hidden in his brown eyes.

"Hmm?" he asks, his eyes roaming over my face.

"I said…" I don't remember what I said.

His lips.

They're dark pink and full.

The scruff on his cheek is in dire need of shaving, but it gives him an edgy look that sets my nerves on fire.

"I missed you," I murmur.

"You already said that."

"I'll say it a thousand times," I tell him.

He smirks. It's maddening. And hot.

"Where are your glasses?" he murmurs, his fingers once again stroking through my hair.

"Over there."

"Do you need them?"

I just need you.

"Not right now," I whisper.

His dark eyes drop to my lips again, making my heart stammer in my chest. *I have a boyfriend. I have a boyfriend. I have a boyfriend.* I can chant it all day long in my head, but my body forgot. All it knows is Jordy. My Jordy. Here in my arms. Handsome as ever. All man and incredibly hot. Alive and well and smiling.

He shifts one of his large hands to my hip. His fingers are so long, they curl around my backside, nearly touching my ass. A thrill races down my spine. His thumb brushes over my bare skin above my bikini bottoms.

"Kelsey told me you'd be here swimming," Jordy says. "I wore trunks I borrowed from Roan."

He starts to step back, but I can't let him go.

"I could swim," I mutter. "Take off your shirt."

His eyes darken and his jaw tenses. "Let go, Roux."

"I can't." My words come out as a painful whisper. "I'm afraid if I do, it'll all be a stupid dream."

His hand smacks my ass in a playful way that makes my pussy throb. "It's not a dream. I'm here." He grips my wrists and gently forces me to release his neck. When he brings our hands down between us, he doesn't let go. "I'm not going anywhere ever again."

I nod, fighting back tears. He releases me to kick off his shoes and peel off his shirt. I shamelessly ogle all of his tattoos and bigger muscles. Jordy Martinez was always hot and I harbored a crush on him, but he's reached new levels of gorgeous. It's almost too much.

"Jordy?" Charlotte asks, her voice shaking. "You're back?"

"Yep, little mouse. I'm back."

"Little mouse?" she bites out, cocking her hip to one side, making her boobs jiggle. "What the hell?"

I've always been a little jealous of my best friend and how guys look at her. And even though I don't see that Jordy is looking at her any other way than an annoying little sister, a flare of possessiveness ripples through me.

"You're the rat's kid sister. Little mouse is nicer than little rat."

Penny snorts out a laugh. "I kinda like little rat."

Charlotte swats at her. "Don't be a bitch. We legit just made up three seconds ago."

"We're going swimming," I state, interrupting their banter. "We have a lot to talk about." I plead with my eyes for Charlotte to understand that I need time alone with Jordy.

Her blue eyes dart between me and Jordy, before landing

back on mine. "Penny and I were going to go down to the snow cone stand at the park."

"We were?" Penny asks in confusion.

"Yep. Want us to bring you guys something back?"

"Cherry," both Jordy and I answer at once.

Charlotte's eyes gleam with delight. "You got it. See you in about thirty minutes."

They throw on their cover-ups and snag their shoes before walking off, leaving me alone with Jordy. Now that I have him all to myself, I want to spend the rest of our time hugging some more.

If only you were this into your boyfriend, things wouldn't be so strained.

I cringe thinking about Kayden. Having Jordy here is going to be a huge complication. I shove those thoughts away and grab Jordy's hand. He lets me tug him to the river. It's cool, but it feels good when we step into it. When I get waist deep, I dunk myself under, needing to cool off completely. Eventually, I have to come up for air.

"I missed this place," Jordy says, staring off down the river.

I drink in his beautiful form. The way the water droplets run down his shoulders. How his now-wet hair is slicked back. The sharp line of his jawbone. He's just so lickable.

"This place missed you," I reply, my voice breathy.

He turns to regard me, heat flashing in his dark eyes. My nipples are hard from the cold water but grow harder when he glances down at them.

"Jesus, Roux," he grumbles before diving into the water.

I frown, crossing my arms over my chest. What was that all about? Irritated at his abrupt attitude, I glower at him as he swims farther into deeper water.

Asshole.

With a sigh, I start swimming after him. The currents are always strong, but we're used to them. True river rats we are. When he realizes I'm following him, he starts swimming back.

A predator in the water.

Dark, hungry eyes.

Approaching like an alligator ready to take a bite.

Ravenous. Territorial. Fierce.

He swoops an arm around me, tugging me to him. "Don't want you getting sucked into the Columbia River." The nearby river that Hood River meets has much stronger currents and is far more dangerous to swim in.

I allow him to drag me flush against his hard body. He's hard everywhere. Even his dick, which is pressed to my thigh. Every time Kayden rubs his erection on me through our clothes, a silent request for sex, I'm annoyed.

I'm anything but annoyed right now.

Slowly, I wrap my legs around him, my eyes locked on his.

"Roux," he chokes out. "Fucking Roux."

His palm rests possessively on my ass, squeezing gently. Is this how it's supposed to feel? Like you're going to spontaneously combust unless you can devour the one who makes you feel so alive?

"Jordy," I murmur, shamelessly rubbing my body against the hardest part of him.

He curses, resting his forehead to mine, and closes his eyes. "I've been in prison for far too long. I haven't... I haven't fucked anyone in forever, Roux. Don't do this to me. Please."

His words cut me deep. Do what? Hold him? Hurt

burrows its way inside me, carving out a place to hide and live. The rejection is colder than the river water, chilling me to the bone.

He is not your boyfriend, Roux.

You have one of those, dumbass.

"Sorry," I croak out. "I just… Sorry."

His nose rubs against mine. Our breath commingling, our mouths inches apart. I run my fingernails through his hair along his scalp, desperate to touch him anyway. He angles his head closer, inhaling my breath as it blows from my mouth. His lips nearly brush against mine, sending zings of desire straight to my core.

Overcome with the need to kiss him, I tilt my head so that our lips do touch. I press a kiss to his lips. And then another. It's the third one I realize he's making no moves to kiss me back. His body grows stiff as he shuts down. He turns his head to the side and carefully extricates me from his body.

"That…" He sighs and pinches the bridge of his nose. "That was a mistake."

I recoil at his words. "What?"

"You're fuckin' seventeen, Roux. My best friend's sister. Just because I'm horny as hell, doesn't mean I need to make out with you, Little Hoodlum. I'm sorry. You're just the first thing I've come across." His words are icy cold and cruel. "I need to get laid. And not by you."

I suck in a sharp breath. "Fuck you."

"Stop," he orders. "Don't be a child about this."

I haul off and smack the shit out of him. "Don't be an asshole about this." My hand stings from the force I hit him with. I doubt it even registered to him. His dark eyes are fiery and intense as he pins me in place with one look.

"You caught me at a weak moment." He shrugs. "After this weekend, I'll get laid and then things can go back to normal. It'll be like old times. Me, you, and Roan."

I scoff at him. "Things aren't like they once were. Now we have Hollis and Char and Kelsey." I poke him in the chest. "And my boyfriend."

He scowls, fury flashing in his eyes. "Boyfriend, huh? Roan didn't tell me you had a boyfriend."

"Probably because he's been my secret boyfriend for a while now." I smirk at him. "I think you know him."

Poke the beast, Roux. Excellent idea.

"So help me," Jordy growls, "if you're referring to Kayden fucking Ramirez, I'm going to make your life a living hell."

He wants to hurt me?

I can hurt him right back.

I'm no longer the innocent girl he remembers. I grew claws when he left me here to fend for myself.

"At least he actually wants to fuck me," I spit out at him.

I don't wait for his reply, swimming back to the shore as fast as I can.

Screw Jordy.

He can't destroy my life by leaving me and then destroy it again by coming back.

"I'm going to kill him," he calls out behind me.

His words chill me to the bone because I know them as truth. He's killed for me four times before. What's one more?

CHAPTER SEVEN

Jordy

'M HALFWAY TO DRUNK. OFF THREE BEERS. FUCK. I SCRUB my palm down over my face, trying and failing to hear what Cal is saying. Apparently he and Terrence are having the time of their lives off at college. Those two idiots haven't grown up at all, fucking everything that moves.

Roan, on the other hand…

His smile is serene as his fingers run through Hollis's hair. Hollis, who's sitting at his feet and nursing a beer, is happy as a lark. Husbands. What the fuck. I'm not a homophobe, I just don't understand what Roan ever saw in the rat. He's a total prissy dork. I mean…to totally go from manwhore who fucks every chick at our school to full-on gay was hard to comprehend. Yet, here we are. Hollis not only hooked my best friend, but he got him to put a ring on it.

And they're so fucking happy.

I'm envious of them, even if I don't understand it.

"No offense, Hollis," Cal says, his voice slurring slightly, "but I'd totally fuck your sister."

Hollis groans. "Have fun in prison."

"Say hi to Dad," Roan chimes in.

The reminder that she's seventeen, like Roux, is a kick to the balls. What was I thinking? I almost fucked Roux Hirsch in the goddamn river. Holy shit.

"What about Tara or Tayla or whatever the fuck that girl's name is? She's eighteen now," Terrence offers. "You could keep your asshole safe."

Cal snorts. "Was your asshole safe in prison, Jordy?"

"Why don't you grab a bottle of water?" Roan grits out. "You're being more than your usual dickhead self."

"Naw," I mutter. "It's fine. If we don't joke about it, who the fuck are we? Certainly not Hoodlums." I down the rest of my beer. "Nobody came after my ass because I'd beat the fuck out of them. And your dad had my back."

Roan's brows furl, but I can tell he's relieved to know Jace was looking after me.

"Do you guys ever feel like losers still partying here with all these goddamn kids?" Terrence asks, tossing his empty beer bottle at some douchebag near the fire.

"We're only here to keep an eye on shit," Roan reminds him. "Roux and Charlotte seem to like hanging out with these assholes. And some of these assholes think it's okay to deal like this is their goddamn property. All we're doing is reminding them they don't run this town, we do."

Everyone sobers at that statement.

"Is that baby Cuntingham?" I ask, nodding my head to the fire. "He's fuckin' little mouse?"

Hollis groans. "She's my sister. I'd rather not imagine her fucking anyone if that's all right with you."

"Ryan Cuntingham almost got his ass kicked a while back," Cal says with a laugh. "He's kept in line since."

"Yeah? What for?" I tear my gaze from Cuntingham by the fire to my best friend.

"For being a dick," Roan says with a shrug.

"Or, he was sending a message back to his older brother," Terrence teases like he's a goddamn gossipy girl. Fuck, I've missed these guys.

"What sort of message?" I ask.

Roan drains the rest of his beer and tosses it toward the fire. "Tyler wants to fuck my husband."

"Oh my God," Hollis groans. "Seriously? This again? He was being nice. He doesn't want to fuck me."

"I've seen the way he looks at you, man," Roan grumbles in annoyance. "I'll lay his ass out if he even thinks about acting on his fantasies."

"He can't have me, rat lover." Hollis twists to look up at Roan. "I'm yours."

They kiss and I watch them. Again, envious. Not because I want to dick down some dude, but because I want to have that connection with someone.

A giggle pierces the night air.

Her giggle.

My dick twitches at the memory of Roux wrapped around me, kissing my lips. Fuck. That took self-control not to shove my trunks down and claim her in that river. I would've been so fucked, though. Not only is she underage, but she's Roux. Little fuckin' Hoodlum. So untouchable it's not even funny.

"You living at home?" Terrence asks me.

I cringe as I think about the way my mom shook her head when I stood on the porch. No. She turned me away after she tossed a bag of my belongings at me. It was only fair when I did the same to her and Dad when they tried to visit me. That

59

fucking hurt, but I was determined not to have to beg Juno for a place to stay. I was going to figure it out on my own, but Roan and Hollis wouldn't have any of it.

"Nah, he's gonna stay with us until he gets on his feet," Roan says. "He's family."

If he only knew how close I got to fucking said family, he'd murder me.

"What?"

The voice carries over the partygoers' laughter, waking my cock much to my disgust. Roux traipses up the porch steps of the cabin where we're all spread out in lawn chairs. She crosses her arms over her chest, only serving to push her perky tits up, making them threaten to spill from her sundress. I shamelessly check her tits out before tearing my gaze away. Maybe I ought to find that black-haired skank everyone was joking about earlier.

"Jordy's gonna take the couch," Roan reveals. "That okay with you?"

Her fiery glare burns into me. "What does it matter? It sounds like it's already a done deal."

"It matters," I bark out. "If you don't want me there, I'll find another place to stay."

She walks over to me, scowling. "Whatever. I don't care."

Liar.

"Hey, Roux-Roux," a deep voice calls out. "A bunch of us are heading over to Zac's. You wanna come hang with us?"

I'm out of my chair before I can think better of it, my hands fisted and ready to pummel Kayden Ramirez. "Get the fuck out of here."

His boyish grin fades as he glares back at me. "What the hell, man?"

Roux grips my arm, her nails digging into my flesh. "Stop."

Kayden's eyes rake down to where she touches me, fury flaring in his eyes. I flash him a smug grin. One that says, "Your girlfriend's pussy was on my dick hours ago." He hears the unspoken message loud and clear.

"Roux. Can we talk a second?" he hisses, his body thrumming with barely contained rage.

She releases my arm and pats my chest. "Just stop, Jordy."

I watch her as she walks down the steps toward her secret boyfriend. The same boyfriend I'm going to fucking destroy. They can pretend all they want, but everyone knows they're together. He crowds her like he can claim her just by standing near her.

She's not his.

Fire burns in my veins.

"I need a drink," I grumble, never taking my eyes off them.

Roan is at my side, gripping my shoulder. "I thought part of your parole was you weren't to drink."

I shake him off. "You gonna tattle on me, bro?"

"Fuck off," he grunts. "Let's go see what we can find in the cabin."

Several shots later and I'm halfway to plastered. I'm queasy and the world keeps spinning. Roan is nearly as fucked up as I am. We're not always the best influence on each other. With his arm slung over my shoulders, we head back outside. Roux is still talking to Kayden. They seem to be having an argument. I laugh because it's funny. I hope they break up so I don't have to break his neck.

"They're still together," I blurt out. "Been together this whole time."

"What the fuck?" Roan roars. "Fucking seriously?"

"Yep."

Roan charges down the porch steps, rage fueling him forward. Because I can't let my best friend get hurt, I storm after him. Kayden, the cocky bastard, lifts his shirt, showing off his piece.

That motherfucker.

Roan screeches to a halt, the reality of the situation sinking in. "You're fucking carrying?"

Kayden lets his shirt drop back down and pats Roux on the ass. "See ya around, babe."

Uncaring that this asshole has a fucking gun, I rush him, my fist swinging hard. I clock the motherfucker right in the jaw, knocking him the hell out. He slumps to the ground and his gun hits the dirt. I pick it up and charge through the woods and to the beach. With a grunt, I heave it as far into the river as I can. It splashes and I laugh.

"You're such a dick," Roux yells as she stumbles along the sand toward me. "I hate you!"

She's beautiful tonight with her dark hair twisted messily on top of her head. Her glasses are perched on her nose and her features are screwed up into an angry expression. With each step, her tits bounce and her dress rides up her thighs. I'm so fucking horny for her. When she reaches me, she tries to slap me. I grip her wrist hard, twisting it behind her back. I grip her jaw with my other hand, forcing her to look up at me.

"You're not allowed to hate me, Little Hoodlum."

"I can do whatever the hell I want!"

I squeeze her face, making her lips pucker out. "Anything you want, honey, but not that." I relax my grip and run my thumb over her plump bottom lip. "Now say you're sorry."

"Fuck you," she snaps.

I sure fucking wish.

"You and Ramirez are through. Understood?"

"He's my boyfriend. You can't force me to break up with him." Her amber eyes flash under the light of the moon.

I lean forward, enjoying the way her breath hitches at my nearness. "You don't want him like you want me."

"I can't have you," she whispers.

"You can't," I agree. "But that doesn't make you want him any more. If anything, it makes you resent him."

"You don't know how I feel." Her eyes well with tears. "You know nothing about me anymore."

I release her and then gently brush a strand of hair from her face, tucking it behind her ear. "I know you love Fruity Pebbles. And dumb chick flicks. I know your eyes turn dark copper when you're worried. I also know your lips quirk up on the right side when you're amused. I know you couldn't care less about sports, but always cheered your brother on like it was your favorite thing to do. I know your favorite color is navy blue. I know you hate having to be tutored but are thankful for the opportunity. I know you write poems as therapy for all the fucked-up shit your mom put you through. I know—"

"Please stop," she begs, tears racing down her cheeks. "I can't take this."

I pull her to my chest, hugging her and kissing her hair that smells like coconut with a hint of rum. "Okay, Little Hoodlum. Just know that time may have passed, but I still know you. The real you."

She relaxes in my hold. "I'm so mad at you, but I'm glad you're back."

I stroke my fingertips up and down her spine, soothing

her. Greedily, I inhale her scent and memorize the way she feels pressed against me. "I'm glad I'm back too."

"You need to be careful," Roux says, her hot breath tickling my chest through my T-shirt.

"Why's that?"

"Kayden's not some kid anymore."

I bristle at her words. "Neither am I."

"He carries a gun," she says in frustration, pulling back to look up at me.

"Used to." I smirk. "Now it's sitting at the bottom of Hood River."

Her nostrils flare. "And he'll just get another one. But now you've put a target on your back. You don't want to mess with him."

"Are you afraid?" I demand, the fierce need to protect her consuming me.

"For you."

"I can handle myself."

"Your track record for that is really shitty," she grumbles. "If I promise to stay away from him, will you do the same?"

"I can handle that."

She lets out a heavy sigh. "Okay. I need to get back there and check on him."

As she starts to walk away, I can't stop myself from taking her hand and squeezing it. Her fiery eyes search mine out, silently questioning what sort of games I'm playing with her. Truth is, I don't know. I can't have her for myself because she's too young and forbidden territory, but I want her anyway.

"What do you want?" she rasps out.

The only answer I have is her name. I tug her back toward me, my other hand seizing her hip. "Only one thing."

"What is it?" Her head tilts up and her eyes flash with such vulnerability, my heart cracks down the middle.

"Something I can't have."

"Maybe you could have it." Her whispered words set my soul on fire.

"I can't."

"Maybe…"

I lean forward, stealing a chaste, forbidden kiss. "I can't. I won't. Don't make me. Please don't make me."

She tugs her hand away from mine and touches her lips I just pecked. "You worked your whole life to make sure no one hurt me." She pulls her fingers from her lips and presses them to mine. "And yet here you are, hurting me more than anyone has in my entire life."

Her words shred me.

"Roux…" I trail off, my voice husky with emotion.

"Good night, Jordy. I guess I'll see you at home."

This time, when she walks away, I let her. I watch her leave me with such an overwhelming longing inside my chest, I think I'll suffocate.

I hurt her.

Worse than anyone.

I'm a fucking monster.

CHAPTER EIGHT

Roux

"**C**OME WITH US," KAYDEN BITES OUT, SPITTING out more blood. "It's not a request."

His friend Zac snorts out a laugh that boils my blood. If Jordy heard him talk to me this way, he'd be nursing a broken nose too.

"I can't. Roan said no."

Kayden's dark eyes dart back to the campfire where the guys are back at their posts, standing guard over the entire party like they're the Kings of Chaos rather than Hoodlums.

My brother has a possessive arm slung over Hollis's shoulder, glaring into the fire. Cal's hands are in some girl's hair as she works her way down his body, but his eyes are lingering at where Ryan and Charlotte are talking. Terrence's attention is on one of the freshmen getting mouthy nearby, his shoulders tense and ready for a fight.

Then there's Jordy.

He sits in a chair, sipping on a beer, with his legs spread apart and his gaze locked on me.

"It's because of him, isn't it?" Kayden asks, drawing my attention back to him. "Jordy?"

"W-What? No," I blurt out, my tone a little too defensive. "You know how Roan is. He's overprotective."

"He's not your dad."

I bristle at his words. "No, but he's doing the best he can to look after me."

He softens and lets out a sigh. "I'm sorry." His hand lifts and he toys with a strand of my hair. "I'm just stressed and I don't need the Hoodlums giving me shit."

"What are you stressed about?"

"Just some shit my brother wants me to do." He flashes me a devilish grin as he grabs my hand, pulling us behind his car that's hidden in the shadows. "Nothing for you to worry about, Roux-Roux." He pulls me to him, his palms roaming over my ass. "Your only job is to give me a kiss."

I used to melt over his sweet words whenever he'd blow me off about what's going on with him. Now, I find them irritating.

"Why are you carrying a gun?" I demand, slightly pushing away so I can see his eyes.

He scowls. "I told you I'm doing shit for my brother."

"I don't like it. It's dangerous. You could get hurt."

"Nah," he says, flashing me a smug grin. "That's what the gun's for. So I *don't* get hurt."

"Can you please stop provoking the Hoodlums?"

"Me?" he bites out. "They fucking started it and you know it. We were just fine until they decided I'm not good enough to date you."

He starts to kiss me, but I duck out of the way, ignoring his pouty frown.

"You're all bloody." I lean back in to peck his cheek before pulling away. "Drive safely and text me later."

"Tomorrow we'll go party somewhere else. Figure out a way to sneak out since they won't let you come with me," he says, taking my hand. "We haven't had much time alone and I miss you."

"I'll try," I offer, though I know it'll be virtually impossible now with Jordy home with us.

"Try what?" Ryan says, walking over to us with Charlotte tucked under his arm.

"Nothin', man," Kayden replies. "You still want some candy?"

Ryan stiffens. "No."

I dart my eyes back and forth between them. Kayden gives him a knowing grin before patting Ryan on the shoulder and leaning in. He whispers something to him and I don't miss the fact that he slips something into Ryan's pocket. Ryan nods.

"We're headed to the party at Zac's," Charlotte tells me. "You sure you can't convince Roan?"

"Hollis let you go?"

"Hollis isn't my dad," she bites out.

I flinch at her words. She's off. Her head is leaned against Ryan and she pets his chest like he's the softest pillow in the world.

"Maybe you should stay with me," I say, stepping close to take her hand.

"Don't be a cockblocker," Ryan snaps at me.

"Don't be a dick," Kayden barks at him.

"I want to go with Ryan," Charlotte tells me. "Stop worrying so much."

"Can I talk to you for a second?" I start to tug her away from her boyfriend, who glowers at me, but she stops me, shaking her head.

"I'm sorry Roan's being a dick and won't let you go, but I never get alone time with Ryan. He's my boyfriend. I want to spend time with him." She sighs. "I love you, Roux. I'll call you tomorrow."

Ryan shoots me a triumphant grin before leading Charlotte away from me. I hate that Hollis hasn't forbidden her to go like Roan did me. But I guess their situation is different. My brother has pull over me. Hollis has no pull over Charlotte.

"I'll keep an eye on her," Kayden promises. "She's my friend too."

I give him a quick hug. "Thank you."

He tries to kiss me again, but I sidestep it, his kiss landing on my cheek instead. I get a grumble but then he saunters off, calling out for Zac. With a heavy sigh, I turn and head back to the party to go find Hollis. Charlotte may not have to answer to him, but I still think he should be aware of where she's going.

As I approach, I don't see Jordy, Hollis, or Roan.

Cal's getting his dick sucked by Tarrin. He's such a man-whore and she's a slut. Gross. Terrence laughs when he sees me glaring at them.

"Best you go on, Little Hoodlum," Terrence calls out. "The grownups are doing grownup things."

Tarrin, spurred on by his words, starts slurping and bobbing like her life depends on it. I roll my eyes, ignoring those two.

"Where'd the guys go?" I ask, climbing up the steps onto the porch.

"The wives went to their tent to fuck like bunnies," Terrence says and snorts out another laugh. "The convict is in the cabin taking a leak."

Yuck.

I don't want to think about my brother and Hollis fucking. Making my way past Terrence, I head inside to find Jordy. He's sprawled out on the pullout sofa, staring up at the ceiling, his eyes hooded.

"Hey," I mutter.

His body tenses and his eyes snap to mine. "Thought you left."

"Roan doesn't want me to go. Plus, I told you I was going to check on him, not go with him."

"Is he hurt?"

"He'll live."

"Pity."

I let out a heavy sigh. "You should behave so you don't get your ass thrown back in prison."

"Come here," he orders, patting the bed beside him.

A thrill shoots down my spine. "Okay."

Kicking off my shoes, I make my way over to him and then sit down. He hauls me to his chest, hugging me to him.

Several long seconds pass, my heart hammering in my chest. Neither of us speaks or moves. When the racing in my heart slows, I tentatively touch his pectoral muscle over his shirt. His nipple is hard and I can't help but run my fingertip over it.

"Roux." The warning in his voice makes every muscle in my body quiver.

"Hmm?"

"Just let me hold you."

"That's it? You just want to hold me?"

"That's all I can do."

I slide my palm lower, rubbing over his ridiculously hard abs. His breath hitches. I tease my fingertips along the hem of his shirt that's ridden up, stroking the hair of his happy trail.

"Roux," he rasps out, his voice a guttural growl.

"I'm just cuddling," I say in the most innocent tone I can muster. "I missed you. That's okay, right, Jordy?"

He groans, his breathing growing heavier. I don't move my hand from the small sliver of skin between his belt line and shirt. I'm not blind to the way his cock strains against his shorts.

"Does your boyfriend know you're cuddling with me?" he asks in a husky tone. "Is he going to shoot me?"

His words chill me to the bone. "Don't say stuff like that."

"I think you like playing dangerous games," he rumbles. "First by dating that piece of shit, and now by pushing the limit with me. Are you trying to get hurt?"

"We're just cuddling," I retort.

"And you wish you were cuddling my dick," he says in a smug tone. "If I asked you to peel your little panties off and climb on my cock, you would. Boyfriend or not, you'd fuck me, Roux, because you want what you shouldn't. You want something dangerous."

Turned on by his words, I slide my palm down, but before I can reach his dick, he grips my wrist hard.

"But I'm not some douchebag like Ramirez," Jordy growls. "I'm here to protect you at all costs. Even if that means protecting you from me."

I jerk my hand from his grip and start to climb off the bed, but he pulls me to him, my back flush to his chest. His powerful arm curves around my middle, holding me in his protective embrace. He nuzzles his nose in my hair. All the anger that surged up inside me has melted away as I allow myself to be held by this man. I've missed him so much.

"Everything feels so messy," I whisper. "Since you came back." Tears flood my eyes and spill out, soaking the bed below.

"I'll clean it up," he assures me, his hot breath tickling my hair.

His cock is hard behind me, but unlike Kayden, he doesn't rub it against me. Jordy simply holds me like I'm the most important thing in his world. It's confusing and infuriating, and also incredibly satisfying.

"You confuse me," I whisper.

He kisses my head. "I confuse myself."

"Was my dad nice?"

A laugh barks out of him. "Nice? Your dad? Not the word I'd use to describe him."

I twist around to face him. His eyes are nearly closed and he smells like liquor. It makes me wonder if I could get away with kissing him.

You have a boyfriend.

That I don't like. Not like this.

For the first time since I started dating Kayden, I come to the conclusion I need to break up with him. It's not fair to either of us. He wants to have sex and I don't want to. Not with him at least.

But with Jordy?

I always loved him. Like a brother. But now… Now everything is different. He's always been so hot, but I've never been affected like this. I practically melt at his touch and hang on his every word. I crave to touch every part of him and have him touch every part of me.

I want him so much.

"What word would you use to describe him then?" I ask, my lips close to his.

"Total dickhead." He chuckles. "He looks after his own, though."

"You were his?"

He opens his eyes, his dark browns pinning me. "We're family, Roux. Always have been. Always will be."

I don't think family lies tangled up this way, eager to get naked and kiss.

"I'm still a virgin," I whisper. "I know I made it seem like I wasn't before, but I am. I don't want you to think I'm a ho like Tarrin, though Kayden probably wishes I were."

He spreads a possessive palm over my ass, squeezing. "You're worth waiting for. When you're ready to have sex, it should be on your terms, not some horny-ass thug who just wants to bag a virgin."

I'm ready.

But not with Kayden.

If Jordy would give me the time of day, I'd let him do whatever he wanted to me. With Jordy, it feels safe. Comfortable. Like home.

"I'm ready," I breathe, brushing my lips against his. "Kayden's just not the right one."

Jordy brings his face closer to mine, kissing my jaw. "The right one will be worth it. Whenever it happens. Just hold out for the right one." His lips trail a searing line along my jaw. "Don't give it to *him*."

I tilt my head up, groaning when his lips part and he kisses the side of my neck. His tongue flicks out, sending currents of desire right to my core. I let out a moan, my fingers biting into his bicep. He sucks the skin on my neck gently. Shivers ripple through me. His tongue drags back up to my jaw and he nips me there.

This is the most erotic thing I've ever experienced in my life.

My body begs for his touch, trembling and whimpering in need.

His palm slides down my outer thigh until he meets bare skin beneath the hem of my dress. Slowly, he drags the material up, his fingertips leaving a trail of fiery heat. He sucks on my neck again, this time a little harder. Our breathing is heavier and each hot breath on my flesh turns me on further. I'm squirming with desire. I want him to strip me and claim me.

He pulls my thigh up over his hip. A draft of air flutters over my wet panties, making my cheeks burn with heat. His mouth opens wide, like he's trying to devour me. Teeth scrape over the pulsing vein in my neck. I whimper, wanting him to bite me. Instead, he sucks me hard, to the point of pain. I cry out, inching my leg higher up his hip, needing friction. Needing him. He slides his palm up under my dress, teasing his fingertips under the edge of my panties on my ass.

"Jordy's passed out!" Terrence booms from the other side of the door.

I fly out of Jordy's arms. He reaches over to tug my dress down before pulling the blanket up over me. My heart is hammering in my chest. This thing happening between me and Jordy feels good, but I'm under no delusions that Roan will be okay with it.

Roan will freak.

And if Terrence or Cal or Hollis were to find us doing what we were just doing...

I don't want to know.

Jordy just got back. The last thing he needs is all the Hoodlums hating him. He needs support and love.

Terrence walks into the cabin, stumbling and cursing. When he sees us in the bed, he cocks his head. "We fuckin' Little Hoodlum?"

Jordy growls. "*We* aren't doing anything. I don't like Roux out there alone. I'm keeping her safe."

Not a lie.

Not completely.

"Hmph," Terrence says, kicking off his shoes as he heads our way. "Scoot your asses over. I'm not sleeping on the floor and Cal took Tarrin Hooker to my tent."

"Fine, but your drunk ass is sleeping next to me, not Roux," Jordy growls. "Understood?"

Terrence laughs as he crawls into bed, playfully cuddling Jordy from behind. "If you wanted some ass, sweetheart, all you had to do was ask."

Jordy rolls his eyes but lets his friend pretend to rut against him. His dark eyes are locked on mine, a storm of brewing emotions. Guilt. Anger. Lust. Confusion. He doesn't try to kiss me or touch me, but he doesn't look away from me.

"Go to sleep, Roux," he murmurs, stroking his fingers down the length of my arm.

"I'm not tired."

His dark eyes fall to my lips and he lets out a heavy sigh. "Please."

"Shhh," Terrence groans. "I'm having sex dreams about Jordy's ass. Stop interrupting, kiddo."

Jordy laughs and it's infectious. Both Terrence and I laugh too. With my soul a little lighter at hearing Jordy's rare laugh, I relax and my eyes flutter closed. A few times I pop them back open to find Jordy's stare never wavering.

I don't know what's happening with us, but I don't want it to stop.

CHAPTER NINE

Jordy

I WAKE WITH A SPLITTING HEADACHE AND TO THE SOUND of people arguing. Reluctantly, I crack my eyes open. Terrence is no longer in the bed, but Roux is. The purple hickeys on her neck are a harsh reminder that last night was not some fantasy or dream.

It. Was. Real.

Fuck.

Roan is going to murder me.

And as much as that thought makes me sick to my stomach, I can't look away from her. With her dark lashes on her apple cheeks and her plump lips parted as she sleeps, she looks like a fucking angel.

I'm in too deep.

Staying with them is going to be too difficult. I don't trust myself. Every time I've been near her, I can't keep my hands off her. What happens when I lose all resolve? I'll take her virginity and make her mine.

Sick, Jordy.

Wake the fuck up, man.

But I can't. All I see is her and how goddamn much I want her. Even if I somehow could wait until her birthday to have her, it doesn't change the fact she's Roux. My best friend's little sister. It's part of the bro code: Don't fuck little sisters.

What about love?

I've been loving Little Hoodlum for as long as I can remember.

Not this kind of love, but the powerful kind that would mean walking into traffic if it meant it would somehow save her. Sure, maybe before I was a stand-in big brother of sorts.

Now?

Everything's changing and I don't know how to stop it. I'm not sure I want to stop it. I want to give in to these urges between us and claim her so fuckfaces like Kayden Ramirez can't.

She's too perfect.

Too fucking pretty.

Too innocent for the likes of people like him.

Mine to protect and love.

Holy shit, I'm so screwed. This isn't right. It's fucked up.

Voices outside begin rising, jolting me from my thoughts. Unease flitters through me. I climb out of the bed and throw on my shoes before heading out of the cabin. As soon as I open the door, I wish I'd stayed in bed.

Renaldo motherfucking Ramirez and my goddamn brother.

Looking chummy as fuck and ready to kill the Hoodlums.

"Yo!" I call out, dragging the attention of all five men.

Hollis is lingering off to the side, his brows furled

together in concern. I lock eyes with him and dart them to the cabin. *Roux.* My unspoken word is heard loud and clear because he slips past me, closing the door behind him.

"Holy shit," Juno says, holding his arms out. "Get over here, little brother."

I walk over to him and hug him. Renaldo slaps my back.

"We were just looking for you," Renaldo says. "Been lookin' all over, in fact. 'Bout time you check in."

"Check in?" I step back, crossing my arms over my chest. "For what?"

Roan's expression is murderous. "I told them you have a job lined out at a restaurant in town. One your parole board wants you working at. But apparently they don't give a shit."

Terrence and Cal glower at Renaldo and Juno. The air is thick with tension. Over me. And my motherfucking girl is on the other side of that door. Worry over her clouds my every thought.

"What're they gonna pay you over there, Jordy?" Renaldo asks. "Minimum wage? So you can wash fuckin' dishes? Come on, man. You know where the real money is."

Juno nods, grinning at me. "Same work as before, but we're growing. The Ramirezes and the Martinezes are business partners now."

I grit my teeth and grunt at him.

"Like Romeo and Juliet, man," Renaldo says with a laugh. "Your side and mine haven't exactly been friends, but we're married now, bitch."

My brow lifts and Juno snorts.

"We're not fuckin' homos," Juno says, shaking his head. "It's figurative. This shit we're doing—the money we're making—it's fucking romantic."

"They both died in the end," I remind them, pleased with the fact I remember something from high school.

Renaldo's gaze darkens. "Not this time."

"They'll lock my ass back up if I violate my parole," I say through clenched teeth. "I can't chop cars for you, man."

"Naw," Renaldo growls. "I need you keeping eyes on my brother. Make sure no one's giving him any shit. He's just a kid."

I scrub my palm down my face. "I'm not exactly your brother's biggest fan."

"Kayden doesn't get a choice in the matter," Renaldo growls. "I need someone I can trust keeping tabs on him and making sure he doesn't get his ass capped. You feel me, man?"

"Yeah, I feel you." I meet his hard stare. "And if I say no?"

He cracks his neck and Juno scowls.

"You won't," Renaldo spits out. His eyes drift to the Hoodlums. "Because if it's not you, it's one of them. I'd rather it be you, but I'll recruit any one of these guys. Even the blond one that pussed out and went inside."

Yeah fucking right.

The rat wouldn't last a second working for Renaldo.

"Jordy," Roan rumbles in warning.

Ignoring him, I nod at Renaldo. "I'll keep an eye on him when I can, but I'm not his goddamn babysitter. I have shit I have to do to keep my ass from getting locked up. If he needs a babysitter, then you need to stop giving his ass shit to do."

Renaldo's eyes flare with rage, but he nods. "Fair enough. You're on call, though. He's to text you when he's doing any big deals. I want you there. Eyes the fuck on him. Understood?"

"It's not like I have much of a choice," I spit out. Because

79

if it's not me, it's them, and I refuse to let my friends get pulled into Renaldo's bullshit.

His grin is wolfish. "I always knew you were smart."

"Are we through here, 'cause I want to get the hell out of here and shower?"

Renaldo pins me with a hard stare. "Yeah, kid, we're through. For now."

They head back for Renaldo's suped up Tahoe, taking the tension with them. It isn't until they start the engine and drive off that Roan lays into me.

"What the actual fuck, man?" he roars, shoving me.

I get in his face so our noses are touching. "You know what the fuck."

Panic flashes in his amber eyes. "Please don't alienate yourself again. Please."

"Roan…" I close my eyes, resting my forehead on his. "I just…I'll do anything if it means keeping them away from you and Roux."

Roan grips my shoulders, squeezing before he pulls me to him for a fierce hug. "We do this together, brother."

"We can't."

"We. Can. Just… Just give me time to work some things out." He releases me and frowns at me. "I want updates on everything he makes you do. We're brothers. Do not cut me off again to try and protect me. I can't deal with this shit again. You fucking include me and we figure it out together."

My chest aches at the prospect of letting him into this fucked up world I'm still attached to. "Roan, I don't know—"

"That's right," he growls. "You don't know."

"We could kill them," Terrence suggests like he's recommending his favorite pie at the diner. No big deal. "Bury them here on the campgrounds. No one will ever find them."

Tempting.

Hollis steps over to us, no longer in the cabin. "It's amazing you Hoodlums lasted this long without my help. Too much brawn and not enough brains."

Roan laughs. "Watch your mouth, rat."

"Not today, Satan." Hollis smirks. "I have an idea."

"On where to bury the bodies?" Terrence asks, perking up.

"Less brutal, but still effective," Hollis says. "I need to make a call, though. Get me what you can on Renaldo."

I gape at Hollis, shocked as hell. "Who is this guy?"

"My husband," Roan says with a cheesy-ass grin. "I taught him everything he knows."

Hollis's ear is pressed to his phone, but he must overhear because he shoots us the bird before walking off.

"For the record, I don't like this one goddamn bit," I state, crossing my arms over my chest.

Cal slings an arm over my shoulders. "Too fucking bad, bro. We're here for you. Can't let your dumbass get sent to prison again. You're too pretty to go back. You have douchebag college dickhead hair now. Someone'll make you their bitch for sure."

I shove him away, laughing. "I fucking hate you."

"You love my ass and you know it." He grins at me.

"Speaking of college. These two fuckfaces will go back in a week, so they're useless," Roan says, shoving Cal into Terrence. "But Hollis and I will be here. We'll figure out a way to get Renaldo off your back and Kayden away from my sister."

I flinch at the mention of Roux.

As if on cue, she pokes her head out of the cabin. With messy hair and a sleepy face, she's fucking adorable as hell. My gaze falls to the purple hickeys on her neck and I freeze.

Shit.

"What the fuck, Roux," Roan snarls, no longer in a playful mood. He stalks over to her, pushing her hair aside. "Who did this? Kayden?"

Her eyes dart my way, making Terrence snort. "He's my boyfriend," she screeches, her voice shrill. "That's what boyfriends do."

I should tell him.

It was me.

I'm fucking addicted to your sister, Roan.

All I can do is stare at her pretty, purple neck.

"You're not allowed to see him," Roan growls. "Ever. Fucking. Again."

She lifts her chin, meeting his angry glare with a fierce scowl of her own. "Fine!"

Roan deflates, shooting the rest of us Hoodlums a confused look. I try not to smile, but fuck if I'm not happy about the idea of her not seeing Kayden. She catches my smile and her cheeks turn pink.

So beautiful.

And young.

Fuck.

While she and Roan bicker, I try to remind myself of the fact she's just a teenager. It guts me I can't have her. I'm fucking obsessing over it.

I know the law.

If I hooked up with Roux and anyone found out, I'd go right back to prison where her dad wouldn't be so welcoming this time. He'd beat me to a bloody fucking pulp and then eat my goddamn soul or some shit. You don't fuck the meanest guy in prison's baby girl.

I need to stay out of prison to keep her safe.

And I can't do that if I fuck her.

A bone-deep sadness settles inside me, weighing me down. Her amber eyes are pinning me, reading my goddamn mind before I have to even say the words. I'm practically dripping with resignation.

"I need to go," I mutter. "Terrence, can you give me a ride?"

I ignore Roan calling out for me or the way Roux's stare bores into me.

Don't look.

Don't fucking look.

As soon as I get into Terrence's car, I can't help but drag my eyes up to seek her pretty face out.

Heartbreak and anger.

I fucked up.

Again.

It's better this way.

As we drive away, I pull out my phone and text Samantha.

Me: I need to see you.

CHAPTER TEN

Roux

H IS STUFF—A SMALL, RATTY BACKPACK—SITS IN ONE corner of our living room, but Jordy's intense presence is missing. He hasn't come to the garage apartment since he blew out of the campground this morning. I don't know where he's gone and I don't know how to get in touch with him.

And I have no one to talk to about this.

My fingers hover over the phone, considering if I should tell Charlotte my woes. We're not exactly happy with each other right now. Once I found out she was alive and well this morning, I sort of went off on her. Normally, she would argue back, but she was strangely quiet. It makes my chest ache. I don't understand this girl she's become lately. Hell, I don't understand myself.

The apartment is empty. Hollis is visiting with his mom and Roan is at work. If they had big plans of keeping me locked away in my tower, they're doing a terrible job. I could go anywhere right now and no one would care.

The only place I want to go, though, is right into Jordy's arms. If only I knew where that was.

My phone buzzes, dragging me from my thoughts.

Charlotte: I'm sorry for being a bitch last night and today. I love you.

I smile and type out a reply.

Me: I love you too.

Charlotte: Come over. Let's get ready together. Hollis just left to take dinner up to the station. Mom, Aunt Karen, and Penny just left to have dinner with Mike. I need my bestie. Don't make me show up to Zac's party alone.

Roan doesn't want me going to that party, but he's not exactly here to stop me.

Me: I'm going to break up with Kayden.

She sends me about a hundred wow-face emojis.

Charlotte: Get over here now, sis. We have so much to talk about.

Me: Be there in five.

I'll probably get my ass handed to me by Roan, but I'm not going to worry about that right now. My best friend needs me and I need her.

And I seriously need to break things off with Kayden.

"Gross," Charlotte complains. "Tarrin was just blowing Cal last night. She won't be happy until she's had the dick of every man in this town in her mouth."

Sure enough, Tarrin is on her knees, giving head to some guy who appears to be a few years older than us. I make a gagging motion with my finger that has Charlotte laughing. Tonight, she looks like her usual self. Flawless and effortlessly beautiful. Charlotte is charismatic and confident. It's just who she is.

"Hey, babe," Ryan says, popping up beside us, a predatory glint in his eyes as he roams his gaze up her body in appreciation. "About time you got here."

All her confidence wilts right in front of my eyes.

I don't like the sudden change in her.

Her shoulders hunch, her head bows, and she leans toward him. If I weren't staring right at her when he showed up, I would've missed the entire transformation. It's weird. I don't think she even realizes how weird it is.

"Roux, will you be okay if Char and I get alone for a while?" He pins me with a hard glare, daring me to say no.

"Actually, I want to hang with you guys if that's okay." I smile sweetly at him, knowing he's pissed. Screw him.

He grits his teeth. "Twenty minutes is all we need."

Charlotte speaks up, aiding him. "Didn't you need to tell Kayden something?"

I deflate at her words. "Yeah, but…"

"We won't be gone long," she rushes out. "Promise. We can make fun of Tarrin together in a little bit."

Reluctantly, I nod. I can't force her to stay away from her creepy boyfriend. Not if she doesn't want to. And I do need to speak to Kayden.

"He's in the basement. It's crazy down there," Ryan warns. "Be careful."

Like he cares.

"Meet you here in half an hour," I tell Charlotte. Then, I give Ryan a pointed look. "If you're not here, I'm coming looking for you."

She laughs as she pulls Ryan away. "We'll be here."

As soon as they disappear down a hallway, I go on a hunt for Kayden. This party has a lot of the usual Campfire Chaos subjects, minus the Hoodlums, and a lot of older guys I don't recognize. They're not people my brother and Jordy went to school with either.

They're harder.

Scarier.

Sketchy.

A couple of guys standing in the kitchen wearing matching red bandanas eye me up like I'm a piece of meat. Yikes. Maybe coming to this party was a bad idea. I rush past them to the open door to the basement. Music thumps loudly from downstairs. It's dark down there aside from some strobe lights blinking in tandem with the bass. Several people make out on the stairs and I'm pretty sure one couple is having sex. I finally make it to the bottom, my eyes squinting against the blinking lights to try and find Kayden.

Ahh, there he is.

Looking like the king of his domain, perched on the back of a sofa with girls hanging all over him. Disgust roils through me. He's not exactly doing anything with them, aside from not pushing them away, but it irritates me anyway.

As though I have room to talk.

I let Jordy freaking Martinez give me hickeys last night.

At the memory of his mouth on me and how that made me feel, I flush. Heat burns across my flesh, making me crave him all the more. It just drives home the fact I need to break things off with Kayden. When I reach him, I can tell he's high as hell. His lids are hooded and he has a lazy smile on his face. He's shirtless and the two girls kneeling on the cushions on either side of him pet his ripped chest in appreciation.

I stand right in front of the sofa between it and the coffee table, glaring at him until he realizes who I am. His dark eyes latch onto mine. At first, he grins wider, seemingly pleased to see me. Then, he remembers his predicament.

He snarls out something to the girls, swatting their hands away. Both of them pout when he reaches for me. I shake my head, walking off. I'm not talking to him about anything with those two lingering. I've nearly reached the stairs when two strong arms hug me from behind.

"Hey, Roux-Roux." Kayden nips at my ear through my hair. "Missed you, baby."

I struggle against his hold to no avail. "Let me go."

"Don't be mad," he begs. "You know it's not like that with them. They're just flirting, but I never act on it. You're my girl."

Not for long.

I tug against him, trying to extricate myself from his arms. All I manage to do is pull us away from the stairs to the dark corner. I spin around in his arms, hoping to put some distance between us. He grips my biceps, pinning me with his hips. There's no mistaking how hard he is in his jeans. With the strobe light behind him, I can't see his face. Just the outline of his head. He leans forward like he might kiss me, but then freezes.

"I want to break up," I yell out over the music.

One of his hands lets go of my arm to travel to my neck. When his thumb brushes over my hickey, I stiffen.

"Who the fuck did this?" he demands, his breath hot and in my face.

"Did you hear me, Kayden?" I bite back. "I want to break up. We're over."

His thumb presses hard against the hickey, which coincidentally happens to be over the big vein in my neck. It makes me dizzy and I suck in a ragged gasp of air.

"That hurts!"

He squeezes my arm while simultaneously pressing against the hickey. I was angry, but now fear is trickling down my spine. Kayden wouldn't hurt me, would he? The bruises I feel forming where he's touching me state otherwise. Panic crawls up my throat and tears spring in my eyes.

"Kayden," I croak out. "Stop."

He relaxes his hold before crashing his lips to mine. I'm shocked by the kiss and am helpless to push away from him. I manage to get my palms to his bare chest so I can push him away. He doesn't budge because he's stronger than me. Turning my head to the side, I tear my lips from his, my heart frantically racing in my chest.

Kayden's mouth finds my ear. "Who did you let suck on your neck, Roux?"

I'm sure as hell not telling him the truth.

"Was it Jordy?" he accuses.

I shake my head in vehemence. "S-Some boy on the basketball team," I lie. "I was drunk. It didn't mean anything."

"Did you fuck him?"

"What? No!"

He grabs a handful of my hair, smashing his lips back to mine. His hips grind against me and he moans in my mouth. I freeze in his arms, hoping like hell this'll be over soon. He tastes like hard liquor and is practically thrumming with whatever's running through his system.

This was a bad idea.

I do not want to lose my virginity in a basement with a fucked-up boyfriend who's pissed because I let someone give me hickeys.

Fear has me searching for the boy I was helplessly head over heels for months ago.

"Kayden," I whimper against his lips. "I'm scared."

He stops kissing me to release his firm hold on me. I'm hauled into his arms as he hugs me tight. Tears threaten, but I blink them back. I hug him, hoping he'll snap out of it.

"You're my girlfriend, Roux," he says against my ear. "I can't lose you. I *won't* lose you."

I don't have an answer for him. Nothing I say will matter. Not when he's acting like this.

"We're not breaking up because you made a mistake," he tells me, his voice deep and fierce. "We're made of tougher stuff than that. Just like those girls flirting with me was a mistake. I should have told them not to touch me."

I remain silent, wondering how pissed Charlotte will be when I beg her to take me home.

"Let's get out of here, baby," Kayden says. "I think we just need to take that final step. So you will realize how much I mean to you. I already know you mean the world to me, which is why I want to make love to you."

A tremble shudders through me. The thought of getting into bed with him, especially after tonight, has bile creeping up my throat. I need to leave. If I can't find Charlotte, then I need to call Roan and have him come get me.

People start shouting from behind Kayden, interrupting our intense moment. A fight has broken out. Kayden yells, rushing into the fray because it seems like maybe it's one of his friends involved. I take this opportunity to get the hell out of here, taking the stairs two at a time. When I burst out of the door and into the kitchen, I ignore the thugs and make a beeline toward the hall I saw Charlotte and Ryan disappear into.

I push into a few doors, grossed out to find people having

sex in each room. One room has a full-on orgy going on and I turn away, closing the door behind me.

Wait.

I pause.

Not Charlotte. She's with Ryan. I think she loves him for some unknown reason. Unease claws at me. Slowly, I twist the knob and turn it, peeking my head back in. Charlotte is completely naked as Ryan fucks her. His friend Isaiah is stretched beside them, groping my best friend's tit. Some other guy I recognize from school is naked, stroking his cock on the other side of the bed.

I'm stunned.

I knew she was having sex with Ryan, but I didn't know she was having orgies with his friends. It's then I realize she's not contributing much. None at all, in fact. I burst through the door, fury burning through me.

"Charlotte!"

She doesn't move. Isaiah smirks at me, as he pinches her nipple. Ryan groans, flexes his ass, and then pulls out.

"What's happening?" I shriek, rushing over to Charlotte. "What have you done to her?"

Ryan scowls at me, as he throws on boxers over his dripping dick where the condom is thankfully in place. "She's blissed out of her mind. Mind your own fucking business, Roux."

"You can't have sex with someone who's passed out!" I yell, shoving his stupid friend Isaiah away from her.

Ryan grabs my arm hard, yanking me until we're face to face. "She was pretty fucking into it moments before you showed up. Not my problem if she passed out right when I was nutting. Leave us alone, bitch."

I smack him hard with my free hand. "Let me go."

He shrugs, releasing me and finding his jeans. "Go," he tells his two friends. "I'll deal with her."

Isaiah flips me off as he passes. The other guy flashes me a flirtatious grin. I shove him when he nears. They both laugh and walk out of the room. Ryan has tossed a blanket over Charlotte's naked body.

"I'm turning you in," I hiss. "This is wrong."

His lip curls up. "When she wakes up, she'll tell you she consented to all of this. I said mind your own goddamn business."

"I'm calling the cops," I threaten.

He laughs at me. "When she comes to, and she will, she'll admit we were having fun. Your friendship, which is already on the fucking rocks, will be destroyed." He takes a threatening step toward me. "My dad's a cop. I know everyone at the station. What do you think's really going to happen?"

I stare at him in horror. He's so confident nothing will happen. That this is absolutely okay.

"You might be above the law," I seethe, "but you are not above my brother. And he will not be okay with what you're doing with his sister-in-law."

Fear glints in his eyes.

Roan will beat his ass.

"Leave," I hiss.

He finishes yanking on his clothes, his jaw furiously working. "You're gonna regret this, Roux."

"Get the hell out of here!"

As soon as he storms off, I yank my phone from my pocket and call Roan. He's going to be pissed, but he'll be even more pissed if I don't call him. God put big brothers on this earth for a reason. They're here to get their little sisters out of heaps of shit.

I'm standing in the biggest heap yet.

CHAPTER ELEVEN

Jordy

UNBELIEVABLE.

After checking into El Juarez Restaurant for my lame-ass dishwashing job, I took care of some shit, including meeting up with Samantha at her hotel. I'd barely made it into Hollis and Roan's place when someone knocked on the door. Juno showed up with one of his goons, gave me a pimped-out navy-blue Camaro, and told me an address. I'm barely out of the pen, and I'm back to the same old bullshit.

I can't exactly tell Juno and Renaldo no, though. It could be worse. They could be asking me to chop cars or deal drugs. Right now, all they want is eyes on baby Ramirez. Since he's all kinds of in love with my fucking girl, it shouldn't be too hard.

My girl.

In another life.

She's nothing but my best friend's little sister.

I have to remember that.

When I reach the address, the street is lined with cars. I've barely parked and am climbing out when a familiar purple Mustang zooms past me.

What the fuck is the rat doing here?

I storm after him and have to run when he takes off toward the house.

"Yo, rat, where the fuck you heading in such a hurry?" I call out.

He comes to a screeching halt and whirls around. "Thank fuck you're here. It's Charlotte and Roux. Roux called Roan flipping the hell out earlier."

I stalk past him, no longer annoyed to be here but on an eager mission to find them. The place is filled with a bunch of motherfuckers eyeing me the wrong way. They're all carrying. I can see it in the way they watch me. I must put off some "don't fuck with me vibes," though, because no one messes with us.

"She said in the second bedroom on the right," Hollis says, ushering me down a hall. "This way."

We find said door, but it's locked.

"Roux! It's me and Jordy!" Hollis calls out, banging on the door.

The next moment, the door flings open. Roux looks like hell. Scared out of her mind and sobbing. I don't think twice about yanking her to me in a protective embrace. Charlotte sits on the bed, her hair messy and her eyelids drooping.

"I told her I'm fine," Charlotte slurs.

"You don't look fine, little mouse," I bite out. "You look like total shit."

She flips me off. Hollis sits down beside her and starts snapping at her about being irresponsible. Beneath all his anger, worry ripples from him.

"What happened?" I ask, raking my fingers through Roux's hair and tugging her head back so I can look at her.

She swallows, drawing my gaze to her hickeys. "She says she wanted it, but, Jordy, I walked in on them doing stuff to her while she was passed out."

I frown and press a kiss to her forehead. "Who, Little Hoodlum?"

"Ryan and Isaiah and a kid named Gunther, I think."

"Want me to kill them?"

Her nostrils flare. "Don't even joke about that. Not after…" She trails off and her lip wobbles. "I want to go home. Can you please take me home?"

Fuck, I would kill to claim her plump lips and promise her everything will be okay.

But I can't.

"Let's get out of here," I bark out to Hollis.

Hollis tugs Charlotte out of the bed, but she's incredibly unsteady on her feet. Her brother scoops her in his arms, surprising the hell out of me, and nods at me for us to leave. Roux breaks away from me to grab Charlotte's shoes and purse.

People stare at us as we leave the party. I follow them to Hollis's Mustang and hold the door open while Hollis sets Charlotte into the front seat.

"Take her home," I tell him. "I need to take care of something."

Hollis's jaw clenches. "You can't beat them up, man. There's like fifty of those assholes in there who look scarier than you. Bad idea."

"I'm not beating anyone up," I growl. "I'm going to check on some things. I'll meet you at your mom's after."

"I'm staying with you," Roux says, tugging on my T-shirt.

"No."

She starts to argue, but Hollis backs me up, his voice dripping with big brotherly authority he no doubt learned from Roan. "Get in the car, Roux. It's not up for debate."

"Be careful," she mutters to me before slipping into the back seat.

"What she said," Hollis grumbles.

As soon as they drive off, I head back inside. I'm on a mission to find Cuntingham and knock his teeth in. He's nowhere to be found, but baby Ramirez shows up looking like a fucking shirtless gangster.

His jeans are hanging low on his hips, showing the band of his white boxers. The kid is cut, but I could stomp his ass without breaking a sweat. Unfortunately, I have to play nice with this idiot. It's going to be difficult when I know he's had his tongue down my girl's throat and who the fuck knows what else since they've been together.

Not my girl.

Still my something.

Not fucking his.

"Where's Cunningham?" I demand at the same time he asks, "Where's Roux?"

I crack my neck, ignoring the crowd of losers who come to stand behind him. Most are about his age and I could take them if I had to. "Roux went home with Charlotte. Now where the fuck is that piece of shit?"

Kayden's eyes narrow, anger flashing in them. "Did he do something to Roux?"

"No, man, but he did something to her best friend. I want to talk to him." And by talk, I want to fucking head butt him.

"He's out back," Kayden says. "Cody, bring him here."

A lanky kid—Cody—ambles off on a hunt for that motherfucker. I pop my knuckles, my furious glare never leaving Kayden. I may have to watch over him, but I don't have to like his ass. As I wait, my eyes skim over the crowd. I spot Renaldo's crew easy with their red bandanas. It's a few guys wearing Nike sweatbands that stand out like sore thumbs. Some of Alejandro's crew used to wear that shit. A less obvious way to state they were a part of a gang without bringing attention from the cops.

"What the fuck?" Cuntingham bellows as he storms toward us. "Who the fuck…" He trails off upon seeing me. His lip curls up and he sneers at me. "What are you doing here, convict?"

I don't flinch. I don't react.

After a long beat of silence, making him wait so I can watch the panic slowly slide over him like a fog, I lick my tongue over my upper teeth and lift my chin at him.

"You like to fuck unconscious girls?" I ask, my voice low and deadly.

Kayden stiffens, anger bursting from him in hot waves. "What the fuck? You said that shit wasn't for—"

"Back the fuck up off my nuts," Cuntingham snaps at Kayden. "You don't know shit, man. She wanted to try it."

Kayden's jaw clenches.

"Why the fuck are you so worried about my girlfriend anyway?" Cuntingham snarls, turning his jealous rage on Kayden.

Maybe it'll be more entertaining to watch them beat the fuck out of each other.

"She's my girlfriend's best friend," Kayden snaps. "That's why. You fucked up, Ryan. Get the hell out of here."

Cuntingham shakes his head like a spoiled child. "You can't kick me out. Half these people are *my* friends, not yours, douchebag!"

Kayden steps closer, getting in his face. "And the other half belong to me, motherfucker."

"We have an agreement," Cuntingham hisses, his nose bumping Kayden's. "You choose this fuckface over me and that agreement goes the fuck away."

What agreement?

Kayden tenses. It must have something to do with Renaldo.

"I don't have shit with you," I grind out, causing Cuntingham to turn around. "This is for little mouse."

My fist slams into his gut, making him groan and double over. I want to bash his fucking face in, but I know who his dad is. I'm not getting sent back to prison for breaking the nose of a cop's son.

"Y-You," Cuntingham chokes out.

I don't give him a second to get his words out. With a growl, I snatch him by the hair and drag his pussy ass out of the party. He cries out like a bitch when I toss him outside and into the yard like yesterday's trash. Turning on my heel, I head back into the party.

"Isaiah and Gunther?"

Two guilty as fuck dudes freeze. I don't have to do anything except glower at them. They rush out of the house without argument.

Kayden easily calms the group like he was born to command people, much like his brother. He barks out a few orders and the crowd disperses.

"Renaldo sent you to babysit me because some Rockfords

are here." His jaw clenches, irritation present in every tick of his facial muscles. "I can handle a few fucking Rockfords."

"I just do what I'm told." I shrug. "Is Cunningham going to be a problem?"

"Nope. He owes me. We have a deal. He keeps his dad and the cops off our asses, and I keep him and his crew supplied." His head cocks to the side, studying me with obvious distaste. "Are *you* going to be a problem?"

You better fucking believe it, asshole.

"Guess we'll find out," I say instead.

His jaw clenches. "I don't need you here watching over me. I have this shit handled."

I don't sense any threats, so I'm sure as hell not staying. With a clipped nod his way, I turn on my heel and head out the door. I've barely made it over the threshold when baby Ramirez calls out to me.

"Stay away from my goddamn girlfriend or I'll cut your throat," he bites out.

He could try.

I offer him my finger and saunter away from his bratty ass.

"If I found out it was you who left those hickeys on her neck," he yells after me, "I'll make you pay."

I reach my car and turn my head to look at him. He stands in the yard, a new gun in his hand at his side and a murderous scowl on his face. With all the hatred I can muster, I sear my glare into him.

He's a fucking kid.

I will destroy him if I have to.

And seeing that he's involving Roux in all his bullshit, I might just have to.

"You know I can't stay away from her." I lick my bottom lip, smirking a little. "She's my best friend's little sister." I laugh. "I'm going to see her every goddamn day. All goddamn day. Hell, I might even bump into her at night on the way to the bathroom."

He storms my way, raising his gun at me, pointing it right in my face like he actually has the balls to use it. I don't flinch, just eye him up like he's a piece of shit stuck to my shoe.

"Touch her, motherfucker, and see what happens. I don't give a fuck what sort of agreement our brothers have," he snarls. "I *will* kill you."

Not if I kill you first, little boy.

"Bye, baby Ramirez."

I climb into the car and peel out, sending gravel spraying all over that idiot. When he raises his weapon and fires into the sky, I laugh.

Then, cold dread settles over me.

This kid is an angry little shit and has his claws deep in my girl.

He's a problem. A problem I absolutely need to deal with.

CHAPTER TWELVE

Roux

CHARLOTTE'S MOM, KELSEY, IS LIKE THE MOM I never had.

Sweet. Loving. Caring.

Of all the years I've known her, she has always been calm and collected. Not once have I seen her lose her shit. Until now.

"You've lost your damn mind," Kelsey seethes, her body trembling as she shakes a finger at Charlotte.

Charlotte wears a bored expression as she yawns, her eyes darting to the clock. "It was just a party. Roux overreacted."

Hollis snaps his head her way. "She didn't overreact. That dickhead took advantage of you."

"He's my boyfriend," Charlotte snaps, tears welling in her eyes. "I love him. What we do in the bedroom is none of your damn business."

"You're seventeen, baby," Kelsey says, her voice softening. "It's absolutely my business."

Charlotte turns her white-hot glare my way. "This is all

your fault. Since when did you become a narc? I thought we were closer than that."

Guilt hits me like a ten-ton pile of bricks. I shrink back from her words. It breaks my heart hearing her talk like this.

"I'm calling Dad," Hollis says, cutting through the thick tension with a loaded statement of his own.

Charlotte gapes at him, her bottom lip trembling. "I thought you weren't talking to him."

"We talk," Hollis grits out. "Just because I haven't forgiven him for what he did when he found out I was gay doesn't mean I still don't want a relationship with him. He's my dad too."

"Don't call him," she pleads.

Kelsey nods her head at Hollis. "I don't know what to do anymore," she says to her daughter. "Maybe your dad can get through to you."

I know of all the things Kelsey could do to her, calling Char's dad is the worst. Not because he'd be mean, but because she's a daddy's girl. Even with him all the way in Vermont, she has him wrapped around her finger. She and Penny both do. Whatever they want, all they have to do is call and it's suddenly theirs.

Charlotte starts to cry and I ache to go to her. Instead, I curl my arms around my waist, fighting tears of my own. Kelsey gives me a sad, knowing look. She knows what this is doing to our friendship.

"Dad?" Hollis says. "Yeah, I know it's late. My stomach is fine." A pause. "It's Charlotte." He pauses again. "Hold on. Let me put you on speaker phone."

Charlotte shoots me a horrible glare. One that will haunt me in my dreams. She's never looked at me with such hatred. My gut hollows out as tears leak freely down my face.

"Princess?" Garrett says, his voice tense with worry.

"Hi, Daddy." A sob from Charlotte. "I'm sorry."

"Don't be sorry. Just talk to me. Tell me what's happened."

Kelsey sits beside Charlotte and tries to take her hand, but she swats it away.

"I have a boyfriend. We did some stuff. Now everyone is on my case. I'm sorry, okay? Can we just drop it?" Her bottom lip trembles. "I'm fine."

"Is your mother there?"

"Right here," Kelsey says with a tired sigh.

"I'm booking a flight and coming to visit," Garrett states. "From the stuff Hollis told me this morning, and now this, I think my presence is needed."

I shoot Hollis a questioning look. He shrugs it off.

"You have work," Charlotte says sadly, though I notice the hopeful gleam in her eyes. She misses her dad so much.

"Work isn't my primary concern, honey," he says softly. "You are. I'm going to fly out there and we'll work everything out. Okay?"

"Okay," Charlotte croaks. "I'm sorry."

"Stop saying you're sorry," Garrett replies. "Just be good and stay with your mother until I get there. Can you do that for me?"

Tears race down her red cheeks and she nods. "I can. I miss you."

"Miss you too, sweetheart. Hollis, take me off speaker."

Hollis mashes a button and then disappears with his phone.

"Why don't you go upstairs and shower?" Kelsey says. "We can talk after you've cleaned up."

Charlotte tries to stand, but her legs give out. Kelsey

frowns. My brows scrunch with worry. When Charlotte notices my expression, she goes off on me.

"Stop looking at me like that, Roux! Like you're better than me! Like your boyfriend isn't a damn gangster!" She swipes angrily at her tears. "Why are you even here? You're not wanted. Leave. Leave!"

Kelsey tries to calm her shrieking. I stand up, stung by her words, and start for the front door.

"Don't walk home," Kelsey calls out. "Just wait for Hollis. I'm going to get her upstairs and into the shower."

With Kelsey to lean on, Charlotte manages to stand up. She may still be fucked up on drugs, but her anger cuts through the haze like a knife.

"I hate you," she whispers. "So much."

Kelsey shakes her head. "She does not. She's just upset."

"I hate her!" Charlotte shrieks. "She's trying to ruin my life!"

Needing an escape, I turn on my heel and run out the front door. As soon as the warm air hits my face, I burst into tears. I sit down on the front step and hug my knees to my chest.

What's happening to my life?

I don't recognize it anymore.

It's not fun or silly or hopeful.

It's dreadful and scary and sad.

I cry until I hear the rumble of an engine. A navy-blue Camaro pulls into the driveway and the headlights cut off. The door swings open and Jordy climbs out.

Big, strong, loyal Jordy.

He takes one look at me and strides across the lawn on one mission.

Me.

I cry out when he grabs my arms, hauling me to my feet and into his arms. He hugs me tight, nuzzling my hair. At least if my world is going to break apart, Jordy can hold me together. Gently, he strokes my hair and whispers assurances that I feel more than hear. It isn't until we hear the front door open, that he pulls away.

"How did it go?" Hollis asks, coming down the steps to stand beside us. I can feel the heat of his stare as he takes in how Jordy still grips my hands.

"Fine. I kicked Cuntingham out of the party. His loser friends too." Jordy nods at the house. "How did it go here?"

"Dad's coming," Hollis replies.

"Same dad who ran you out of Vermont?" Jordy asks.

"Same one. He's working on his issues," Hollis says with an exhausted sigh. "Are you going to take Roux home? I wanted to talk to Mom about this stuff. But if you have somewhere to be—"

"I can take her," Jordy grunts out, interrupting him.

Hollis sweeps his eyes over us once more before turning on his heel and going back inside. Jordy tugs me toward the Camaro. He opens the passenger side door and waits for me to get inside before closing it. As I wait for him to join me, I skim my gaze over the expensive interior. I'm not sure I want to know how he got this car.

Probably same way Kayden got his.

Sickness roils in my belly. Jordy gets in the vehicle and fires up the engine. The drive to our apartment at Mike's is only a minute or so away. We remain in silence until he parks in the driveway.

"Come on," he grunts out, reaching over to pat my thigh. "We'll talk inside."

I follow him up to the garage apartment. He makes his way into the kitchen and starts to rummage around.

"Grab a shower, Roux. I'll fix you something to eat."

I nod and escape his intense presence. Everything about Jordy is so heady and intoxicating. He makes me forget about all the bad stuff and only focus on him. Problem is, I can't afford to forget about the bad stuff. I need to fix it.

After a quick shower, I pull on some of Hollis's old sweatpants he gave me and a hoodie that used to be Roan's. The clothes swallow me, but they're comforting and warm. I find Jordy in the kitchen, at the stove, making something that smells too good. No one cooks anything good at our house. Mostly, we reheat whatever stuff Karen or Kelsey make and send our way.

Needing to touch Jordy, I make my way over to him, hugging him from behind. He's tense at first, but relaxes in my arms. I love the way he smells. A hint of citrus mixed with a slight leather scent. Considering I've never seen him with leather or a bag of limes, I wonder if it's just his unique smell. Regardless, it's my favorite. I think it always has been.

"Whatcha cookin'?" I ask, gently running my palm along his hard abs over his T-shirt.

"Grilled gouda and tomato sandwiches."

I scrunch my nose, pulling away to peek around him. "Did you rob a Whole Foods while I was in the shower?"

He laughs. "Nope. Surprisingly, your brother had this stuff on hand. Not sure why since all he knows how to do is make white people grilled cheese he probably learned from his old man."

White people grilled cheese?

Jordy's mom is Mexican, but their dad is white. He's

always claimed his Latino roots only while pretty much ignoring the fact he's a product of both Hispanic and Caucasian parents.

"They've been working out a lot lately and have been eating strange things," I admit. "But Roan still makes the best grilled cheese ever."

Jordy rolls his eyes as he plates two sandwiches. I grab us a couple of cans of Pepsi from the fridge and sit down with him at our small kitchen table. The sandwich is rich and savory, something I wasn't expecting. I groan because it's really good.

"That was an mmmm," Jordy says with a knowing smirk. "Told you."

"Don't tell Roan," I say while chewing. "Keep this between us."

His eyes darken, roaming down my face to my lips. "We'll have to. Otherwise he'll kill me."

We're not talking about grilled gouda and tomatoes anymore.

Conversation ceases to a halt as we eat our late dinner. My mind drifts to Kayden and how he scared the hell out of me. Then, how my fears ratcheted even more seeing Charlotte passed out with three guys around her.

"This was good," I murmur as I stand. "Thank you."

He follows me into the kitchen, also depositing his plate into the sink. I turn and face him, gnawing on my lip. His dark brown eyes skate down to my neck and his nostrils flare. Absently, I touch the tender spot that was worsened by Kayden's brutal grip.

"About last night," Jordy starts. He lets out a frustrated sigh. "I'm sorry. I was drunk, but that's no excuse."

"I liked it," I whisper, stepping closer. "A lot."

His jaw clenches when I tentatively reach up to press my palm to his chest. The thundering of his heart thumps against my hand. He rests his own hand over mine.

"It shouldn't have happened for so many reasons, Roux. So many reasons."

Stung by his words, I frown. "What reasons?"

"For one, you're underage. I could go back to prison for what we did."

Cold dread runs through my system. "We didn't have sex," I croak out. "Cuddling isn't against the law."

"No, but the things we did…"

"We didn't even kiss," I hiss. "Stop it. You're doing it again. Retreating into yourself in an effort to save me. I'm sick of it."

I start to pull away, but his hand flies to my hip, pulling me flush against him. His fingers thread into my damp hair and he tugs my head back.

"I can't have you, Roux." He leans down and presses the softest kiss to my lips. "At least not yet."

He didn't say never.

I part my lips, begging for more than a peck, but he pulls his head back. A storm of emotions brew in his dark eyes. I can feel how much he's attracted to me by how his erection presses into me. But this boy has the strength of a saint and he doesn't act on any of it.

"When?" I whisper.

"You know when."

Eighteen.

March, not August.

I'll die from want.

"I broke up with Kayden." I study his face for a reaction. He gives off nothing aside from the flash of triumph in his eyes. It makes my heart flutter.

"He didn't seem like someone who'd been broken up with when I saw him."

I shudder, remembering what Kayden said to me. How he'd hurt me and told me we weren't broken up. "He said no," I admit. "A fight broke out and then I left."

"If you want to break up with him," Jordy growls, "that's your choice, not his. What the fuck is his problem?"

"I don't know, but he's not the same guy I started dating in March."

"Because he's a fucking thug."

"Which makes me scared for you," I breathe, my eyes burning with tears. "What if he…"

"He won't do shit to me," Jordy assures me in his usual arrogant tone. "I won't allow it."

I hope that's true. I don't want to worry about Kayden's jealousy getting out of control and him hurting Jordy. I would die if something happened to Jordy.

"I love you," I blurt out.

He grins, boyish and handsome. "Love you too, Little Hoodlum."

But not like he thinks. I loved him growing up like he was a brother. Not anymore. The moment I saw him behind that glass at the prison, something inside me shifted. I haven't been able to think of anyone, especially Kayden, since.

Only Jordy.

And when he showed up at the river, I'd been completely consumed by him. Waiting until I turn eighteen to see if we can pursue this burning desire between us feels like an eternity. I waited three years, though, for him to get out of prison. What's seven more months to have him fully?

"Charlotte hates me," I tell him, resting my cheek on his chest. "She told me as much."

"She'll get over it."

"No, she won't."

He strokes my hair. "If your brother can get over the fact I nearly drowned his then-wannabe-boyfriend, then Charlotte can get over you trying to protect her from a gang of douche-bags. Just give her some time."

I think about going to school next week for my senior year and not having my best friends by my side. Without Charlotte and Kayden, everything will be like it was before the English family moved to Hood River.

Lonely.

Desolate.

Horrible.

"I don't want to be alone," I murmur, mostly to myself.

"You're not alone. You have me. You always have."

CHAPTER THIRTEEN

Jordy

THE HAUNT'S "WHY ARE YOU SO COLD?" BLARES through the AirPods Cal gave me. I'm thankful to drown out the noise of the cooks at El Juarez, who have been talking nonstop about pussy. Don't get me wrong, I'm a pussy man, but I don't want to hear about it twenty-four-fucking-seven.

Especially when all I can think about is one girl.

And just how sweet her pussy will be.

One day.

Fuck.

Roan is going to murder me.

Shoving those thoughts out of my mind, I spray down another plate. This job isn't so bad. It's my first full week here. Mondays are slow, but Tuesdays are their biggest night for Taco Tuesday. All week, I either worked or hung around Roan's place, watching movies with Hollis and Roux since it was their last week before school started back up. I'd managed to avoid any babysitting jobs for baby Ramirez and didn't have to see Juno or Renaldo. I also didn't see much of Roan, because he works his ass off, though we did manage to hit the gym a couple of times together with Cal and Terrence before they fucked back off to college.

I still can't believe Roan's a fireman.

Pride courses through me. For as much shit that Roan has gone through in his life, he deserves to be happy. And if putting out fires with the guy who's banging his husband's mom makes him happy, then I'm happy.

My phone buzzes in my pocket. I dry my hands off to check my messages.

Juno: Kayden's meeting some Rockford guys today after school. Traitors. They think they deserve to wear red. Make sure he doesn't get jumped by those sketchy motherfuckers.

I groan because I fucking hate watching this kid. But it's better than the alternative—chopping cars—and they're leaving the Hoodlums out of it. That's all that matters.

Cal texts me next, chasing my bad mood away.

Cal: Terrence doesn't think I can bag the dean's daughter. I told him not to insult me.

Me: How old is the dean's daughter?

Cal: Legal. You know I won't touch them unless they can vote.

Unlike me.

Fuck.

Me: Don't die.

Cal: I'll try not to. T and I made it back to campus. Hit us up though if you need us. We'll be there in a few hours. Hoodlums always have each other's backs.

I send him a thumbs-up emoji—which he hates with a fucking passion—that earns me about fifty middle finger

112

emojis. I'm still laughing and about to pocket my phone when someone taps my shoulder.

I'm tense as I turn, only to deflate at seeing the owner.

Bob Gonzalez.

His real name is Roberto, but he told me when I started, he likes to go by Bob because no one fucks up how to pronounce it. I can't fucking say Bob with a straight face, though. Bob is a guy who wears a brown suit, has a comb-over, and sells insurance.

Not a Mexican with face tattoos, a few gold teeth, and a gray and black beard that goes to his goddamn belly button.

"What's up, *Bob?*" I smirk because I can't fucking help it.

He grunts, swatting me upside the head and knocking one of the AirPods into the floor. "Don't be a smartass, kid. Someone's here to see you."

My first thought is elation.

Roux.

Then irritation because I don't want the cooks looking at her.

"A girl?"

Bob snorts. "No. A cop."

Oh, fuck no.

"I don't do cops," I snarl, picking up the AirPod and pocketing it.

"Calm your tits, boy," Bob says with a boisterous laugh. "He's a regular. Says he knows you. Just wanted to see how you're doing."

My eyes drift to the loser on the grill who's staring off into space, probably dreaming about pussy. Frederick, I think his name is. "He's about to burn that meat."

Sure enough, he starts to curse when the meat smokes. Bob

grumbles in irritation, stalking over to Frederick to do damage control. I walk over to the door into the dining room of El Juarez and peek through the small round window.

As soon as I see him, I recognize him.

Captain Scott Fitzgerald and Officer Jessica Kline.

They were two people who testified on my behalf at my trial. If it weren't for Fitzgerald calling me off the ledge that night, I might have turned that gun on myself. Kline was the one who pulled Roux out of there, promising me she'd be safe. I owe it to them to at least say hi.

With a sigh, I take out my other AirPod and shove it into my pocket before pushing through the door. As soon as Fitzgerald sees me, he grins, motioning at his table for me to take a seat. I pull a chair out, flip it around, and sit backward to face them.

"Hey," I grunt.

"Good to see you, kid," Fitzgerald says. "How are you holding up now that you're back in the real world?"

Working for a gang and almost fucked a teenager.

"Fine." I force a smile and nod at Kline. "Officer Kline."

She laughs. "It's lieutenant now."

"Congrats on the raise. It's great seeing you two and all, but this is my first full week on the job. *Bob* back there might be pissed if I'm out here shooting the shit while on the clock."

Fitzgerald chuckles. "Roberto and I go way back. He's a cool guy. Someone you can trust." He cocks his head to the side. "Do you have anyone like that, son?"

I thought I could trust my parents, but they've both ghosted me since I've been released, which feels fair since I did the same thing to them.

At least I have the Hoodlums.

Even the little one.

"Yeah, I have people."

He nods in approval. "I spoke to Samantha."

I stiffen, my eyes dragging through the restaurant of people to see who's around. Fitzgerald, the smart bastard, picks up on it immediately.

"I've already made sure we were safe to talk candidly," he assures me, though he lowers his voice. "She said you have an appointment with Tom."

My heart hammers in my chest. I hate that Samantha runs her mouth so much, but she's my attorney. Everything she does is to help me.

I give him a one-shouldered shrug. I'm not admitting to anything.

Fitzgerald's lips press into a firm line as he studies me. He has that way about him. With his salt-and-pepper hair and concerned eyes, he plays the part of worried dad well. But he's not my dad. My dad is working himself into a grave at the tire factory, trying to forget his son killed four men and went to prison for it.

"You're not alone, Jordy. You never have been. When you finally realize that and start to rely on other people, you'll see. It can only go up from here."

I'm barely out of the pen and I'm getting in fights, driving a stolen car, and am so close to sticking my dick in Roux.

Shit can only go down from here.

"Break time's over," I grunt, giving them both a nod. "See you around."

"You will."

His promise makes my blood curdle. The last thing I need is a cop trying to be buddy-buddy with me. I don't even want to know what Renaldo would do.

Fuck.

Why can't my life just be normal?

I'm minding my own business, pulling hot plates out of the dishwasher, when Bob checks in on me again.

"Frederick quit," Bob says, scowling. "What do you know about cooking?"

"A lot more than doing dishes."

His eyes skim over my work. I spent the better part of my first day of work last week fixing the disorganization the last dumbass who worked here left for me.

"You ever cooked on a big grill?"

"No, but I cooked at OSP for whiney-ass inmates. Also been cooking with my mom since I was little."

He nods. "You're fired from dishwashing and hired as a cook. Tomorrow grab an apron and shadow me. I need someone reliable."

How he knows I'm reliable after one week of work is beyond me. I do, however, need this job to keep my parole officer happy.

"Yeah, man, I can do it."

He opens his mouth to say something when we're interrupted by a waitress named Sheila. "We need a mop!"

Bob slaps me on the shoulder. "Today you're still a dishwasher. Go clean that shit up."

I roll my eyes at him but do as I'm told. Once I have the mop, I saunter back out into the dining room. The lunch rush is over, so the crowd is thinning out. A brunette woman, sitting in a booth with her back to me, is fussing over a toddler in a booster seat beside her. An empty glass sits on the table and the mess has been cleared away there by Sheila. The floor is still soaked.

With my head down, I start mopping. The woman gasps, drawing my attention to her.

"Jordy?"

I let my eyes skim over her face. "Sidney."

She's stiff as she takes in my appearance. I'm not exactly a revered hero in this town. Especially not to her. I used to be such a dick to Sidney.

"Got knocked up, I see." I guess I still am a dick to Sidney.

She scowls at me. Sidney's always been beautiful with her bright green eyes and shiny brown hair. She's also a bit of a skank, especially where my friends are concerned.

"Don't be rude. I'm married. We have a son together." She crosses her arms over her tits that have grown. It's then I realize she's barely showing, pregnant again.

"Who the fuck married you?"

"Fuckfuckfuck," the little kid parrots.

Whoops.

"Sebban, sweetie, that's a no-no word."

"Nononono."

"Who's the dad?" I know the kid sure as fuck isn't mine. I never fucked Sidney, though she tried to get me there on more than one occasion. He's not dark-skinned like Terrence. But those eyes…

"Gio," she says with a huff. "Duh."

"Hmph."

"Don't hmph me, Jordy. I see you judging me. I'm not the same person as before." It's then I take in her appearance. She was always trash like the rest of us. Poor as fuck, but at least had good looks on her side. Now, she really is different. Seemingly more mature and put together.

"Gio took his certifications. He's selling insurance now. Does really well. If you need car insurance, he could hook you up." She sighs. "He wanted to go into finance and go to college, but with the baby, that wasn't an option."

"Does the nerd still drive a minivan?"

She rolls her eyes but lets a smirk tug at her lips. "God no. I made him trade that in the second we were married." A genuine smile tugs at her lips. "He's a good dad, you know. I know you guys used to give him hell in high school, but Gio's a good man."

Guilt niggles at me. We were all such dicks to poor Sidney. All she wanted was attention and for someone to love her. None of the Hoodlums had it in us to love her. Glad the nerd stepped up. She's not a bad person and it looks like he really pulled the good parts out of her.

"Stay-at-home mom?"

She bristles. "Yes. Have a problem with that? I want to go to dental school to be a hygienist, but Sebban needs me. He's busy and likes to hide. I don't think a babysitter could keep an eye on him like I do."

"My mom stayed home with us when we were little. Not knocking it, Sid." I finish mopping and then lean the handle against a vacant table. "I'm sorry I was a dick to you back then."

Both of her perfectly sculpted brows fly up and Sebban starts chanting my newest fuck-up.

"You're sorry?" She laughs, shaking her head as though she can't believe it. "I guess what they say is true. Prison really can change a man."

"What eye color does Gio have?" I ask, boring my stare into her.

Her face blanches. "Brown. Why?"

"No reason."

"The kid's not yours, Jordy," she hisses. "We didn't screw. Stop being so defensive."

I steal one more glance at the kid. "Thank fuck. I do not need a kid right now."

Sebban grins at me and then throws his sippy cup at me. Little bastard is nothing but an ankle biter and already sticking up for his mom whether he realizes it or not. Good kid.

"You should come to Campfire Chaos," I tell her. "Catch up with the Hoodlums. Like old times."

Her face burns bright red and she scowls. "I'm a married woman with responsibilities now. I'll pass."

"Consider it. I bet Roan and the guys miss you," I challenge.

"I don't miss them," she throws back.

I leave her be.

For now.

God only knows I have enough shit on my plate.

CHAPTER FOURTEEN

Roux

HATE SCHOOL.

Always have, always will.

When I finally manage to escape this prison, I won't be going to college. Roan will freak, but I don't care. He knows how hard school has always been for me. It's not that I don't try, because I really do. It's because my brain muddles when it's time to make sense of what I've learned. If the teachers would give me my tests verbally, I'd probably ace them all. There's just something about staring at the paper that gets confusing.

Karen—or Principal Frazier to everyone else—says I have a learning disability, but I even shut down when I've been tested for that. She's made special allowances now that I'm at the high school. I'm given reduced homework compared to the others. I'm allowed breaks during tests and can ask questions. All sorts of crutches to help me pass.

And I still barely keep my head above water.

My senior year will be more of the same.

"Miss Hirsch," Mr. Ewing says when the final bell rings. "Can you stay back for a minute?"

I nod and then skim my eyes over to where Charlotte is sitting. She won't look at me or speak to me. We're going on over a week of not talking. It's not a phase. She won't get over it like Kelsey thinks. It guts me.

Today, Charlotte was glued to Ryan and his inner circle. A girl named Rena has buddied up to her. Isaiah and Gunther—the two guys also messing with her that night—hang out with her and Ryan like nothing ever happened.

I guess I shouldn't have butted in after all.

The class leaves, all of them eager to go home. It makes me wonder if Kayden will be in the parking lot when I finally make it out of here. He'd tried to pick me up for school this morning, but I ignored him to climb into Hollis's car. I know Kayden was pissed, but we're broken up. No matter how hard he tries to deny it.

Mr. Ewing clears his throat, drawing my attention his way. He's a few years older than Roan. Definitely cute if you're into the tall, lean-built, nerdy professor type. I like him because he loves poetry and has already assigned us some poems to read. I may fail his class, but at least it'll be one of the few classes I'll enjoy.

"I spoke to Ms. Frazier," he says as he stands from his desk and walks over to where I'm sitting. He sits on the edge of the desk across from mine. "She said you needed some modifications for my class."

I nod, no longer embarrassed by the spiel. This haze has followed me through my entire school career. "They usually give me extra time to take the tests or let me ask questions." I puff out a sigh. "Though it'd be easier if you'd read the questions to me and just let me answer them." I let out a laugh because that's something they never allow.

"Okay."

I jerk my head up. "Okay?"

"I can do that. Not during class because of the other students, but we can make arrangements for verbal testing after class since this is the last period of the day."

I grin at him. "Really? Thank you!"

"Your GPA isn't anything to write home about," he jokes, "but I read what you turned in today. It was a good poem."

"I love poetry," I say with a sigh. "I love that it doesn't seem to have order or make sense. Kind of like my mind. I have tons of it stuck to the walls in my room."

He smiles. "That's something we can relate on. I started a book of poems."

"Like Atticus?"

"If only I could be that successful. Maybe you could give me some feedback one day."

I'm shocked. Teachers never want feedback from me. Mostly I'm an annoyance—someone they have to work extra hard for.

"Mr. Ewing, I'd love that."

"Call me Wes." He smirks. "When we're alone, of course. The other students have different rules."

His words make my stomach twist in a strange way and I don't know why. He's just being friendly. Still, I have a small bout of nerves suddenly.

"Okay," I mutter. "Sounds good, er, Wes."

He chuckles, scratching at his jaw. "Don't sound so horrified. I'm just a regular guy like your brother. How is Roan these days? He played basketball with my brother Brody."

"He's well. Mostly, he works for the tire factory, but he also volunteers for the fire department. Married now."

"Married, huh? I never took him for the type to settle down with some girl, but I guess when you find the one—"

"A man."

His brows lift. "Oh?"

"They're happy."

"That's all that matters." He nods and motions to the door. "Your boyfriend is waiting."

I snap my head to find Kayden loitering, looking like I kicked his puppy. Grinding my teeth, I gather my bag and shake my head.

"He's not my boyfriend."

Mr. Ewing—Wes—flashes me a knowing smile. "See you tomorrow, Miss Hirsch."

"Roux." I smile and give him a small wave. "Bye, Mr. Ewing."

As I make my way over to Kayden, he's glaring at Wes. I roll my eyes, shoving past him and into the hall. Ignoring him, I head for the stairwell.

"Roux!" Kayden calls out. "Jesus, slow down. I want to talk to you—to apologize."

"There's nothing to talk about," I grumble, taking the stairs down quickly.

He grabs my arm, stopping me. "Roux-Roux." His lips are pouted out and his brows are furled. This act used to work. It got him his way with nearly everything where I was concerned. "Please don't shut me out."

I scowl, shifting on my feet. "What?"

"Forgive me."

"It's not that simple."

"But it is, baby. I was fucked up that night. I didn't mean to get so rough with you. That party was dangerous and I let it get out of control. It wasn't safe for you to be there." He steps closer, running his knuckle along the side of my throat that no longer bears bruising or hickeys. "I'm so sorry."

"Apology accepted. Can I go now?"

He runs his fingers through his hair, messing it up. "I want us to get back together."

"Look," I say with a sigh. "You need a girlfriend who'll be intimate with you. I'm just not ready for that."

Never mind the fact that I won't ever be ready.

With him.

Now Jordy, on the other hand...

I can wait for Jordy. He'll be worth the wait.

"I don't need that," he murmurs, dipping low so his face is near mine. "Just you, Roux-Roux. Kissing you is enough."

He starts to kiss me, but I pull away. I expect anger since he's been acting like a twat lately. Instead, his features crumble.

"I really fucked this up." His voice is hoarse, like he might cry. "Roux, baby, let me make it up to you."

"Kayden," I say in exasperation. "I need space." I've barely made it to the bottom of the stairs, when he grabs my hand, pulling me to him. I jerk my hand free, but he's undeterred, stepping closer.

"Fine. I'll give you space, but then I'm going to win you back. You'll see. I can be romantic." He flashes me a flirtatious grin that used to make me weak. "Prepare to fall back in love with me."

He walks backward down the now-empty hall, grinning at me. Eventually, he makes it to the outside doors and leaves. I let out a heavy sigh filled with frustration. It's then I get the creepy sensation I'm being watched.

I swivel around, looking down both hallways and back up the stairs. Nothing. No one. I'm about to head out the door when someone coughs. A man. I creep over to Mrs. Duffy's classroom. It's empty, with the lights out, and she's no longer in it.

"You're not supposed to be in there," I tell the man who's standing near the whiteboard with his back to me.

He's definitely a teacher, I think, based on his dressy suit. The guy is probably Mike's age. Older, but not too old. He checks his watch and turns toward me, smiling. "Pardon me."

"Are you a teacher?"

His lips thin out. "No."

"A parent?"

"No."

"You're a cop," I breathe out.

He blinks hard at me. "I'm not a cop."

"What's your name?"

His jaw clenches. "Tom."

"You're being creepy, Tom."

At this, he laughs. "Duly noted." He cocks his head to the side. "I couldn't help but notice you having a fight with your boyfriend."

"He's not my boyfriend."

"Er, friend. Are you okay?"

"I'm fine. He just thinks we're something we're not."

"I see. Take care, miss. Stay away from pushy assholes." He smirks. "And creeps."

"I'm trying," I grumble, "but you guys are so plentiful in this town."

"I'm not from this town," he argues, a smile in his voice.

"Maybe you should go back where you came from."

"You're not as weak as I thought." He takes a step toward me and I take a step back.

"I don't know who's been telling you I'm weak or how you even think you know me, but that's super creepy."

"I'll work on my creepiness. I didn't realize it was so obvious."

I've backed myself almost to the bank of lockers. Tom remains hidden inside the dark classroom.

"Very obvious, but I think God made creeps be obvious, so people like me could stay away."

"Pretend you never saw me, Roux."

I cringe at him knowing my name.

Weirded out by that fact, I take off running down the hall, bursting out the side door. No one chases after me, but try telling my racing heart that. I run my way over to a crowd of kids that have formed in the parking lot around two cars. Kayden's and someone I don't know.

Kayden's lost his T-shirt and stands there in a tank, his arms spread open in a taunting way. Hard to believe just a few minutes before, he was giving me the saddest eyes ever and trying his damnedest to romance me. Now he's back to being a thug.

No, thank you.

I scan the parking lot for Hollis. He said he'd pick me up, but I don't see his familiar purple Mustang. My eyes do, however, stop on a navy-blue Camaro.

"Boo."

I nearly jump out of my skin. "Jordy!"

He sidles up beside me, careful not to touch me. It's been driving me crazy. Aside from a few hugs this week, he's kept his distance.

I can wait.

I can wait.

I brush my fingers against his. Apparently I can't wait.

"I missed you." I peek up at him and smile. "How was work?"

He gives me a lazy, half smile. "Missed you too, Little Hoodlum. Work was fine. Got a raise and a promotion."

"What?!" I squeal and throw myself into his arms, uncaring if anyone sees. "That's amazing!"

He tries to shrug it off. "It's just from dishwasher to cook."

"But you love to cook." I grin, inhaling him. "This is exciting."

His dark eyes roam down to my lips. "I guess it is."

"Tonight, we're celebrating."

He pulls away and turns his attention on the crowd. It's then I realize he wasn't supposed to pick me up.

"You're here to give me a ride?" I ask, frowning. "Where's Hollis?"

"Nah, just a job." He nods at Kayden. "Make sure his dumb ass doesn't get shot."

He ended up telling me this week that Renaldo is making him keep tabs on Kayden. I don't like it a bit, but it's better than chopping cars, which he told me was the alternative.

The guy Kayden was taunting seems to back down, nodding at him. They do the dumb guy thing where they sort of shake hands and sort of hug. Then, the guy leaves. Kayden then starts laughing with some of his friends.

"I think he's fine. Want to get snow cones? The stand will only be open a couple more weeks." I'm already texting Hollis to let him know Jordy's picking me up.

His eyes dart to the dispersing group for a second before latching back on mine. "Yeah, let's get snow cones. He can handle himself."

Jordy motions for me to walk with him. His hair is still wet from his shower after work and he smells strong like limes. I wonder if he tastes tangy too.

I'm just about to climb into Jordy's Camaro when I feel eyes on me. Not creepy ones. Angry ones. I turn in time to see the look of disgust on Kayden's face when he sees who I'm getting in the car with.

Screw him.

Jordy is Roan's best friend. I have nothing to feel guilty over.

My mind can't help but wonder, though. If Kayden gets super pissed about me being in the same vicinity as Jordy, I can only imagine what sort of meltdown he'll have when I finally get Jordy to kiss me and claim me as his.

I have seven months to worry about that.

Maybe by then he'll have a new girlfriend.

If not, I'm in serious trouble.

CHAPTER
FIFTEEN

Jordy

ONE OF MY FAVORITE MEMORIES OF ROUX WAS when she was just a kid and we all went out for snow cones after swimming all day. Cal and Terrence were being dipshits, shoving each other, and Roan was brooding over his mom. Roux was happy as a lark with her grape snow cone.

Until Cal shoved Terrence into Roux and the snow cone splattered all over the sidewalk.

She'd tried so hard not to cry, though her bottom lip wobbled hard. Roan offered her his, but he's the only one who likes the pineapple flavored one. Both Terrence's and Cal's were nearly gone. And mine was cherry.

But that day, I handed her my snow cone and we kept on walking. She didn't gripe about cherry, even though it wasn't her favorite, and quietly ate it. When we made it to the bus stop, she hugged me and said cherry was her new favorite. I laughed it off, but it was the truth. From then on out, she never got grape again. Always cherry.

Seeing her sit across from me at the picnic table in front

of Slim's Shady Cones, I can't help but notice how much she's evolved into the woman she is today. Sure, there's an innocence in her big amber eyes, but I don't think that'll go away with age. It's just a part of her. One of the reasons I'm so drawn to protecting her—to protecting that innocence. Aside from not being eighteen yet and somewhat sheltered by her brother, Roux is very much a woman. And I'm not just talking physical appearances, though when I saw her the first time after three years at OHP, I was absolutely drawn to her womanly body.

Something about her calls to the male parts of me that crave to pull her to me and keep her there. She's not a piece of ass to be used and tossed away. Roux owns so many bits of my heart that it may as well belong to her. What started as a bond between friends—albeit an age gap—has evolved into something deeper. Something physical. Romantic.

I feel like shit for thinking it, but Roux and I have been tumbling toward an "us" since I saw her for the first time in the flesh after my release. An instant chemistry. A connection that, threaded with our already unique bond, has become something fiery and unstoppable. I want to pin her down, strip her, and claim her as mine. It takes everything in me to hold back from doing just that.

"What?" Roux asks, one corner of her lips quirking up on one side. "Do I have something on my face?"

She absently darts her cherry-stained tongue out to lick across her bottom lip. I track the movement as curls of desire wind their way straight to my cock.

"Nope," I grunt. "Everything looks perfect."

Her cheeks blush and she smiles.

I'm craving to pull her over the table and into my lap when my phone rings, thwarting my nefarious agenda.

"Hello?"

"Hey, sweetie," Samantha purrs into the phone. "What are you doing?"

I glance over at Roux and let out a sigh. "Nothing. What's up?"

"I need to see you."

"When?"

"Right now." She lets out a breathy laugh.

"I can't. I'm busy." I zero in on the way Roux wraps her lips around the spoon. "Really busy." Because I could watch this all damn day.

"Doing what?" Samantha huffs. "Don't worry, I'll meet you at your place."

She hangs up and I pocket my phone, unease slicking over me like oil.

"Is everything okay? Who was that?" Roux asks as she finishes up her snow cone.

"My attorney, Samantha."

"What did she want?"

"To see me."

"About what?"

I shrug. "You ready to go?"

She frowns at my blowing her off but nods. We toss our trash and climb back into the Camaro. In ten minutes, we're back at her apartment. I can tell she's pissed because she bolts from the car, storming up the steps. I climb out and stalk after her. She's barely made it inside the apartment and dumped her bag when I grab her from behind, pulling her to my chest.

"What's wrong?" I demand, nuzzling my nose in her hair.

She shrugs, giving me a taste of my own medicine.

"Did it ever occur to you," I murmur as I pull her hair off

her shoulder and swoop it around to the other side so I can have access to her neck, "that I don't tell you stuff because it's better for you that way?"

"Did it ever occur to you that maybe I don't want to be left out of the loop when it comes to you?" she bites back.

I press a kiss to her neck. My hands settle at her waist. "I just want to keep you safe."

She swivels in my arms so that her perky tits are pressed to my chest. Her palms skim over my shoulders, up my neck, and into my hair where she threads her fingers.

"Maybe I don't want to be safe. Maybe I just want to be with you and know all the dirty, ugly details." She pulls my head down until we're just inches apart. "I'm a big girl, Jordy. I can handle a helluva lot more than you think I can."

Fuck, I want to kiss her.

So much.

My gaze skims over her wet, red lips, wondering how she would taste if I devoured her right now. *Like cherries.* "Roux..."

She stands on her toes, her lips brushing against mine for a ghost of a peck. I slide my fingers into her hair, angling her head to where I can finally claim her. It's not smart. It's really fucking stupid. But right now? I don't care. Her lips part and I meet them with my own lips. I don't have time to swipe my tongue across hers when someone bangs on the door.

Roux squeaks out, nearly jumping out of her skin. I let out a groan as I pull away from my girl to answer the door.

"Samantha," I state, both annoyed and relieved she stopped what was quickly happening yet again between Roux and me.

"Jordy, honey," she greets, flashing me a wide grin. "We need to talk."

I run my fingers through my hair and sigh. "Sure. Come in."

Roux comes to stand beside me, making the hairs on my arms stand on end. It's like she's always charged with electricity and I can't help but get shocked by her. Absently, I place my hand on the small of her back.

"Would you like something to drink?" I ask Samantha.

Samantha's smile falters as her eyes dart back and forth between me and Roux. "I'm okay. Thank you." She pins me with a firm stare. "We need to speak. In private."

I don't want Roux to leave my side, but this is a necessary conversation with Samantha.

"Roux…" I start, my voice gruff.

"I get it," Roux snips, shouldering past me. "For my own protection."

Roux storms out of the house, slamming the door hard behind her. Samantha's sculpted brows fly up and her lips thin out.

"What?" I grunt, hating her uncanny ability to tear apart what's going on inside my mind.

"I'll take that drink now. Make it something hard."

I stalk into the kitchen and start flinging open cabinets looking for Roan's liquor stash. When I come up empty, I settle for a couple of beers and pop the caps off. I exit the kitchen to find Samantha perched at the kitchen table, opening her laptop and already making herself at home.

"What's so important it couldn't wait?" I demand, setting a beer down and pushing it toward her. I sit opposite of her and glower her way.

"I thought it was just prison that made you grumpy. Turns out, it's your personality." She laughs, making her boobs, which are nearly spilling from her blouse, jiggle. "Oh, Jesus, Jordy. Take a joke already."

"I'm not in a joking mood." I cross my arms over my chest, my eyes drifting to the window, searching for Roux. "Is this going to take long?"

She sips her beer before setting it down and tapping her nails on the glass bottle. "Before we get to what I came here for, I want to know something."

"You know everything there is to know about me." I take a long pull of my beer as I give her a one-shouldered shrug.

"Are you fucking the teenager?"

I choke on my beer, sending some of it running down my chin. I slam the bottle down on the table and wipe my face off with my palm. "What the fuck, Samantha?"

Irritation flashes in her eyes. "If you are, that's a problem. Really huge problem."

"I'm not." But I want to be.

"See," she snips, "the way you say it, I don't exactly believe it."

"It's none of your business."

"It's absolutely my business. You're my client, Jordy."

"I'm not fucking her," I growl.

"If you were, you can't ever do it again." Her words are firm and commanding. "If you haven't, don't. And if you're thinking about it, stop. You thought killing four men to defend that girl was bad? Try being an ex-convict who sleeps with an underage girl. You won't be a hero, Jordy. You'll be a villain. Any progress you made to get here"—she waves a hand in the air—"will be destroyed."

"I said I'm not fucking her." My words are filled with venom. "Don't mention it again."

She purses her lips and shakes her head. "One more thing and I'll let it go."

I narrow my eyes, my jaw clenching.

"When it does happen, and for your sake, I really hope it's after she turns eighteen, understand that she's young. Girls like her are wishy-washy. They want what they can't have. Right now, that's you. And after she moves on, because she will, I implore you to not lose your shit over it."

"She's my best friend's little sister," I say out loud, because I need to fucking hear it.

"And, unfortunately, that won't matter."

She's right. It won't.

I was so close to devouring my sweet little Roux only moments ago. It will happen. My thread of self-control is too thin.

"You don't know me," I utter.

"I know your type," Samantha says with a tired sigh. "You forget I'm a criminal attorney. I've seen and heard it all."

"I can't mess up. I have to be here for them. I won't touch Roux."

Lies.

If Samantha hadn't shown up, I would've already had Roux beneath me whimpering.

"You're going to have to try harder at convincing both of us. I'm not the only one who doesn't believe you." She shakes her head, a frown of disappointment on her face. "Moving on. Let's get to this."

CHAPTER SIXTEEN

Roux

HIS ATTORNEY IS HOT.

Long, tanned legs. Silky blond hair. Big tits.

And a bitch.

I could see the way she looked at Jordy. As though he were a bone with some meat she wanted to suck off. After the soft kiss we'd shared, I was certain things would have gone down differently than they did.

That I'd be a part of his world like I always wanted to be.

Instead, he sent me away.

Dismissed me so he could talk to his attorney. They're probably getting naked as we speak. I let out a snort at my poutiness. Jordy is a lot of things—angry, fierce, vengeful—but he's not cruel. He wouldn't lead me on just to fuck his attorney when she showed up. I'm just pissed that he sent me away. It means he's still protecting me, and we both know what happened the last time he tried to protect me.

A car turns onto our street and heads toward our house. It's unfamiliar—a black luxury vehicle. Maybe a BMW, though I can't tell from this far away. It pulls into the driveway, stopping just a few feet from where I'm sitting on the bottom step outside our garage apartment.

Three car doors open and I recognize everyone immediately. First, I see Hollis climb out. Behind him, Penny follows, though I wish it were Charlotte. It's the driver who surprises me.

"Mr. English?" I say, rising to my feet.

I've only met their dad a few times. He's always been nothing but business when he visits. I know the girls have gone to stay with him at the hotel before whenever he's in Hood River. They usually leave with shopping bags full of gifts. The last time he came to visit, Charlotte left with a cherry-red Audi TT RS. I can tell Penny's already sporting new tennis shoes and Hollis has a new hoodie.

Must be nice to have a dad who spoils you rotten.

"Hello, Roux," Mr. English says as he approaches. "I've told you to call me Garrett."

"Sorry," I mumble. "Where's Charlotte?"

Garrett's jaw clenches. He and Hollis exchange a look I'm not meant to interpret. "She's off with her boyfriend."

Penny makes a motion with her fist and mouth like she's mimicking a blow job. My cheeks blaze with heat as I stifle an inappropriate giggle.

"Roan's not here," I tell Garrett.

"We're here to talk to Jordy," Hollis chimes in, tugging at a strand of my hair. "Is he up there?"

"With Samantha," I say icily.

Garrett's brows lift and Penny snorts out a laugh.

"His attorney," Hollis tells his dad. "Come on."

Penny and I follow Garrett and Hollis up the steps. At one time, Garrett was bigger than Hollis, but ever since Roan and Hollis got on their freak gym kick, my brother-in-law has bulked up. Garrett is handsome for an older man and could probably land someone like Samantha if he wanted, but he's clearly still pining over their mom.

Good luck, buddy.

Kelsey's boyfriend—and my legal guardian, Mike—is obsessed with her. Spoils her rotten with dinners and presents and stupidly sweet gestures. Garrett, according to Hollis, cheated on Kelsey. His loss, too. Kelsey is kind and gorgeous and the mother of his children. Garrett really screwed up.

We make it to the top of the steps and enter the apartment. My eyes skim right over to where Samantha is leaned across the table showing Jordy something on her computer. The way she looks at him grosses me out.

"Oh," Samantha says, jerking back. "We have visitors."

Jordy's dark eyes land on his favorite place—my lips—and then lazily skim down my front, leaving fire in the wake of his stare.

Garrett introduces himself to Samantha as Jordy stands. He makes a beeline over to me, his body thrumming with the need to touch me. I reach for him and he moves like he might take my hand. At the last second, his hand flies up to rub at the back of his neck.

"Girls," Garrett says, cutting through the crackling energy between Jordy and me. "Can you run along so the adults can talk?"

Jordy winces and I recoil, fuming at his words.

"I'm staying," I bite out.

Garrett frowns, shaking his head. "Go to your room."

I gape at him in shock. Samantha wears a satisfied smirk. Hollis has the sense to look guilty but doesn't intervene.

138

When my eyes land back on Jordy's, his eyes take on that dead look he gets when he shuts me out.

"Come on," Penny says, taking my hand.

"I want to stay," I whisper to him.

"Go with Penny." He nods at my bedroom before turning his back on me.

Fire bursts up inside of me, but before I have a chance to yell at him, Penny is dragging me through the living room. She has to shove me into the room and then closes the door behind her. Hot tears of anger flood my eyes, streaking down my cheeks.

"Seriously?" I hiss. "They act like we're little kids!"

"Daddy's meetings are always boring," Penny says. "Trust me, we dodged a bullet."

She nosily starts picking up picture frames, reading poetry pieces, and peeking in drawers. That's Penny for you. Always lurking and noticing things.

"Is Char really with Ryan?" I demand.

"Yeah. He's such a dick, too. No one but me ever sees it either."

"I see it," I offer. "You think she'll ever break up with him?"

Penny's features darken. "Right. As if the all mighty Ryan Cunningham would allow that. Oh, heavens," she drawls, "what will the other policemen think if Papa Cunningham's son gets dumped by the school's queen? What a scandal!"

"Why do they even care?" I mumble, irritated over the whole situation.

"Same reason they cared back home. The popular people have to mate with each other. It's some weird evolutional bullshit. Makes the merry world go round."

"Hmph."

She laughs and it's not a usual sound from Penny. "I'm the grumpy one, not you. They really have your panties in a wad today."

"I hate that Jordy treats me like a kid."

"You are a kid."

"Shut up. I am not."

"You're literally seventeen, Roux."

"I lost the opportunity to be a kid when my mom decided heroin needed her more than her children," I bite out. "I grew up a long time ago. Not all of us have a rich daddy we can bat our lashes at to get what we want."

"Right. You're an adult. Totally sold me after that toddler fit you just threw." She smirks. "Seriously."

I hate when she's right.

"Have you ever wanted someone you're not supposed to have?" I ask, frowning.

She laughs. "I once had a sex dream about the black Hoodlum."

"You had a sex dream about Terrence?" My eyes are wide with shock.

She rolls her eyes as she sits on my bed. "It wasn't like *that*."

"Fine. Tell me about how it was then."

"He was fucking some blond chick on the bleachers while I was playing basketball. They were being so noisy. I kept missing the baskets and I was so pissed at him. I'd just stormed his way, ready to throw the damn ball at his face, when a little kid came running out of nowhere. I got distracted helping the kid walk down the steps. When we reached the bottom, the blond chick was gone and Terrence was up there watching me." She shivers. "Kinda creepy, huh?"

I nod. "That's not technically a sex dream, though."

"There was sex in it. I was there. It was a dream."

"Hmph."

"You're full of those today," Penny says, her stare roaming over me. "Are you crushing over Jordy?"

I wince at her words.

This thing with Jordy is so much more than a crush. It's not unrequited, either. It's bone-deep. Maddening. Burning through my veins like liquid fire. I can taste the want for him on my tongue. The buzzing need vibrates continuously through me.

It's not a crush.

It's an annihilation of my emotions.

"Oh," Penny says with a frown. "You're in love. Gross."

"Love's not gross. Your brother's in love. So is your mom. Probably Charlotte too."

Penny lies back on the bed, staring up at the ceiling. "Hollis and Roan are the cutest thing I've ever seen. It's gross watching Mike maul Mom, but she laughs a lot, so I tolerate it." Her gaze hardens. "Charlotte isn't in love with Ryan. She's scared of him."

I tense at her words. "You think she's scared of him?"

Penny sits up on her elbows, giving me an exasperated huff. "He's a controlling bastard. Of course she's scared. Charlotte has always been…trusting. Ryan is the type of guy who exploits that sort of thing."

"Can you tell your parents? Maybe they'll make them break up."

"You already tried, remember? And look where that got you. My parents are scared too. After what went on with Hollis, Mom is trying to be the superhero parent and Daddy is trying desperately not to fuck up again with one of his kids."

Penny lets out a dry laugh. "Charlotte will be stuck with that douchebag until he dumps her for someone else."

"I wish she would talk to me," I murmur. "I could try and reason with her."

"It's not her you have to reason with."

Ryan is who we need to break it off.

And he's having too much fun being her puppet master.

"Everything will change soon, though," Penny says in a cryptic tone.

"What? Why?"

Her blue eyes glitter. "Daddy's moving here."

"What? Seriously? Garrett's a big-time surgeon in Vermont, though."

"He's tired of it, he said. He wants to be here. To open his own family practice so he can be closer to us." Her lips curl up into a wicked smile. "Daddy can only tiptoe for so long. Once he sees how Ryan treats her—I mean really sees—we won't have to worry about Ryan dumping her. Daddy will make it happen."

"She'll hate him," I remind her.

Penny shakes her head. "There's a lot you don't know about my dad. He's connected. It doesn't matter where he's at, he is connected to everyone who's important. Watch. Within a month of moving here, he'll be playing golf with the mayor and rubbing elbows with the police chief."

"Oh."

"Yeah, oh. Daddy will destroy Ryan and he won't know what hit him." She smiles victoriously. Then, her smile falls. "Why do you think Mom bailed? She won't admit it, but I think she was worried Daddy would turn the whole town against her."

142

"Your dad sounds like a real asshole."

"Sometimes it's beneficial to be the biggest asshole in the room. Or, in this case, Hood River."

"This town has enough assholes," I grumble.

"What's one more?"

I let out a heavy sigh. "Yeah, what's one more? Will you tell Charlotte I love her and miss her?"

"She knows," Penny says, giving me a rare smile. "She plays your dumb songs you love all the time ever since you guys broke up."

My heart clenches painfully in my chest.

"I'll be here for her when she comes to her senses," I tell her, my voice cracking.

"I think she knows that. Let's just hope she comes to them before she does something really stupid."

CHAPTER SEVENTEEN

Jordy

SLEEPING ON THE COUCH SUCKS.

Sleeping on a thin-ass mattress at OHP with a cellmate who snores really fucking sucks.

I'll take sleeping on a lumpy sofa at my best friend's place any day over prison. It's probably five or six in the morning. The apartment is silent. Just me and my damn thoughts that never seem to shut off.

She's pissed.

That's the thought that keeps rolling around in my head. I had shit to deal with when Samantha arrived, and I needed for Roux to not be a part of it. It's better this way. Safer. Of course, she took it personally.

After everyone left, Roux didn't show her face again. I'd knocked on her door, but she didn't open it. At some point, Roan came home and checked on her. I saw him bring her a sandwich for dinner. It killed me not to go in there and talk to her.

But I can't.

Samantha reminded me I can't start anything with Roux.

I just fucking can't. Oregon's laws are strict when it comes to age of consent. As much as I want Roux, it just can't happen.

Not yet.

One day, though, I'm going to claim that girl.

Someone pads into the kitchen and turns on the light. I sit up, hoping it's Roux, but instead see her brother. Roan is wearing a pair of sweats and no shirt as he sleepily starts a pot of coffee. I climb off the couch and head to the bathroom to take a piss. By the time I make it back to the kitchen, the coffee is brewed and he's already poured me a cup.

"Hey, man," Roan greets, rubbing at his eye with the heel of his palm. "You're up early."

"Can't sleep."

"You and me both." He sighs heavily. "Fucking arsonists."

"Oh yeah? Someone set something on fire?"

He nods, a scowl marring his features. "One was a warehouse two days ago. Last night was a house down on Fourth Street."

"The fuckin' ghetto, man," I say with a snort. "Those houses need to go anyway. They did you a favor."

"Tell the bodies we found inside that," he says, his face somber. "They were most likely dead first and the fire was to cover the murders up. It's been a big fiasco. Feds are involved."

I perk up. "Oh yeah? Must be a big deal then."

"It's looking that way. Keeping everyone busy at the station. Mike's being a total bitch about it too."

"For being a huge, burly ass dude, he sure does whine a lot."

He sips his coffee, his amber eyes locking on me. "Hollis told me Garrett's moving here." He closes his eyes and his nostrils flare. "So help me, if he tries to mindfuck my husband

145

again, I will murder him." His eyes pop open, blazing with fire.

I chuckle and set my mug down on the counter. "Garrett's not so bad. I get he was a dick back then, but he seems cool."

He rolls his eyes. "You two best fucking buds now?"

"Nah, your old man's my best bud," I joke.

He laughs. "Asshole."

We carry our coffee over to the kitchen table and sit down. I yawn, wondering if I'll be able to steal a conversation with Roux when she gets up or if she'll continue to avoid me.

"Your thoughts are so loud I can damn near hear them. Are you worried?" Roan asks, his pierced eyebrow lifting in question.

I scrub my palm down my face. "Yes. I don't like being involved with Renaldo any more than I have to be."

His brows furrow and he nods.

"Hey," I utter. "Spoke to Sidney yesterday."

He flinches and his face sours. "Cool, bro."

"Don't be a fuckhead."

"What do you want me to say?"

"Have you seen her lately?"

"Nope. Don't have any desire to either." He grips his coffee mug with such intensity his fingers turn bright white.

"I thought Hollis was her friend," I say, cocking my head to the side.

His grin is wolfish. "I keep him too busy for friends."

"Gross, man," I grumble. "I don't need to think about you fucking the rat."

"Would you prefer to imagine when he fucks me instead?"

"I hate you," I say with a laugh. "Seriously. I thought they were friends."

"As soon as Sid and that dorky bitch started dating, she ghosted on everyone, Hollis included." He shrugs. "Hollis was bothered by it, but he had me and the other Hoodlums. Believe it or not, he makes friends with just about everyone he comes in contact with."

It feels like a lifetime ago when I hated his fucking guts and wanted to drown his ass.

"We gave him such shit," I mutter. "That's all your fault, you know."

"Like I was supposed to know I was into him," he says in exasperation. "All I ever knew up until he showed up was chicks. Shit got weird as I figured out what the fuck was going on with me. Sorry I dragged you along with me."

"All that matters is you did figure it out. The rat's cool in my book. I promise I won't try to drown him ever again." I place my hand over my chest over my heart and flash him a wicked grin.

"I taught his ass to swim," he reveals. "Don't touch my husband or I'll cut your balls off."

I wonder if his sister is off-limits too and what the fuck he'd do if he knew I'd touched her...

"Backtracking to your days before the rat," I say, leaning in to make eye contact with him. "You haven't seen Sidney? At all? Like around town?"

All humor fades from his face. "What is your obsession with Sidney? You always hated her. Three years later and suddenly you're wanting to reminisce about her? Drop it, man."

"She has a kid."

"Yeah," he grumbles. "So what? I heard she and the nerd have another one on the way too."

"Have you seen him?"

"The nerd?"

"No, moron, Sebban."

His eyes sear into me. "Nope."

"You should catch up. Have dinner with them."

"Jordy…"

"Roan," I bite out. "Just… I think you should see the kid."

His face pales. "I don't like what you're fucking insinuating right now."

"I'm not insinuating shit. I'm just saying you should invite them to Campfire Chaos or say hi. Just one meeting, man."

He's still scowling at me when Roux walks into the kitchen. I lean back in my chair, my eyes darting over to her. She's wearing shorts that show off her skinny legs and an oversized hoodie. Her hair is messy, but she's still cute as hell.

"I'll say hi," Roan agrees. "You gonna back off and not mention it again?"

I pretend to zip my lips. He visibly relaxes before standing up to go greet Roux. She squeals when he tickles her and then they start chatting about everything they didn't get to talk about last night. She mentions her English teacher is really cool. He tells her about the arsonist. I take note she doesn't look at me or mention snow cones or the fact I picked her up. Nope. It's like she's pretending I don't exist.

"I'm going to grab a quick shower. I can make you something when I get out," he tells Roux.

She laughs, the sound melodic and enchanting. "I'm grown, Roan. I can pour my own cereal now."

His smile for her lights up the entire apartment. "We can pretend you're still a needy-ass ten-year-old who can't reach the top cabinet." He pokes at her with his finger. "Oh…that's right. You still can't reach the top cabinet."

"Get lost, dickhead," she grumbles, fighting a grin.

He laughs. "Don't say dickhead."

"I'm about to call you a lot more than dickhead if you don't take that cheesy smile away from me," she playfully gripes. "It's too early for your nonsense."

He messes up her hair and then jumps out of the way before she can swat at him. As soon as he disappears into the bathroom, I rise from the table and stalk into the kitchen where she's unsuccessfully trying to reach for the cereal box. I crowd her from behind, lifting my arm easily to grab the box. Her body heat warms the front of me. It takes everything in me not to pull her to my chest and nuzzle my nose in her hair.

"Looking for this?" I ask, lowering the box in front of her.

She jerks it from my hand and slams it down on the countertop. As she starts to step away, I slide an arm around her waist and indulge in inhaling her sweet scent.

"Can we talk?" I murmur.

"What's there to say?"

"Well, for starters, I'm sorry I made you angry."

"It is what it is."

Gripping her hips, I turn her around to face me. Hurt shines from behind the lenses of her glasses in her coppery eyes that won't exactly meet mine.

"Roux, I'm sorry." I lean forward and kiss her forehead. "Please look at me."

This stubborn girl refuses.

Gently, I grip her jaw, tilting her head up. Anger chases away the hurt as she glowers at me. So fucking cute. I rub my thumb over her lip.

"You make my life difficult," I rumble. "You know that?"

She scoffs. "Likewise, buddy."

Without thinking, I drop down and press a kiss to her lips. It's as natural as breathing. Her fury has melted away as she smiles prettily at me.

"You're so beautiful," I murmur. "It's hard not to do the things I really want to do to you right now."

She shivers, biting on her plump bottom lip. "As much as I want those things with you, I can wait for them. Waiting for you will never be the problem, Jordy."

"But?"

"But you shutting me out is a huge problem." Her eyes shine with unshed emotion. "I won't let you tear my heart out again."

Guilt slams into me. "Roux…"

"No," she whispers. "You want me. Us. Then you need to let me in. I'm not your best friend's little sister that you're bound to protect by some bro code. I'm yours. But I won't be halfway yours. And shutting me out with whatever is going on with you is only allowing parts of me in. I deserve to be more than a sliver in your life."

Fuck.

When the fuck did Little Hoodlum grow up into this gorgeous, intelligent, mouthy woman?

"Roux," I murmur.

Her amber eyes turn hard. "What did Samantha want? What did she say?" The challenge gleams in her eyes. There's only one answer here. The truth. And if I don't give it to her, she's going to hate me.

"Let me take you to school," I murmur, ignoring the question.

She untangles herself from my arms and storms away from me, sucking the warm air along with her, leaving me cold and empty. "What did she say, Jordy?"

"Baby," I rasp out, reaching for her. Aching for her. Needing her.

A tear streaks down her cheek and she shakes her head. "I'm not your baby. I'm nothing to you until you let me in."

She waits for what feels like an eternity, when in reality it's only a minute or so.

"I want to let you in," I murmur, "but—"

"It's not safe," she interrupts. "Heard you loud and clear. Goodbye, Jordy."

With those words, she leaves me alone. The finality in her words is gutting.

CHAPTER EIGHTEEN

Roux

T HE CLASS LOOKS AT ME, SNIGGERING, AS I CARRY IN Kayden's newest gift. A small bouquet of carnations. Navy blue. How he even got flowers in my favorite color is a mystery. I'll admit, Kayden has been going through great lengths all week trying to win me back. And if this were one of my romance novels, I'd think the gestures were sweet and swoonworthy.

In the books, though, the guy trying to win the girl back isn't a wannabe gangster.

She's also not hopelessly in love with someone else.

So, as sweet as his gifts are, I can't ever be the girl Kayden wants me to be. We were always better as friends. I set the bouquet on the edge of my desk and sit down for my last class of the day. My eyes drift to where Charlotte's desk is.

What's happened to her?

She's no longer the beautiful, confident, vibrant girl.

Ryan has destroyed all the good parts of her.

In her place is this shell of my best friend. Her once golden blond hair hangs in limp, almost greasy waves over her shoulders. Dark circles that almost look like bruises are a common look under her dead eyes these days. She normally glows, but lately she's pasty white. Skinnier than usual. Shaky. I don't know how to help her and it kills me.

I try to make eye contact with her, but she's purposefully looking anywhere but at me. Eventually, she yawns and lays her head down on the desk.

As Wes enters the classroom and starts distributing the test, I think about Jordy. All week, ever since I gave him an opportunity to come clean to me and he didn't, I've avoided him. It's difficult since he lives with us, but I manage.

Jordy is the most stubborn man I know. That's saying a lot because Roan is really stubborn too. But Jordy would rather go to prison than give in. It scares me to death. I absolutely can't lose him again. Three years was three too many.

As Wes nears, he winks at me, sets the test down on my desk, and continues walking. He told me he'd give me the written test along with everyone else, but that he'd officially grade me on the verbal one after class. To sort of use it as a study guide until then and as a way not to have attention brought on myself for not taking the test along with everyone else. I appreciate that he's looking out for me and not giving the other kids ammo to ridicule me over.

Rather than looking over the test, I glance back at Charlotte. She's sleeping. Not taking her test. This isn't her. She's the girl who wants to be a doctor. Who aces everything. I hate Ryan for this.

The class is over all too quickly. Wes frowns when he collects Charlotte's test, shaking his head. She didn't even write her name on it. Dread consumes me. She doesn't seem upset as she stands when the bell rings. Quickly, she grabs her bag and bolts. I stare after her, hating that I don't have my best friend at my side.

The door closes with a soft click and Wes gives me a sad smile.

"Are you okay?"

Tears well in my eyes and I blink several times to make them go away. "Yep."

"I'm not blind, Roux," he says, sitting in his desk chair and rolling it over to me. "Is it your friend? I couldn't help but notice you staring at her the whole hour."

A tear leaks out and I swipe at it. "I'm just worried about her."

"I'll talk to her about retaking her test," he says. "Maybe she's just having an off day."

"It's not an off day, though," I whisper, hating that I'm about to unload my woes to my teacher. "Ever since she started dating this guy, she's not been herself. He's toxic." My chin wobbles. "I miss my best friend."

He reaches forward and gives my thigh an affectionate squeeze. "I'm sure it's just a phase." His smile is gentle. "She'll need you whenever she gets past that phase."

Wes removes his hand from my leg but remains so near I can feel his body heat. The close proximity makes me slightly uncomfortable. I know he's just being nice, though. I'm making more out of it than it really is.

"Ready to take the test?"

"Ready as I'll ever be."

His eyes lock on mine as he asks the first question. My cheeks heat at his intense attention on me. All of my answers come out breathless and shaky. Rather than being annoyed with me or making fun of me, he simply smiles. Playfully nudges me with his knee when I stammer.

"Relax, Roux," he says. "You're done."

A rush of air escapes me. "Oh yeah?"

"Yeah." He grins wide and boyish. "You aced it."

"Really?" I don't ace tests. I usually barely skim by with Cs. "No way."

He laughs. "Yes way. I'm so proud of you."

His praise means a lot and I can't help but smile back. Roan is going to be so happy when I tell him.

"Thank you," I tell him. "You have no idea how good it feels to actually make an A on something."

"Some students just need a different approach," he affirms. "We've found yours. Don't worry. I'm on your side. You'll get through my class with an A."

I glance at the clock. I'd told Hollis I'd be late after school since I was having to take my test. I'm to text him when I finish.

"I should get going." I start to stand, and Wes rolls back in his chair. He seems nervous. "Are you okay?"

He rubs at the back of his neck, a shy smile playing at his lips. "This is going to sound stupid."

"What?"

"You were probably just saying it to be nice, but I really do value your opinion on my poem book. I wanted to see if maybe you wanted to grab coffee after we leave here and look at it." He barks out an anxious laugh. "You can say no. I know it's weird. I'm your teacher."

"No, I want to," I rush out. "Let me just text my brother-in-law that I'll catch a ride home."

Wes grins. "I can run you by your place after."

It's a little awkward that my teacher and I are going out for coffee, but I try not to read too much into it. He's not much older than Roan and Jordy, so it's not like it's gross or anything. And I'm not interested in him that way. Not that I think he's even remotely attracted to me. It's fine. Might be strange to others, but I really do want to read his poem book.

Wes rolls his chair back over to his desk and gathers up his things. I pack up my own stuff and pick up my flowers.

"Who's the lucky guy?" he asks as he comes to stand beside me, car keys in hand. "The guy who was waiting for you last week?"

"Yeah, that's my ex. We broke up, but he really wants to get back together."

"Teenage boys are dumb," he agrees. "I remember being that age. Not realizing something good when I had it in my grasp."

His comment makes me squirm.

"I love these flowers, but I'm not taking him back." I'm in love with someone else. "He's persistent, though."

"I can see why." He flashes me a flirty grin.

I laugh away his comment and wonder if maybe I'm making a bad decision going to have coffee with Wes.

But what's the alternative?

Go home and sulk because my best friend hates me? Cry into my pillow because Jordy won't let me in?

It's just coffee and poetry.

Wes and I walk to the staff parking lot. He drives a white Jeep. It's the only car left in the lot at almost four in the afternoon on a Friday.

"The handle is funky," he tells me, rushing ahead to open the passenger side door. "There you go."

I blush furiously at his gentlemanly gesture. "Thanks."

He shuts the door. I set the flowers and backpack on the floorboard, but keep my purse clutched in my lap before pulling on my seat belt. After he deposits his bag in the back seat, he settles in the front seat. He unknots his tie and yanks it off, shoving it into the cup holder.

"Been waiting to do that all day," he says with a chuckle as he grabs a pair of sunglasses from the dash, swapping out his glasses for them. "Worst part of teaching is wearing a tie."

"Does Ms. Frazier enforce a dress code on you guys too?"

He groans. "I think it's punishment for all those years I gave her hell. Back before she was a principal and taught Algebra. I fucking hate math."

Like a typical guy, he drives like a bat out of hell out of the parking lot. In this moment, he reminds me of a Hoodlum. Older, rebellious, fun. I relax because I'm a Hoodlum too.

We drive past all the familiar haunts. No Starbucks or Panera for us.

"Hood River's coffee sucks," he reveals when he notices my confused face. "Rockford has a place called Josie's. It's technically a bookstore, but the complimentary coffee's great. I stumbled across it while hunting for a poetry book for class. You'll love this place."

He takes us to the next town over and to the small Main Street there. We park in front of a tiny bookstore.

"The door. I'll get it," he says, reaching across me to grab the handle. "Gets stuck all the time." His arm brushes across my breasts and I turn a million shades of red.

The door gets flung open and he climbs out. While he fishes something out of his bag in the back seat, I suck in a few breaths of air. *Don't be so awkward, Roux!* I get out and shut the door before following him up the steps.

The bookstore is empty and smells old. It's cram-packed with books. I love it. He walks over to a self-serve coffee area. While he sets to making two coffees, I browse the store. An old woman sits behind the counter, her nose in a book. She doesn't bother to greet us, which is fine by me.

"Here," Wes says, handing me a mug of coffee. "I'll show you the best spot."

I follow him into another room. Behind a tall bookshelf is a love seat facing a window at the back of the building that overlooks a greenbelt of trees. He sets his coffee down on the table in front and plops down. I sit beside him and sip my coffee.

"Don't look so nervous," he says, smiling. "I'm the nervous one. What if you hate my poetry book?"

"I doubt that," I say with a laugh.

He angles his body to face me, leaning an elbow on the back of the love seat. "You haven't read it yet." He sets an iPad down in my lap. "This is nerve-wracking."

His own nervousness surprisingly helps settle mine.

"I'll be gentle," I assure him. "Let's see if you're as good as Atticus."

"Maybe I *am* Atticus," he says with an impish grin. "Has anyone ever seen his face?"

I swat at him before settling in to read his book. From the first poem, I grow absorbed in his raw words that seem to bleed onto the page. As I read, I manage to gulp down my whole cup of coffee. He disappears to make more, this time returning with a plate of cookies too.

"These poems are really good. Really good, Wes."

He sighs heavily. "Really? God, you scared me. You're so quiet."

"I'm obsessed with these. They're all so unfiltered. Like you get a glimpse into the writer's soul." My cheeks heat. "Your soul."

His smile widens. "You've made my day. I've been reluctant to let anyone read them."

"You need to publish this book and let everyone read them. They're seriously that good."

I kick off my shoes and pull my legs up under me, relaxing as I read. A particular poem called The Broken One reminds me of Jordy. I read over it three times, hating how my heart hurts.

Why must everything be so complicated?

I want Jordy and Jordy wants me.

Simple.

"We'll be closing soon, kids," a woman says, making me jolt.

I can no longer see the greenbelt outside. Just my reflection in the dark window. And Wes's. He's staring at me as I read. Slowly, I glance over at him.

"You have a lot of poems," I murmur. "Sorry I lost track of time."

He chuckles, patting my foot. "I thought I wanted feedback, but you getting absorbed and ignoring the world gives me all the feedback I need."

"I could keep reading these, but I should get back home." I dig through my purse and pull out my phone. Since it was on silent from being at school, I completely missed a bunch of texts from Hollis and Roan. A few calls too. My phone buzzes in my hand with a text.

Roan: You better be dead, because if you're ignoring me on purpose, I'm going to kill you.

Crap.

Me: Sorry! Was studying and lost track of time.

My phone rings immediately and I can't ignore it.

"Hey," I squeak out.

"Don't hey me, Roux. Where the hell are you?" Roan demands, his voice taking on that fatherly quality when he tries to be the boss of me.

"I told you," I grumble. "Studying."

"With who? Where are you?"

"A friend." Not a lie. "In Rockford."

A beat of silence.

"Get home."

"On my way."

I hang up and glance over at Wes. Guilt swims in his eyes. It's not his fault my brother can be an overbearing dick.

"Sorry, but I have to go now." I let out a frustrated sigh. "Maybe we can do this again sometime soon."

"I'd love that." He takes my phone from my hand, his long fingers brushing over mine. "Here's my number. Text me later and I'll send you some other poems I wrote."

Okay, then.

My teacher just gave me his number.

Not weird. Not weird at all.

Except he's looking at me like a guy looks at a girl when he likes her. Maybe this whole coffee and poetry thing was a bad idea.

"I know I'm your teacher," Wes says as though reading my mind, "but I'm just like your brother. Not some creep. I know you're going through some stuff with your friend. If you need someone to talk to about it, I'm a great listener. It's the least I could do for you putting up with my forcing you to read my poetry book."

We both laugh.

I'm lacking in the friends department at the moment. It's kind of nice having someone to talk to and they're not shutting you out. Charlotte, Kayden, and Jordy have all pushed me away in some capacity.

We gather our stuff and Wes guides me out to his Jeep, his palm on my lower back. I shiver at the touch but try not to read too much into it. He's just a nice guy. I wait for him to open the car door for me and then climb inside.

On the drive home, Wes prattles on about how he's going to try and get his poetry book published. I completely agree with him. If a publisher were to pick him up, he could be every bit as popular as Atticus. Before we know it, we're arriving at my place. He parks and gives me a sad smile.

"I had fun. As inappropriate as it probably was. If you won't tell, I won't tell." He laughs and makes a playful motion of zipping his lips.

"I had fun too. See you Monday."

"Call me, Roux. I'm serious. Don't suffer in silence."

I give him a nod of appreciation before I grab my stuff. He reaches over me again to grab the door handle, leaning in so close I can smell him. Coffee and cologne. His nearness makes me feel awkward. Like I'm doing something bad that I shouldn't. He gives me a crooked grin before pulling away.

"Bye," I murmur before rushing out of the Jeep.

He peels out of the driveway—typical guy—leaving me shaking my head and grinning. I stop dead in my tracks to see the dark, shadowed figure standing beside the stairs.

"Do you want to tell me why in the fuck you just came home late with Wesley fucking Ewing?" Roan's voice drips with fury.

Oh, shit.

"Not really," I snap, storming toward the stairs.

"So help me, Roux. Stop and talk to me or I'm going to lose my goddamn mind."

"It's none of your business!" I shout. "I'm almost eighteen. My life is my life."

"The hell it is," Roan yells back. "And when you're fucking around with a teacher, I have every right to stick my nose in your damn business."

My face heats. "I'm not fucking around with my teacher! He's my friend!"

"Yeah, real fucking friendly, Roux. Teachers aren't supposed to buy you flowers and take you on dates."

"These are from Kayden," I shriek. "And it wasn't a date. It was coffee. He's the only person around here who doesn't treat me like a child."

"I bet," Roan snarls. "Listen to yourself. He doesn't treat you like a child because he wants to fuck you. Wake the hell up."

"I hate you," I hiss, storming up the stairs.

"And I hate that you're sneaking around," Roan bellows, stomping behind me. "I won't let you do this shit. Not with him."

"What shit?" I demand, spinning around to face him. "It. Was. Coffee."

"Just get inside," he growls.

"Why? So you and Jordy both can team up against me? Like old times? Remind me that I'm just the kid and you two know everything?"

"Jordy's not here."

"Where is he?"

"With Samantha at her hotel."

A sharp pain stabs me right in the heart, sucking the breath from my lungs.

"W-What?"

"You can listen to his lecture later. Right now, you have to put up with mine."

I stumble away from him and into the apartment. Hollis is in the kitchen cooking something that smells healthy and boring. I dump my backpack and flowers onto the kitchen table, rushing toward my room with my purse in hand.

"Roux," Roan snaps. "We're not done."

"I can't deal with you right now," I utter, hating that tears are flooding down my cheeks. All I can think about is Samantha. Beautiful Samantha. With Jordy. My Jordy. In a hotel room.

"Roux." His voice is softer. "Listen…"

I shut the door behind me and lock myself in my room. With a sob, I fall face first onto my bed. Before the tears have fully dried, I text Jordy.

Me: It must be nice to turn your feelings off whenever you feel like it. Apparently I'm incapable.

Thirty minutes pass and he never responds.

I find Wes's number and text him.

Me: Do you have any poems about hating everyone?

He responds immediately.

Wes: Want to talk about it?

I hit dial on his number and spend the rest of the night unloading every heavy emotion that's weighing down on me. Maybe it'll inspire him to write more poems. Regardless, it's nice to talk to someone about what I'm feeling. He listens without judgment. Doesn't treat me like I'm too young to feel all that I feel. Just listens.

CHAPTER NINETEEN

Jordy

THE STOVE SIZZLES AS I TOSS THE MEAT AND vegetables around for the order I'm working on. My head is elsewhere. To last night. My meeting with Samantha. Roux's text that came out of nowhere. By the time I got home last night, everyone was in bed, and I swear to fuck I heard Hollis and Roan going at it.

I'm not gay, but I also haven't been laid in fucking forever.

I had to take a shower and beat off to relieve some tension. I'll never admit that two people having sex—even if they're guys—was hot enough that I got a boner. But I don't want a fucking guy. I want Roux. The unattainable. And with every stroke over my hard dick, I thought about her. Kissing her. Touching her. Pushing inside her.

I'm half hard in the kitchen of this damn restaurant because I can't stop thinking about her. Her text bothered me, yet I couldn't find it in me to respond. She thinks I can just turn off my feelings? She's wrong. I feel too much. All I'm doing is channeling them in the right direction. If I let my feelings direct me, I'll be back in jail before I know it.

"Yo, Jordy, you have a visitor," Bob barks out.

I plate the meat and scoop some rice and beans on the side before tossing it in the window for the waitress to grab. When I turn around, Bob is frowning at me.

"Who is it?"

"Renaldo Ramirez," Bob grits out. "And he's bad news. You gotta stay away from him. Can't get involved with that asshole, Jordy. Trust me."

I crack my neck and shrug at him. "Don't know what you're talking about."

He opens his mouth to speak, but the kitchen door gets flung open. Ramirez, the fucking thug, saunters in, his dark eyes assessing the kitchen with disdain.

"Bob tell you I was here to see you?" Renaldo asks, running his tongue over his top teeth and staring at me with narrowed eyes.

"Yeah. I was about to head out to see you."

Renaldo nods and walks over to the register. He mashes a button, sending it popping open. I watch in shock as he raids the machine, stuffing the larger bills into his pocket, and Bob says nothing.

What the fuck?

I dart my eyes to Bob, who won't look anywhere but at his feet. My hands fist, eager to beat the shit out of Renaldo, but I refrain. Barely.

"Tonight, Kayden is meeting with more Rockfords. I want you there. To be his backup," Ramirez says, coming to stand in front of me. "Here. Some gas money." He hands me a wad of twenties. "I said take the fucking money, kid."

I'm not some damn kid he can push around.

Yet, I take the fucking money, shoving it into my pocket.

"You done terrorizing the shit out of everyone?" I ask, smirking at Renaldo.

Not wise to taunt this bastard, but sometimes I can't help myself.

He laughs. "Smartass. Walk me out."

Bob nods at me to obey, which really fucking irritates me. I follow behind Renaldo into the dining room of the restaurant. As I pass some tables, I notice Sidney, Sebban, and the nerd. The nerd husband of hers stares me down, hatred burning in his eyes.

What the fuck did I do to this guy?

Renaldo opens the front door and a guy walks in. Fitzgerald. He doesn't acknowledge me, just tips his head at Renaldo and thanks him for holding the door open. Once Renaldo makes it to his car, he turns to face me.

"You understand this arrangement, right?"

I clench my jaw. "Right."

"In case you need reminding..." He lifts his shirt, revealing a gun tucked into his waistband. "Kayden is my brother. I have shit to do and can't keep an eye on him. Your brother is one of my most trusted guys, which means you're one of my most trusted guys. I don't want anyone thinking they can get to me through Kayden. While this job is easy, it's fucking important."

"I get it. I'll keep an eye on baby Ramirez. Don't need a fucking reminder."

He shrugs. "I think you do."

This party is on Rockford turf. A bunch of fucking losers—mostly teenage bitch boys—waltzing around like their shit doesn't stink. It's annoying and I'd rather be anywhere than here. Anywhere than watching Kayden act like he's the toughest sonofabitch in the room. My thoughts turn to Roux. Always Roux. Since I'm bored to fucking tears watching him work the room, I decide to answer Roux's text from last night.

Me: I don't turn the feelings off. I just turn them off where everyone else can see them. The feelings never go away. Never.

It shows that she's read the message, but she doesn't reply. I let out a heavy, resigned sigh and pocket my phone.

Babysitting this dickhead is so damn boring. There are a thousand things I'd rather do, all of them with Roux. When the dickhead in question catches my eye over the crowd, he saunters my way, a smug grin on his face.

"I really thought you'd try and hook up with her," he says, his face twisting into a cruel smirk. "Guess you have morals or some shit."

"Don't know what you're talking about," I say coolly.

"Right." He takes a long pull of his beer, eyeing me up and down. "Doesn't matter. I've been trying to get her back. I know she'll give in soon. She missed my dick."

His taunts boil my blood, but I don't let him have the satisfaction of pissing me off.

"You almost done here?" I ask. "This shitty party bites."

"Naw, man," Kayden bites out. "I'd rather fuck with you about wanting my girl and not getting to have her. Must be a huge fucking blow to your ego. I bet you're used to bitches falling at your feet. You know better with Roux. She's not like most girls. Has a brain in that head of hers. Did you put a move on her and get turned down? She's not some whore."

"Shut the fuck up," I snarl, losing patience and quickly.

Knowing he's hitting all the right nerves, he grins in triumph. "I'll wear her down and be fucking her by the end of the month."

I shove him hard away from me, sending his beer bottle flying into the crowd. Murderous hatred gleams in his eyes as he gets to his feet and shoves me back. Unlike his scrawny ass, I don't move when he shoves me. I fist my hand, ready to level his ass, when another fight breaks out. Baby Ramirez's crew and several Rockfords. Kayden, without hesitation, charges toward the fight, ready to help his guys. Because it's my fucking job, I follow after him. Kayden holds his own at first, flinging punches left and right. But when three guys crowd him at once, all of them packing heat, I know I have to intervene before he gets his ass shot.

I grab the guy on the left, sucker punching him in the kidney. He groans when I shove him hard to the floor. His buddy swings at me, but I'm quicker, aiming right for the gut. As he gasps for air, I tackle the third guy, wrestling his gun from his grip. It fires, making people scream and rush from the brawl. I manage to rain punches down on his punk-ass face. Ramirez's guys get the upper hand as we kick these Rockfords' asses.

"Party at Renaldo's!" Kayden yells out. "Everyone except these bitches are invited!"

People cheer as Kayden struts around like he's a goddamn king. I can't stand this idiot. It takes forever to round his ass up, but once he's in his car safely headed to his brother's, I bail and head home myself. He's Renaldo's problem now.

It's well after two in the morning when I get home. Everyone is asleep, including Roux. I peek in to check on her. She never responded to my text which I hate, but probably deserve.

"Everything okay?"

I pull my head out of Roux's doorway to look at Roan. "Yeah. Just taking care of the usual shit."

"It's only temporary. Then you'll be free," he reminds me.

"I hope you're right."

He heads back to his room and closes the door. I take a quick shower, throwing on a pair of sweats after. When I exit the bathroom, Roux stands in the hall, her arms crossed over her chest in front of her.

I want to talk to her, but not in front of her brother's door. Silently, I take her hand and guide her to the living room sofa. It's pitch-dark in the room, but I don't need to see Roux. I have her pretty face memorized. As soon as I sit down, I find her hips, pulling her to me. She doesn't protest me, instead straddling my lap and placing her palms on my shoulders. Greedily, I grab her ass, pulling her closer to me. Her breath hitches when her pussy drags over my dick. Her shorts are thin and I'm just wearing sweats. I know she feels every groove of my cock.

"I'm sorry," I whisper.

"You say that a lot."

"You're right, Roux. I do shut you out. I'm an asshole for it. I don't know how to turn that part of me off. The part that would give up everything—my own happiness included—to keep you safe."

"What about my happiness? Sure, I'll be safe from these unknown monsters, but I'm not happy. Not all alone without you."

The thought of her being alone kills me.

I slide my palms beneath her hoodie, touching the warm, bare skin on her back. She leans closer, her lips brushing against mine.

"Renaldo showed up today. Threatening me," I murmur,

169

pecking her lips. "Showed me his gun like I'd fucking forget. That's reason number one, baby."

She rewards my confession with a soft kiss. I caress her back with my fingertips, tracing words I wish I could say out loud into her skin. Her hips move, taunting me with the teasing way her pussy rubs over my dick. It feels so good, I'm afraid I'll nut in my pants within seconds, which would be fucking embarrassing as hell.

"Roux," I murmur, gripping her ribs to stop her from moving.

Her tongue dives into my mouth. It's an explosion of sweet forbidden fruit. Like the cherry snow cones we love, but sweeter. I groan, quickly taking over the kiss and the way she moves over me. My fingers now bite into her hips, dragging her back and forth over me as I slightly thrust up. Our breathing grows heavy as we kiss like it'll be the only time we'll get to. I'm dizzied by the need to have her and yank off her hoodie before I can think through the action. She gasps, but then her lips are back on mine, nipping and sucking and biting. Her naked tits brush against my bare chest, making us both quietly moan.

"Fuck, baby, fuck."

She smiles against my mouth and then pulls away, giving me access to her jaw. I kiss along the bone until I find her ear. I nip the lobe and then run my tongue down her neck that tastes salty from sweat. She whimpers when I suck on the flesh there, eager to mark her again. With her dry fucking me on the couch, I can't think straight. My dick is leading the way one greedy thrust at a time. I'm about to come in my sweats when we hear the bathroom door close.

Roux flies off my lap, leaving me aching with need and

panting heavily. Wordlessly, she grabs her hoodie and starts to bail. I grab her hand blindly and pull her to me for a chaste kiss before letting go. Seconds later, her door closes with a click. I lean back on the sofa, my heart racing and my mind trying desperately to catch up to my actions.

Fuck. Fuck. Fuck.

The toilet flushes and whoever was in there leaves. I wait for about three seconds before rushing into the bathroom. As much as I'd love to go into Roux's room and finish what we started, I know better. I root around in the closet until I find the hidden bottle of lube Hollis and Roan keep in there. After shoving my sweats down, I squirt some lube on my throbbing dick. A groan of relief tumbles past my lips as I stroke my aching length. I can't look at myself in the mirror. Instead, I close my eyes while thinking of Roux. How her small nipples rubbed against me, hard and pointy. The way she would grind herself over my dick. Each lash of her tongue against mine. Within seconds, I climax. My release shoots out, hitting the bowl of the sink. I jerk at my dick until I'm wrung dry. As soon as I finish and the lust fades, guilt takes over.

I can't do this shit with Roux.

My brain reminds me pushing her away for now is necessary. Not only is she jailbait, but she's also someone Renaldo could use against me if he wanted to. I'm not about to give that asshole any ammunition.

I quickly clean myself up and then the sink bowl. By the time I exit the bathroom and head to the couch, the sun is rising. I locate my phone and shoot Roux a text.

Me: I confided in you. You promised you'd wait for me. Is that still true?

I figure she's asleep, but she responds immediately.

Roux: You know it is.

Me: Don't hate me for keeping you at arms' length. I hate myself enough for both of us.

Roux: I've only ever loved you, Jordy. Even when you're the dumbest asshole on the planet and I don't understand anything that goes on in that prison of a mind of yours. You piss me off but hate never crosses my mind. Not ever.

Me: Promise me you'll wait for me. Even if everything feels messy and confusing and like I don't care. I care, Roux. So fucking much. Just trust me.

Roux: I don't have a choice.

Me: You always have a choice.

Roux: Not when it comes to you. My heart decided for me.

Me: Our hearts are on the same team. They always have been.

Roux: Then let's win.

Me: It's my plan.

CHAPTER TWENTY

Roux

A NOTHER PARTY, ANOTHER WEEK.

I'm not interested in going to Zac's party, but I know Charlotte will most likely be there. The fact she's been declining further tells me it's imperative I show up for her own safety. I mentioned to Hollis she's getting worse and he assured me he's working on it with his parents. Not fast enough. I'll have to see if I can talk some sense into her on my own.

I shoot off a text to Jordy.

Me: You going to that party tonight to watch over Kayden?

Jordy: Unfortunately.

I smile because I can imagine his pouty frown. A frown I've kissed away in the dark. Things haven't gotten hot and heavy like they did Saturday night, but he's managed to sneak in to give me a good night kiss each night. No heavy petting, but lots of tongue.

"Are you smiling because we're having a pop quiz?" Wes asks as he drops a paper onto my desk.

I roll my eyes as I put my phone away. "Can we not and say we did?"

His laughter echoes behind me as he finishes distributing the quizzes. Charlotte's at her desk, her cheek on the wood, staring past me as if she's zoned out. My heart aches seeing her this way. When she catches me staring, she scowls and closes her eyes, effectively shutting me out.

Wes tells everyone good luck before sitting down at his desk. My phone buzzes and telling by the expectant look on his face, I know it's him. He's actually been a good friend to me. Listens to me gripe about everything and then offers advice. Mostly, he distracts me with poetry. I pull out my phone and peek at it.

Wes: You should smile more often. If I knew pop quizzes made you grin that way, I would've been tossing them at you all the time.

I discreetly flip him off, earning me a wide, boyish grin from him.

Wes: I should give you detention for that.

Me: But then who would read your poetry?

I playfully bat my lashes at him.

Wes: You're a brat. Speaking of poetry... Want to go to Josie's after school?

Me: Can't. I have to go to a party to keep an eye on Charlotte.

He glances over at her and frowns.

Wes: Should I come with?

Me: No.

His frown makes me feel guilty, but the last thing I need is to show up to a party with my freaking English teacher. No one will understand he's just my friend. Especially not Jordy. Jordy would probably kill him on the spot and wind his ass back up in jail.

Me: Raincheck on poetry. I'll call you tomorrow. I might even read some of what I've written this week.

He sits up and lifts a brow.

Wes: Oh yeah? Feeling inspired?

I think of Jordy's full lips as he kisses me senseless.

Me: Yes.

Wes: What's the name of one of the poems?

I close my eyes, smiling. Then, I type out my reply.

Me: His Lips.

He smirks at me.

Wes: About a kiss?

Me: You'll just have to wait and hear it.

His wink is devilish. And his eyes hungrily rake down my front. It makes me backtrack, rereading through our texts. Surely he doesn't think I want to kiss *him*. He's my friend.

I try not to think about his response and focus on the quiz. My brain jumbles the questions together until I'm frustrated beyond belief. The bell rings, dragging me from my inner thoughts, and I frown at my paper.

Wes gives me a look that says, "Don't leave."

I remain seated as I watch Charlotte drag herself out of her seat. Ryan is waiting by the door and he glowers at me before tucking her under his arm.

Fuck Ryan Cunningham.

Wes closes the door when the last student leaves. He walks over to my desk and picks up my paper.

"You didn't have to attempt this," he says. "I told you I'd give you tests and quizzes verbally."

"I wanted to see if I could do it. Apparently I can't."

He sits down in the desk behind me, playfully tugging at a strand of my hair. "It's fine. I'll go over it now."

I nod, frustrated with myself.

"Relax," he murmurs, one of his big hands moving my hair to the side. His fingers massage one shoulder. I don't relax. After his last comment, it feels too intimate.

Pulling out of his hold, I shoot him a warning look over my shoulder. He winces, horror washing over his features.

"Roux…"

"It's fine. I'm just having a bad day. Can we do the quiz so I can leave?"

I've wounded him. I feel like a bitch about it too. His brows furl and his lip pouts out as he burns his stare into the paper. He clears his throat and shakily reads me the first question. I answer each question easily, and by the time we finish, I feel terrible. He's quiet as he stands and walks over to his desk. Quickly, I gather my things and walk over to him.

"I'm sorry," I blurt out. "I didn't mean to snap at you."

He studies me for a long beat. His hand reaches for me and he jerks it back. "It's fine. I'll talk to you later."

The dismissiveness in his tone guts me. I can't lose my only friend at the moment. It's not his fault I'm stressed over Charlotte and Jordy.

I walk right up to him and hug him, needing him to understand I'm not spooked by his friendliness. He's stiff at first, but then returns the hug. His fingers stroke through my hair. It's relaxing, but that makes me cringe when I think about it too hard.

"I'll call you after the party," I promise. "Maybe tomorrow we can go to Josie's."

We pull apart and he's back to smiling. I'm happy I fixed whatever it was I almost broke. I have enough broken relationships right now to have one more.

The door creaks open and we step apart on instinct, knowing if someone caught us this close they wouldn't understand the friendship we've developed. My head sweeps to the side, thankful to see it's just Kayden.

A seriously pissed off Kayden.

Oh shit.

He storms into the room, his furious glare pinned on Wes. "Let's go, babe."

"Kayden," I hiss. "I'm not your babe."

"You're not *his*, either," Kayden snaps, nodding his head at Wes.

"Stop it." I pin him with a firm stare.

Wes, despite being a teacher and the authority here, doesn't back down. He flashes Kayden a smug, challenging look.

"Stop it." This time, my words are for Wes. To Kayden, I say, "Let's go."

He laughs at Wes, happily threading his fingers with mine. I just need to get him out of here. I'm not sure if he still carries a gun, or even if he does at school, but I'll be damned if I let things escalate between him and Wes. I don't want Wes getting fired or hurt.

I glance over my shoulder at Wes. His jaw works furiously as he watches us leave. I give him a reassuring smile before jerking my hand from Kayden's and stepping into the hallway.

"You can be such an asshole. You know that?" I storm toward the stairwell, not waiting for Kayden.

He catches up to me, slinging an arm over my shoulders. "You love me."

"I don't," I snap. "Not like that."

His face pinches, reminding me of the old Kayden I really did have feelings for. When he's not being an arrogant thug, it's hard not to like him.

"I'm sorry. That was harsh," I say, stopping at the top of the stairs. "I'll go to the party tonight with you."

His eyes light up and he grins.

"As friends," I continue.

"I'll take anything with you at this point," he says, never losing his smile.

"You're so over the top," I say with a laugh. "Seriously, though, I want to see Charlotte. I heard she'll be there."

"She will be. Her dumbass cunt of a boyfriend too." He scowls. "I've been keeping an eye on her whenever I see her at these parties. For you."

"Thank you," I say, exhaling a breath.

We start down the stairs and at the bottom, he pulls me to him, hugging me. I allow the embrace because I miss our friendship. I want him to be like he used to be before Renaldo got his claws dug deep into him.

"I'll keep you safe too," he promises. "I won't drink with you there. No one will touch a hair on your head. Everyone knows Roux Hirsch is Ramirez property."

I pull away, swatting at him. "Had to go and ruin it, huh?"

"Just statin' the truth, baby." He grins at me, which makes me laugh.

Something catches my stare from behind him. In a dark classroom. Tom. Creepy peeping Tom. He holds a finger to his lips. I shiver and turn on my heel.

"Can you give me a ride home?" I mutter, eager to get the hell out of there.

"You never have to ask."

This party is wild like the last one I attended. Lots of people I don't know. Drugs. Alcohol. People fucking in any dark corner they can find. I'm on edge, but I'm on a mission.

Find Charlotte.

Force her to get her head out of her ass.

"Want a drink?" Kayden asks, trying desperately to be the attentive boyfriend.

"No, thanks." I glance around the crowd. "You seen Char yet?"

"They're not here—" he says and then growls. "That motherfucker."

I turn to see Ryan walking in with Charlotte, Isaiah, and some guy I don't recognize. Definitely a sketchy looking dude.

"Who is that?"

"The fucking enemy." Kayden's jaw ticks. "I see how the fuck it is and here I thought Ryan was cool."

"Focus," I say, elbowing him. "We need to get Charlotte away from him. I want to talk to her."

Kayden is focused all right. But on the wrong thing. I can tell he wants to beat some ass. When Charlotte starts to pull away from Ryan and he yanks her hard to him, Kayden bursts forward, not needing much direction after that.

"Dude," Kayden bellows. "Get your fucking hands off her."

Ryan releases Charlotte to face off with Kayden. They go nose to nose, spitting out obscenities at each other. I take it as my cue to sneak Charlotte away. Rushing over to her, I grab her hand that feels bony in my grip and tug her away from them. Her dull eyes flare to life and she hisses at me.

"Get the hell away from me, Roux!"

I'm stung by her harsh words, but I don't relent. "No. You're going to hear me out."

She struggles to pull her hand back, but I'm currently stronger to the surprise of both of us. It's as though she doesn't realize she's been fading away for weeks.

"He's a parasite," I grind out. "He's hurting you and you're letting him."

"Leave me alone!"

"No! You're my best friend, Charlotte. You may have forgotten, but I didn't. I won't let that dickhead kill you!"

"Overdramatic much?" She yanks her hand free and steps back. "You fucked up accusing my boyfriend of those things and then getting my family involved. Friends don't throw each other under the bus. We're nothing now, Roux. I have Ryan now."

"Ryan is an abusive psychopath!"

She slaps me. My best friend hauls off and slaps me. I'm stunned by her striking me, even though it wasn't with enough force to hurt. Char is a bag of bones and gaunt. She couldn't hurt me if she tried right now.

"You hit me," I whisper.

Her blue eyes soften for a brief moment and her bottom lip wobbles. "Stay away from me," she pleads. "I just need you to stay away from me."

With those words, she rushes off into the crowd, leaving me to shatter alone. I touch my stinging cheek, tears rapidly beginning to fall down my cheeks. Swiveling on my feet, I turn and head for the door. On my mad dash for the exit, I nearly run over the man standing in my path. Strong hands grip my biceps, steadying me.

Jordy.

I throw myself into his arms, choking on a sob. He envelops me in a protective embrace, nuzzling his nose in my hair.

"You okay, Little Hoodlum?"

"I am now that you're here for me." I tilt my head up to look at him. "Why are you here for me, though? How did you know I'd be here?"

It all comes crashing down on me.

Right.

He's not here for me. He's here for Kayden.

Ice chills me to the bone as I slip out of his arms and rush out the door. Tonight, the air is cool and it's starting to sprinkle chilly drops. I don't have a car. Since I rode with Kayden, I don't even know where to go right now.

I just need to escape.

The rain starts to pick up, splattering hard on my head and soaking through my hoodie. Droplets land on my glasses, making it difficult to see. I weave myself in and out of cars, eager to get away from the sounds of the party that can still be heard thumping behind me. It grows darker the farther I run. Less cars.

Crunch. Crunch. Crunch.

Footsteps thud over the sounds of rain and now rumbling thunder. The rain starts pelting me, soaking me to the bone in an instant. I look over my shoulder but don't see anyone in the darkness.

Crunch. Crunch. Crunch.

The footsteps quicken, which makes my heart race. I take off running full speed ahead down the dark road. My mind is a blur as I think about Charlotte's hate-filled eyes. Someone grabs me from behind.

I scream, but the moment I'm pulled against the hard body that breathes heavily from exertion, I recognize it.

Jordy.

His smell. His touch. The way he nuzzles my soaked hair, inhaling me.

"Where you running to, Little Hoodlum?"

"Away."

"From me?"

"From life."

"You can't run." He turns me in his arms so we're facing each other. "I'll always find you."

I can't make out all of his features in the darkness and pouring rain, but I never need to see Jordy. I have him memorized. When you know someone your whole life, you don't forget the details of their face.

Like the small, random freckle near his temple. I brush it with my thumb. Or the scar on his forehead from fighting with one of the other Hoodlums when they were younger. I certainly don't forget the way his dark eyes track me no matter where I go. They've always done that, even when he didn't have a romantic interest in me.

Jordy has always cared about me.

The thought warms me as I stand on my toes to seek out his lips. They're cold and wet. I'm to warm them up with mine. Our kiss starts out sweet and within seconds, we're devouring each other like it might be our last kiss. My fingers dive into his wet hair, tugging so he's closer. His arms possessively wrap around me.

He doesn't argue when I climb him like a tree. No, my Jordy assists in my efforts, moving his large hands to my ass and holding me up so I can wrap my legs around his waist. Now that I'm in his arms, he starts walking, carrying me somewhere. I hug onto his neck, needing his warmth and affection as he takes us wherever it is we're going.

We stop in front of a car and I realize it's his. I cling to him, not eager to let go. I know once I do, he'll put distance between us. I hate the chasm that exists when reality sets in. When we're in our fantasy world, we lose track of time and rules, desperate for the other. He leans me against the car, pressing soft kisses to my face.

"Are you okay?" he asks, his voice husky and filled with need.

"I am now."

"Ready to get out of here?"

I close my eyes, hating that Charlotte's gaunt face fills my mind. "She hates me, Jordy."

"It won't be forever."

"How do you know?" I demand, my eyes burning with unshed tears.

"Because your brother hated me." He leans his forehead against mine. "And now he doesn't."

Will time heal this wound Char and I share?

"I hope you're right."

"I am," he murmurs. "Now let's get you home and dry. Hollis just put in one of Kelsey's lasagnas when I left. Roan's home too. Maybe you need a little family time."

Dinner with my brother, his husband, and Jordy?

I could never say no to that.

"Let's get out of here." I kiss him once more. "Thanks for always being there."

"I always will be."

His words flood through me, chasing away every doubt and insecurity. My life might be chaotic and confusing right now, but everything with Jordy feels right. How it's supposed to be. I just have to figure out how to fix everything else.

CHAPTER TWENTY-ONE

Jordy

BOB IS GOING TO KILL MY ASS FOR ROLLING UP THERE late on a Saturday since it's our busiest day, but I can't help it. I'm tired as fuck. Stayed up late shooting the shit with Hollis, Roan, and Roux. It's the most fun I've had in forever. Hollis got drunk and that guy's a funny bastard when he's wasted. Roux wasn't allowed to drink, but for as much as she giggled, she may have well been drunk. Roan's eyes glittered with so much damn happiness.

My chest expands at the realization.

Roan has everything he wants now. Love. His sister. Firefighting. And his best friend. Five years ago, I would've never predicted the outcome of any of this. Everything was so uncertain. Roan fucked and fled. His mom was a cunt who strung them along, barely doing her job as a parent. He had shitty grades and a lack of direction. And I was on a path of destruction myself.

Somehow, though, it all turned out all right.

Or it will be.

Right now, there are some serious fucking issues in the plan that involves me. I'll get them straightened out, but it's going to take some time and patience. Both of which I learned while in prison.

While the three of them sleep, I rush and get ready. I'm in such a mad dash to get downstairs to my car, I almost miss the person leaned against their car parked beside mine.

Unfiltered hate ripples from him.

Again.

"What the fuck is your problem, man?" I demand, squaring my shoulders. "You stalking me now?"

The nerd—Gio—sneers at me. "I came here to ask you the same."

"I'm not stalking you."

"You're stalking my wife," he snarls, storming my way.

This dude is shrimpy. Small and thin and fucking useless. I could knock him out in one punch. I'm not afraid he'll whip my ass, so I stare down at him in a bored way that seems to infuriate him more.

"Why the hell would I stalk Sidney?" I growl. "I don't even like her."

He shoves me with about as much force as Roux. I take a step back, distancing myself so I don't kill his ass.

"You *know* why," he bites out. "And I can't…" His voice cracks. "I can't let you do that. You won't take this from us."

I lift a brow. So he and Sidney both know and don't care? That's as much of a confession as anything I've ever heard.

Too fucking bad.

"Sorry, bro," I say with a shrug, "but I don't know if I can back off from *that*. If you were so worried, why stay here? Why not move away?"

"We have family here. Support. My job. It's not that easy." Heartbreak shines in his eyes. "Please. I'm begging you."

Guilt washes over me, seeping into my pores. I'm not some homewrecking asshole. But I'm also not blind. I can't sit back and ignore something that's not right.

"You may think you're doing the right thing, even if for selfish reasons," I mutter. "It doesn't feel so right to me. You guys should come to Campfire Chaos. Roan was talking about everyone meeting up again. The three of you should make an appearance. Does Sebban like to camp?"

"Don't you ever say my son's goddamn name!" Gio roars.

"Whatever, man. I'm late for work. I'll back off, but inevitably you're going to have to face reality."

"Get fucked." He storms over to his sedan and jumps in. For such a stupid dad car, it sure does peel out and make a shit ton of noise like it's something badass.

Annoyed at this altercation that's making me even later for work, I hurry to my car and climb inside. The drive to the restaurant doesn't take long. I'm rushing to get out and inside when I'm suddenly shoved from behind.

What the fuck?

I swirl around, ready to level Gio's ass if he followed me, but come face to face with Renaldo. His features are murderous.

Oh, shit.

"Renaldo," I grit out.

"Hold him," Renaldo says to two guys who approach.

I tense up, but they're on me before I can escape. The vein in Renaldo's neck thumps hard as his face turns purple with rage.

"One job, motherfucker. You had one job."

He swings a fist, hitting me square in the jaw. I groan as pain explodes in my face.

"You were supposed to watch him," Renaldo snarls. "Not let him get his ass kicked by that cop's douchebag kid!"

Fuck.

Fuck. Fuck. Fuck.

I take another hit to the face. This one, splitting the skin on my cheek. Another hit. My eye starts to swell. Another hit. Lip is busted. Another hit. Black out. Another hit. Wake up, confused. Another hit.

Over and over.

And then I'm on the ground.

Kick after kick after kick.

My spine burns and my kidneys ache. I'm seconds from puking on the gravel. The world spins violently around me, making my stomach churn harder.

Renaldo squats and peers down at me, his head blocking out the morning light behind him. He thumps me in my head, making my throbbing headache worse.

"I don't give people a second chance. I'm not your fuckin' parole officer." His eyes narrow. "But Juno is good to me. And because of that, I owe him one." He spits on me. "One, Jordy. That was your one. Had Kayden been shot or worse, I would've kicked your face in until you were unrecognizable, and they'd be forced to close your coffin."

A groan rasps out of me.

"I'm watching you, Martinez. Your every move. The places you go. The people you see. The bitches you fuck." He chuckles. The sound of it is dark and ominous. "All it takes is one more fuck-up and I'll destroy everything you care about."

I black out and don't come to until Renaldo is long gone. Bob fusses over me, asking what the hell happened. He doesn't offer to call the cops because he can't. If I've learned anything the past couple of weeks, it's that Renaldo owns this fucking town.

And it's going to take more than just me to bring that motherfucker down.

Everything I cook today makes me queasy. The smell of the savory meats and vegetables would normally have me starved by dinner time, but I can barely function without wanting to be sick. Bob wanted to send me home, but the last thing I wanted was for Roan or Roux to wake up seeing me like this. Who the hell knows what Roan would do. I don't need his ass out there trying to fight my battles for me.

A sweet, familiar voice cuts through my haze. I cut my eyes over to the register where Bob talks to Roux. She's handing him an application that's been filled out. Last night she mentioned she needed to get a job, but I didn't think she meant here.

Panic claws at me.

She can't work here.

Not with Renaldo breathing down my neck.

A smile is tugging at her lips until her eyes meet mine. One quick perusal of my beat to shit face, and she's pushing through the door into the kitchen.

"Jordy!" she shrieks, her eyes teary as she looks up at me. "What happened?"

I wince when she touches my bruised cheek. "Got in a scuffle."

Her amber eyes turn hard. Just like Roan's. "Oh hell no. Not now. Not after everything. Tell me who did this to you.

I'm not buying your usual protector bullshit. Tell me the truth."

"Renaldo," I mutter with a sigh.

"Why would he…" she trails off, horror washing over her features. "Kayden? Is he…"

"He's fine. Just got his bitch ass kicked when I left last night."

"Because of me." Her eyes water and her bottom lip trembles. "I'm so sorry."

I cup her face with my palms, frowning at her. "This is not your fault. None of this is your fault."

"You should go to the doctor. Your cheek looks like it might need stitches."

"Nah," I grunt. "I'll be fine. Why are you even here anyway? Not that I mind seeing you."

She nods, gesturing to the wall. "Garrett's buying the building. The vacant space next door is where he's going to open his office."

"He's staying here? Charlotte and Penny will be happy."

Her smile is brief. "Yeah. I think it'll be a good thing having her dad here. Anyway, Hollis and Roan are looking at the space with him. I decided to come over here and apply for a waitress job when I saw the sign in the window. Wouldn't it be cool if we worked together?"

My heart clenches in my chest. Working with her, under normal circumstances, would be fun. Getting to see her more often would be great. But it can't happen.

"I'd like that but not with Renaldo riding my ass. It's not safe, Little Hoodlum."

All happiness fades as understanding dawns on her.

"I want to kill him," Roux seethes. "Can't we go to the cops?"

I grab her hand, leading her to the back where Bob has a small desk wedged into what looks like used to be a supply closet. Quickly, I close the door behind us.

"Listen, baby," I murmur, pressing a kiss to her mouth even though it hurts my split lip. "You can't say shit like that. He has people everywhere. Even here."

Fear shimmers in her coppery eyes. "I didn't think…"

I stroke my fingers through her soft hair. "Just be careful what you say. I'll be fine. I guess I needed the reminder of what a psycho Renaldo is." I close my eyes. "It's not safe for you to be around me. If he knows what you mean to me…" I swallow down that statement. "He can't know."

She hugs me. "I'll be careful. I'm so sorry, Jordy."

"It's okay," I rumble. "Everything's going to be okay. Give me some time to work shit out."

Her head tilts up so she can see me. "I want to help."

"You can't," I growl.

"I'm not letting you go to prison again. And I sure as hell am not letting you die. Tell me what I can do."

Everything in me screams to take her back to the dining room and deposit her into her brother's arms where she's safe. But Roux's not some helpless, scared girl. I know how she grew up. She's had a rough life. The girl is made of tough stuff.

She's a Hoodlum like me.

I draw her close, brushing my lips to her ear.

Whispered words tumble from my mouth. With each word, she hardens, straightens, grows determined.

I guess she's right.

Having people on my team is better than going at it alone.

CHAPTER TWENTY-TWO

Roux

K AYDEN'S NOT HERE.

Every school day, but especially on Mondays, after not seeing me all weekend, he's usually waiting for me by my locker, ready to woo me. Today, he wasn't there. There were lots of rumors going on about what Ryan did to him, but I stayed out of it like Jordy told me to. Jordy said Kayden's okay and not dead or anything. So that alleviates some of the worry.

I make it to the top of the stairwell, headed for Wes's class, when I see them.

Ryan and Charlotte.

The arrogant creep has her caged in against a bank of lockers, one hand above her and his body close to hers as he bitches her out. Her head is bowed, her limp hair hanging in her face. He must sense my staring because he turns, his sadistic grin making me shiver. Slowly, he raises his middle finger at me. Then, he pulls Charlotte to him, kissing her in a possessive way that makes my skin crawl. I hurry to class, hating Ryan with every fiber of my being.

Wes's eyes brighten when I enter the classroom. I give him a small smile before heading to my desk. Quickly, I tap out a text to Hollis.

Me: One day it'll be too late. Ryan will do something he can't undo and Charlotte will suffer the consequences. I thought your dad was working on removing Ryan from her life. It's taking too long.

He responds immediately.

Hollis: Thanks for letting me know. You're a good friend, Roux.

I roll my eyes, hating how even Hollis blows me off. My phone pings.

Wes: You okay?

Glancing up, I find him watching me, his brows furrowed with worry. All weekend he tried to get me to meet up with him at the bookstore, but I spent Saturday and Sunday nursing Jordy after he got his ass beat by Renaldo. Roan was pissed when he'd seen how bad Jordy looked but did nothing in retaliation.

All this patience is not usually a Hoodlum virtue.

But here we are.

Not acting. Not reacting. Doing nothing.

I hate it, but it's necessary because Renaldo is one evil sonofabitch.

Me: I'm fine.

Wes: You're not fine. Stay after class and we'll talk.

Me: Roan will be waiting to pick me up.

Wes: Tell him you have a ride.

His persistence is annoying today.

Me: I can't. Sorry.

I look up to find Wes's eyes. They flash with anger.

"I've decided since half of you failed last week's quiz, I'll do another one. This one is longer." He tears his gaze from mine as he walks over to his desk. "It's difficult, but you can use your book. Think of it as a pre-test. A sample of what the mid-term exam will look like."

Anger swells up inside me.

Is he really giving us a test because I told him I couldn't stay after?

Charlotte enters the room late and falls into her seat. Wes says something to me when he sets a test down on my desk, but I ignore him, watching her as she swipes a tear off her cheek. Seeing her hurting and deteriorating kills me. Wes doesn't even bother giving Charlotte a test. Her head is already on her desk, her eyes closing.

Why won't anyone do anything?

My phone buzzes in my hand.

Wes: Better tell Roan you'll be late. We can do the test at Josie's if you want.

Me: That was a dick move.

He doesn't respond, simply crosses his arms over his chest and sits on the corner of his desk, his eyes pinning me. I let out a sigh of resignation and text my brother.

Me: I have to take a test after school. I'm sure I can catch a ride.

Roan: I'll wait.

Me: You don't have to.

Roan: I know.

Me: How's Jordy?

Roan: Back at work. How are you?

Me: Fine.

Roan: Hollis told me about your text.

Me: They're letting her fade into nothing.

Roan: They're trying to get her away from him. Cuntingham's dad is worse than him. Has the power to make everyone's life a living hell. Plus, you know how Char is. If they forbid her to see him, she'll find a way. Do something drastic. Just let Garrett do what he needs to do.

Me: What exactly is he doing?

Roan: That asshole can be likable apparently. Already super chummy with everyone who's anyone in our shit town. He's going to put pressure on Ryan's dad. Work that angle.

Me: And if that doesn't work?

Roan: Then Ryan's going to get a good old-fashioned Hoodlum ass kicking.

Me: Thank God.

Roan: Good luck on your test. I'll see you after.

I put away my phone to discover Wes blatantly glaring at me. He can be pissy all he wants. I'm pissy too. It was a dick move to force me to stay after with him.

The hour goes by in a hurry and before I know it, the bell is ringing. As soon as it does, Penny pushes into the classroom, her blond ponytail bouncing. Ryan is hot on her heels, his nostrils flaring. The asshole looks like he might want to push around Penny, but Penny isn't some weak girl. She'd probably headbutt him or rip his balls off.

"Let's go, sis," Penny says, ignoring Ryan's brooding presence behind her. "Hollis texted. We're all meeting Daddy at his new office. He ordered pizza for dinner. Thought we could hang out as a family."

This has Charlotte perking up, a rare smile on her face. "Really?"

"No," Ryan barks out.

Penny swivels around, fury pulsating from her. "Nobody asked you, douchebag. Daddy's on his way to pick us up."

Ryan's jaw clenches and he fists his hand like he might hit Penny, but she holds her own.

"Call me as soon as that shit is over," Ryan orders Charlotte. "I'll come get you."

He storms out of the classroom. Penny shoots me a thankful smile before hooking her arm with Charlotte's. The rest of the class has already bailed, so when they leave, Wes walks over to the door and closes it.

"Who were you texting?" he asks.

"My brother." I scowl. "Why are you being an asshole?"

"Me?" he huffs out. "You're clearly upset and need to talk. I know how you like to clam up. I'm just giving you a safe space to vent."

"Maybe I just need space."

He frowns, giving me one of his usual wounded looks that typically guilts me. I'm too upset today to let it affect me. I look down at my desk, waiting for him to start the test. He lets out a heavy sigh and sits in his desk chair. Slowly, he rolls it over to me until he's right next to me, his knee brushing against my thigh.

"Roux…"

"Just give me the test."

He's silent for a beat. "Fuck. I'm sorry, okay?"

"It's fine," I say, "just give me the test. Roan is waiting for me."

Reaching forward, he takes my hand in his. "Please don't be mad at me. I'm sorry. I fucked up, okay?" He pulls my hand to his mouth and kisses my knuckle. "Let me fix this. Fix us."

I tug my hand from his grip. "Wes, we're not an us. You're my friend. But friends don't hold each other hostage."

His face crumples. "I fucked up. Roux, I'm sorry."

"Just give me the test—"

"Fuck the test," he snaps, taking my hand again. "You can have an A. I don't give a shit. I just want to see your smile again. I don't want you pissed at me."

I squirm, uncomfortable with the intensity rolling off him. "Wes, can I go?"

"No," he barks out. I flinch at his word. His gaze softens as he tenderly strokes my hand with his thumb. "I mean, please don't leave when you're mad."

"You're freaking me out," I whisper, my heart in my throat.

"Hey," he croons as he stands. "You never have to be afraid of me."

I'm pulled into his arms and he squeezes me tight. I'm stiff and my heart thunders in my chest. When he nuzzles my hair, it's not like when Jordy does it. This chills my blood. He pets my hair like I'm a kitten. Like I'm his. Teacher's little pet, I suppose.

"Can I go now?"

"No."

I swallow hard, blinking back tears. "Please."

"No." He sighs. "I feel like because I fucked up, now you're going to shut yourself off from me. I can't…I can't lose you, Roux."

I'm not yours.

"I'll text you later," I say, my voice shaking with my lie.

"You're lying," he whispers back.

I close my eyes, swallowing down a terrified sob.

"Shh," he murmurs. "I'm sorry. I fucked up. I fucked up so bad. Let me fix it. I'm just having a bad day. Text Roan and tell him you have a ride. I'll take you to dinner or a movie. We can just relax and hang out." He kisses the top of my head. "Or I could take you to my place. I have more poetry books there." He laughs. "And coffee."

"Maybe another day," I breathe.

"No," he whines. "Today. Please, Roux. I feel myself losing you and I can't. I can't lose you."

His fingers thread into my hair and he tightens his grip, tugging me until I'm forced to look up at him. The guy really is broken up about this. He looks seconds from crying. Guilt assaults me, but fear of his erratic behavior is driving my emotions right now. He rubs his nose against mine and then softly kisses my lips. When I start to pull away, his grip tightens. A whimper of fear escapes me—one he gently kisses away.

"I need assurance we're not over," he pleads, his mouth ghosting over my trembling lips.

"We're not over," I rush out. "I just want to go home."

"You'll text me later?"

I nod, more tears cascading down my cheeks. He kisses them away.

"I don't fall for my students," he murmurs. "You're just different, Roux. You get me in a way no one else does."

I don't get this.

I don't understand him right now.

"I'll text you later," I say. "I swear."

And I will. Anything to get me out of here.

"I'm sorry," he murmurs. "Do you forgive me for acting like an idiot?"

"Mmhmm."

He gives me a boyish grin. "Thank God." He laughs. "I was freaking the fuck out."

I force a small smile. "You can calm down now. Everything is fine."

"It probably needed to happen," he says with a sigh. "To take us to the next level."

"Maybe," I choke out.

His eyes flash as he kisses my lips again. "This weekend tell Roan you're staying with a friend. I'll take you someplace fun. We can have dinner and go out. Then, later, I'll show you how much you mean to me."

"Okay."

"It's a date," he says, beaming. "Great job on the test. You aced it."

I try not to grimace. My heart aches at the realization I've lost yet another friend. "Thanks."

I manage to pull away from his arms to grab my bag and purse. He waits by the door, blocking my path.

"It's so hard having to stare at you every day, Roux, and not obsess over you. You're so fucking beautiful and smart and caring. If I weren't your teacher, I would've publicly claimed you already."

Forcing a smile, I dart my eyes to the door. "Roan's waiting."

"Bye, beautiful."

I close my eyes as he mauls me with a kiss that tastes like a mixture of desperation and obsession. When it's over, I flee from the classroom. Rather than go to the parking lot, I make a stop by the bathroom to fix my face. Then, I head to the office.

"Ms. Frazier?"

Charlotte's aunt feels more like my aunt sometimes.

"What is it?" she asks, immediately sensing my distress.

"I, uh, was wondering if I could change my schedule." I gnaw on my bottom lip. "Starting tomorrow."

"If you're having trouble with one of your classes, I don't mind tutoring you like old times." She smiles. "I'm sure it's nothing that can't be fixed over cookies after school."

As much as I want to confide in her, I don't. If Jordy or Roan gets wind about Wes, they'll freak out. With everything going on with Renaldo, I can't afford that. I just need to fix this and make it go away.

"My last class is with Charlotte. We're not on speaking terms anymore. It's distracting. I can't focus." Not a lie. "Please."

Understanding glimmers in her eyes. "Of course, honey. I'll make the change. You can go to Miss Peterson's class starting tomorrow."

"Thank you."

When I finally make it outside, Roan is sitting in his truck waiting. I all but run, eager to escape this hell hole. His brotherly stare assesses me, no doubt picking up on my distress.

"What's wrong?"

"Nothing. Just asked Ms. Frazier to switch my classes."

"Which one?"

I swallow and level my brother with a hard stare. "My last one."

A million emotions flash in his amber eyes. "Good. Do I need to kick anyone's ass?"

"I took care of it myself."

"Are you okay?"

"Yep."

"Of course you are," Roan says, winking. "You're a Hoodlum."

Damn right.

Hoodlums are tough.

We don't take shit.

He starts to drive off and we pass a parked car. Tom is sitting in the driver's seat, his creepy stare on us. Roan nods at him as we drive.

"You know Peeping Tom?"

Roan whips his head to the side. "*You* know Tom?"

"He's my stalker," I deadpan.

Roan snorts. "Good. Everyone needs a stalker like Tom."

With those words churning inside my head, I wonder where my stalker was when my teacher went possessive boyfriend on me.

"Where are we going?" I ask, shoving thoughts of Wes into the dark corners of my mind.

"To bug Jordy. Maybe he'll hook us up with some free food."

Getting to see Jordy erases every terrible thing that happened today.

"Roan?"

"Yeah?"

"When will our lives stop being so hard?"

He reaches over and takes my hand. "One day soon, Roux. We've earned it."

CHAPTER TWENTY-THREE

Jordy

EVERY TIME I SET A PLATE OF FOOD IN THE WINDOW, I catch Renaldo's glare. He's sitting with Juno and a few other thugs, causing a ruckus. Bob says nothing, clearly terrified of Renaldo. It pisses me off that Renaldo seems to hold power over everyone in this town. I'm about to start on another order when Roan and Roux walk in.

Fuck.

I shake my head at Roan, but he's not looking at me. Renaldo, though, is boring a hole through me. Slowly, he turns around to see who I'm watching. I'll give Roan credit. He doesn't flinch the moment he realizes what he just walked into with Little Hoodlum. Acting as though he's unbothered, he takes a table far enough away from them.

I need to distract Renaldo.

Rushing through the kitchen door, I make my way over to Renaldo and Juno. I crack my neck and level my glare on Renaldo.

"Wow, man," Renaldo sneers. "Someone fucked you up."

I run my tongue over my sore lip. "What do you want?"

"Just checkin' on my boy."

Juno smirks. "Bet you learned your lesson, huh, little bro?"

"Fuck off, Juno," I grind out.

They all laugh at my anger. I'm about to explode. I wish to hell Roan would leave, but it would be too obvious. Plus, my stupid best friend won't leave me to get my ass kicked if he thinks that's where it's headed.

"My brother says you wish you were fuckin' that young thing over there," Renaldo says, losing all humor as he glowers at my girl.

I want to grab his hair and bash his face against the table for even looking at her.

"Your brother is an idiot."

Renaldo studies me for a long moment. "He is, but he's a fuckin' kid. What's your excuse?"

"I don't know what sort of bullshit baby Ramirez whines about when you two are watching the Disney channel together late at night during family time, but he doesn't know shit about me. I grew up with them. I'm not interested in what high school brats are up to. I certainly don't want to fuck them."

Renaldo whistles. "You two. Get over here."

Fuck.

I can practically feel Roan's protective rage pouring over me. Roux comes to stand beside me, between me and her brother. Renaldo looks her up and down, and I'm thankful she's wearing a hoodie so he can't check her tits out. Today she seems messy and frazzled. I'd rather him see her as a young kid than someone fuckable.

"You're my brother's girl?" Renaldo asks.

She straightens. "He wishes."

Juno snorts and the other two guys with them laugh. Renaldo simply smirks.

"He does," he agrees. "He's in love with you for some reason. He misses you."

"We broke up," Roux tells him. "I don't care if he misses me."

"I'm having a party tonight at my place." He licks his teeth and winks at her. "You should come."

Roan steps forward like he might lunge at Renaldo, but a sharp glare from me stops him.

"She's grounded," Roan says, laughing cruelly. "For life. Tell them what you did, Roux."

She crosses her arms over her chest. "No."

"Aww, tell us, little girl," Renaldo taunts.

"No."

Renaldo laughs.

Roux, playing into the weird ass vibe, says, "Kayden really misses me?"

I want to crush Kayden for even existing, but I don't say a word.

"Yeah, kid, he does. Apparently he's a pussy for a virgin. Still a virgin?"

"Yep," Roan growls. "And will stay that way too."

"I want to go," Roux says, glowering at her brother. "To see Kayden."

"You shouldn't have fucking gotten kicked out of class," Roan snaps. "You know grades are fucking important."

Roux turns on the waterworks. "You never let me do anything!"

"Because you're seventeen," I chime in. "And quite frankly, everyone gets tired of you tagging along. I sure as shit hate babysitting. Ask Renaldo. He knows how much I hate that bullshit."

"Fuck you, Jordy," she hisses.

"The little kitty has claws," Renaldo observes, making his crew bowl over in laughter.

"Nah," I say, chuckling darkly. "You're jailbait. Besides, that's what my attorney's for. Least she has tits."

Roan elbows me. "Don't be a dick."

Roux doesn't have to fake the hurt in her eyes. It's natural. She's not a fan of Samantha's to begin with. I know this throws her insecurities in her face.

But I'll do anything to get Renaldo's attention off my girl.

Even if I have to be a dick to her.

"I hate you guys," she snarls, storming off, a sob echoing after as she pushes out the door.

Thank fuck, she's gone.

"I'll be there," I tell Renaldo. "Since Kayden can't do shit without me. Fucking pussy."

Renaldo laughs. "He's just a kid."

"A kid who should be grounded. Like that kid." I nod toward the door where Roux left. "Not trying to be a badass at parties."

"The cop's kid took a cheap shot at my brother," Renaldo grinds out. "I'm going to deal with him."

"Kayden made the mistake of buddying up to Cuntingham." I shrug and laugh. "If you fuck with the cop's kid, the cop is going to come after you."

"That cop won't do shit," Renaldo snarls. "I'll burn his fucking house to the ground."

Roan stiffens.

"Say that a little louder so the whole town hears," I deadpan.

Renaldo's lips curl up into an evil grin. "Who the fuck do you think owns this town?"

The front door opens and some people walk in. Garrett, dressed in a sharp suit, saunters in with a couple of other guys in suits. Hollis's dad doesn't greet us. Instead, he walks right past us, telling the guys with him how he's going to knock down the wall on the other side of Renaldo and his gang to expand his office.

Garrett and the suits make their way to Bob. Bob, clearly uncomfortable with Renaldo's glare on him, fidgets.

"Let's get the fuck outta here," Renaldo says. "I've got shit to do before tonight."

The assholes leave and pile into Renaldo's SUV parked out front. As soon as they're gone, I feel like I can fucking breathe.

"Hey, boys," Garrett says, coming to stand behind us. "Take a walk with me."

The guys he came in with settle into a booth while the three of us walk outside. Garrett takes us next door.

"Used to be a dentist office," Garrett says to me, gesturing at the space. "I'm going to gut it completely and redo it. It'll be perfect for what I need. There's an apartment above the space I'll be looking to rent out if you know anyone looking. Probably have it ready by the spring."

"What do you want?" I ask.

Garrett sighs, scratching his jaw, reminding me very much of Hollis in this moment. "I just wanted to make sure you two were okay."

"Just dandy," I lie.

"Have you seen your face?" Garrett asks, frowning. "I'm a physician. You should have called me."

"I don't need your pity."

"It's not pity…goddammit." Garrett spears his fingers through his dark, golden blond hair in frustration, messing it up. "Where the fuck did Kelsey move my family to? This place is overrun by that Renaldo asshole and his thugs."

"Did you drag us over here to tell us what a shitty place we live in?" Roan challenges. "Because if so, we already fucking know."

Garrett frowns. "No…I…"

"You bought the restaurant too?" I ask through gritted teeth.

"I bought this entire strip of buildings to protect my interests."

Roan snorts. "Come on. Let's go."

"I'm only going to make things better," Garrett calls out to us as we reach the door. "That's all I want to do."

"I don't question your intentions," Roan says, looking over his shoulder. "I just hope no one, especially your children, gets caught up in a war you don't intend to start."

"No one is going to war, son."

Roan growls. "I am not your son, Garrett. And you waged war when you rolled into Renaldo's territory and let it be known that you purchased something that he clearly believes he owns."

Roan's right about that. Renaldo pulls Bob's strings, so he'll be fuming at this new development.

"I won't let that thug or the one seeing my daughter bully me," Garrett calls out behind us. "They're about to learn just how deep my pockets are. How fucking far my reach is."

I sure hope to fuck this guy knows what he's doing, because right now, it feels like he might be making shit worse.

CHAPTER TWENTY-FOUR

Roux

M Y HEART IS IN MY THROAT AS I SPEED WALK down the sidewalk, eager to get away from Renaldo. Roan and Jordy have never thought twice when it came to protecting me. I could practically hear their thoughts.

Get the fuck out of here.

So I bailed first chance I got.

I'm not sure where I'm headed, but when I see a cop car parked outside of a couple of shops, I head that way. A crowd of people are frantically looking around.

"What's happening?" I ask an older woman who's sitting on a bench watching the whole thing.

"Little boy went missing. The momma said she turned her head for a minute and he was gone."

A cold, sick feeling slicks over me. I don't think Renaldo and his guys are in the business of grabbing kids, but it still makes me worry.

"What does he look like?" I ask. "I can help look."

The lady shrugs. Useless.

Pushing through the crowd, I locate the cop. When I

get his attention, I recognize him immediately. It's Captain Fitzgerald. Same cop who was there the night Jordy shot all those men. His brows lift, clearly recognizing me as well.

"A kid is missing? I can help."

He nods and lifts his phone to show me a picture. "His mom sent me this. Brown hair. Brown eyes. Three years old."

"Sebban!" a woman shouts. "Sebban!"

I'm surprised to see Sidney rushing around calling for this child. I give Captain Fitzgerald a nod and then start pushing into shops looking around.

"Sebban! Sebban!"

They said they've turned the candy shop upside down and the gift store next door. No one seems interested in the yarn store, so I head in there. It's quiet and vacated. The owner must be outside looking.

"Hello? Anyone in here?"

I stop and listen.

Nothing.

"I'm going to find you and then tickle you for making us worry," I call out in a playful voice, hoping that will draw the kid out.

A shuffle.

Could have been outside…

Or a cat.

Another sound.

"You're really good at hide and go seek. Your momma isn't that good at finding you."

A small giggle.

My heart races in my chest as I look behind crates of yarn. If I were a kid, I'd definitely like hiding in a place like this. Reminds me when the Hoodlums would play hide and go seek with me at Cal's house. They have a big house on the river near their campground and have tons of places to hide there. I'd wedge myself in the tiniest nook and have them searching for hours until they were worried sick.

I peek behind the register, but it's boring back there. No, if I were a little kid, I'd want to hide someplace fun. Skimming my gaze around the store, I find a trunk full of loose yarn meant for decoration.

Yarn that is slightly moving.

Prowling over to the trunk, I kneel down and say, "Where could Sebban be? We've looked everywhere for him." Then I playfully gasp. "Except one spot. I should check the very last spot."

I reach through the yarn and tickle the toddler hiding there. His squeals of laughter are music to my ears. I manage to pull the kid from beneath the yarn, thankful he's alive and well. His face is red from trying to breathe under all that yarn and his dark hair sticks up in every direction. It's his eyes that have my jaw dropping.

Oh my God.

"Come here," I croon, picking him up and holding him to my chest. "Come here, sweet boy."

"Again!" he cheers. "Again!"

"Let's find your momma first," I say, kissing his sweaty cheek. "Maybe we can play again later."

My mind is racing and trying to do math, which I really suck at, when I burst out of the yarn store onto the sidewalk. I nearly run into Jordy and Roan, who've come to see what the fuss is about.

"What the..." Roan's mouth parts as he darts his gaze between me and Sebban.

Jordy clutches his shoulder as though to keep him standing.

"Sidney's son," I say to him, pinning him with a "what the fuck" look.

"They found him!" someone shouts, sending the crowd our way.

Sidney bursts through them, her face red from exertion and her eyes wild with worry. She snatches Sebban from my grip, hugging him to her.

"You worried Mommy!" she chides. "I was so scared!"

"Again! Again!" Sebban cries out.

Sidney realizes that Roan is gaping at her and sucks in a sharp breath. A sob chokes her. Her head shakes back and forth before she turns, rushing away from us.

"What the fuck?" Roan rasps.

I walk up to my brother noticing how pale he is. He's trembling and I'm glad Jordy is there to keep him standing.

"Is Sebban your son?" I ask, pinning my brother with a firm stare.

He blinks away his daze, frantic amber eyes—eyes that match mine and that little boy's—landing on me. "I...I don't know. I didn't know. How?"

Jordy lets out a sigh. "Must've happened before you hooked up with the rat."

"Do you really think he's mine?" Roan asks, confusion marring his features.

Jordy and I exchange a look.

"Yeah, man," Jordy mumbles. "He looks more like you than he does her, and he certainly doesn't look like the nerd she married."

"But if it's true, why wouldn't she tell me?"

"Maybe by the time she realized it was yours, she was in love with the nerd and didn't want to fuck up their perfect family?" Jordy suggests. "Sure explains why the nerd was all over my nut sack this morning threatening me."

Roan whips around. "What the hell, Jordy? Gio was threatening you?"

"Told me to stay the fuck away from his family. He must know too. She can't exactly hide the fact that kid looks like you and not Gio."

Roan scrubs his hand over his face. "I need to call Hollis. Fuck. I need…"

"A paternity test?" I offer. "If he's ours, don't we have rights to see him?"

Roan's face darkens. "Damn right we do."

I'm shocked at the possibility I might have a nephew, but also nervous for my brother. How will Hollis take this news? And will Sidney cooperate? It sounds like she already refuses to believe Sebban is Roan's.

"Go call him," I urge. "We'll be right here."

Roan pulls his phone from his pocket and stalks back toward the restaurant. Jordy's dark eyes find mine, pinning me in place. His face is bruised and he bears cuts from Renaldo's ass whipping on Saturday, but it doesn't take away from his handsome features. Jordy will always be hot. If there weren't a million people nearby, I'd run right into his arms and kiss his split lip.

"You okay? After what went down back there?" he asks. "I didn't mean that shit."

I smile at him. "I know. You always have my back, even when it doesn't seem like it."

Relief flashes in his eyes. Not sure why he thinks I'd ever doubt him.

"I have to go to that party tonight." Jordy lets out a heavy sigh. "I don't fucking want to, but I have to. And I need you to stay away from Renaldo."

"Don't worry. That guy gives me the creeps."

Jordy starts for me, already claiming me with a hungry stare. I'm seconds from leaping into his arms and kissing him, when someone approaches. Jordy jolts and steps aside to face the stranger, rather than pulling me to him like we both hoped.

"Jordy," Captain Fitzgerald greets.

So, not a stranger.

I shift on my feet, darting my eyes between them. I thought maybe Fitzgerald would be weird around Jordy or treat him like a criminal. Instead, he nods at Jordy, sharing a weighted look with him. Like they're friends or something. And that makes no sense whatsoever.

"Hey, man," Jordy says. "Playing hide and go seek seems below your pay grade."

Fitzgerald chuckles. "Nothing is below my pay grade when it comes to the kids in this community."

We both smile at him because he handled our situation with such care when Jordy shot those men protecting us.

"I'm about to head back to the station. It was good seeing you both," Fitzgerald says. "Maybe one day, we can all have dinner together or something. Catch up." He lets out a heavy sigh. "Not right now because…I'm busy. But later. Sound good?"

Jordy nods at him. "Sure thing."

As soon as he walks off, I frown at Jordy. "Was it just me or was he being weird?"

"All cops are weird."

"Be serious," I say with a laugh.

"He really is busy, I'm sure," Jordy says. "Don't worry about it, Little Hoodlum."

I make a note to bug him about this later when there aren't people milling about. Our shoulders brush as we walk slowly back down the sidewalk toward the restaurant. It'd be nice to hook my arm with Jordy's and stroll around like a real couple, but I know better. We can't flaunt what's going on between us. For one, my brother would flip his shit. Two, I don't know how Kayden and Renaldo would take that news. And finally, it's illegal being that I'm not eighteen yet.

Some laws are stupid.

It's so black and white. No gray area.

I grew up neglected and sometimes abused. Roan and I were forced to grow up at an early age. We saw and experienced things no child should have to. And when everything went down with Jordy killing those gangsters who my mother willingly allowed in our home, we became jaded adults. We lost our best friend to prison and nearly lost each other in the process.

So for the law to tell me I can't be with the man I love—the man who has killed for my family and would do it again in a heartbeat if it meant protecting us—I'm just mind blown. That magical eighteenth birthday won't suddenly make me older and more mature. All that birthday does is signify the difference between me keeping Jordy and me losing him to prison.

It's all dumb.

But no one's going to change their laws for me. I'll just have to wait to make love to him. I'd wait forever and remain a virgin until the day I died if it meant keeping Jordy in my life.

We reach the restaurant just as Roan is hanging up. His eyes are bloodshot and his hair is messy. My brother is a wreck. I rush over to him and hug him.

"Everything okay? Is Hollis mad?"

He pats my back and kisses the top of my head. "No. He…"

"He what?"

"He thinks we need to make sure before we get our hopes up."

"What if Sebban is yours?" I ask, tilting my head up to look at him.

"I never thought about wanting kids. The way we grew up sucked. But…" He sighs heavily and gives me a sheepish smile. "But if Sebban is mine, I want to be a part of his life. Hollis and I obviously can't have kids and the subject never arose until now. He said he supports this and if Sebban is mine, he'll be the best stepdad ever."

We both grin.

"Are you okay?"

"I will be."

"And if he's not yours?" I ask.

"Then it's definitely a conversation Hollis and I are ready to start having."

Looks like no matter what, I'm going to be an aunt.

This shitty day took a turn for the better.

CHAPTER TWENTY-FIVE

Jordy

I EXIT THE BATHROOM AT ROAN'S PLACE TO FIND HOLLIS standing there, waiting to go in. The rat's blond hair is a mess, he has scratch marks all over his recently filled out shoulders, and hickeys coloring his neck. Someone should give those two the memo that they can't physically make a baby, though I'm pretty sure they damn well tried.

He smirks as he shoulders past me. I chuckle and then peek in the cracked door to his bedroom. Roan is sprawled out on the bed panting, with the blanket barely covering his dick.

"You gonna be ready in fifteen or am I going to this party alone?" I ask, my brow lifted as I gesture at the state of undress he's in.

He tosses the blanket away, flashing me his goddamn dick as he saunters over to the dresser. "I'll be ready," he calls out over his shoulder. "Gonna grab a quick shower with Hollis. I had to catch my breath."

Which means we're not leaving for another half hour at least.

I shake my head at him as he passes and heads into the bathroom. Those two fuck like bunnies. It'd be annoying if I weren't so happy my best friend is in love. Hollis has been good to him. I feel bad as hell for letting my anger drive me into pushing him off that bridge that night.

Music plays from Roux's room. I twist the knob and push inside. She's lying on the bed, staring up at the ceiling, her brows furrowed. I close the door behind me and walk over to her.

"You okay?"

She forces a smile. "Yep."

Her phone buzzes in her hand. She reads the text, frowns harder, and tosses it away from her.

"You want to talk about who's upsetting you?" I ask, nodding at her phone.

"Not really. Maybe later." Her bottom lip trembles like she might cry. "If that's okay."

I kick off my shoes and crawl onto the bed with her. She snuggles up against my chest, facing me, blinking the tears out of her eyes. Gently, I stroke my fingers through her hair and admire her pretty face. So beautiful.

Leaning forward, I kiss her plump lips. I ghost my hand along her arm before settling it on her hip. She gasps when I grab a handful of her ass, hauling her on top of me as I roll onto my back. With her dark hair curtaining us in our own little world, we kiss without a worry in the world. As long as I hear that shower going, I'll take my time with her. Her legs are tangled with mine and her fingers run through my hair, messing it up.

Gentle, slow kisses turn into urgent, devouring ones.

Her legs have parted to straddle me and she shamelessly

grinds against my cock. I love having her in my arms. The only thing that feels one hundred percent right in this world. I squeeze her ass through her yoga pants, wishing like fuck I could rip them off her. My hand slides under her shirt so I can touch her tit. She's not wearing a bra, which is hot as fuck. I pinch her nipple, loving the way she groans in response.

The shower shuts off and I know I only have a few minutes before I need to bail. Rolling her onto her back, I buck my hips a few times, wishing we were naked and I were inside her. It still feels good to rub against her in ways that make us both moan.

With a chaste kiss to her nose, I pull away from her and climb off the bed. I shove my feet back in my shoes and try to ignore the way my dick throbs painfully in my boxers. Roux is a disheveled mess and I've never seen her look so gorgeous before. Her cheeks are red and her wet lips are parted. A sliver of her skin is visible on her stomach from where my hand was only moments ago.

"I wish I didn't have to go," I grumble. "I want to stay with you. Fucking Renaldo."

"You have to," she says with a frown. "He hurt you last time and that was because of me. I won't be the cause again. Be careful."

"I'll come give you a good night kiss when I get back," I tell her, my eyes settling on her lips.

"I'll be waiting."

Seems like all we ever do is wait for each other.

With a sigh, I finally leave her bedroom. Roan is dressed and walking out of his bedroom at the same time. I meet his stare, hoping to adopt a bored look.

"Just telling Roux bye," I state. It's the truth.

He narrows his eyes, glancing up at my messy hair, and then nods. "Let's go."

It feels like I dodged a bullet, but I also know my best friend isn't stupid.

I can't swallow down the uneasy feeling that has settled in my gut.

The house is crawling with thugs. Everyone looks at Roan and me like we don't belong. It's true, but what the hell can we do about it?

We find Kayden entertaining a group of guys. His shirt is off and he has a Glock tucked into the waistband of his jeans. A cigarette wobbles between his lips as he animatedly tells a story that has his idiot friends howling with laughter. Several girls linger nearby, ready to pounce on his dick if he'll let them.

Unfortunately, this prick has a hard-on for *my* fucking girl.

If it didn't land me in jail, I'd fuck him up just for thinking he could have her. As though he can sense my thoughts, he spots me through the crowd and imitates a gun with his finger, pretending to pop me in the head.

"Fucking asshole," Roan grumbles.

"Same asshole who wants to fuck your sister."

"I hate him."

"Join the goddamn club."

We ignore them and head over to a keg, helping ourselves to some beer. Kayden pushes past his friends to make his way over to us. He's sporting a black eye, but other than that, he looks fucking fine. I don't know why Renaldo beat my ass ten times worse than Kayden got it from Ryan.

"What's up, kid?" I ask, sipping my beer.

"Did you bring Roux with you?" He looks around for her. "Renaldo said she was grounded, but we know better." He smirks at Roan. "You're her brother, not her dad."

Roan shoves him away. "Keep it up, Ramirez. Jordy here'll take another ass whippin' from your brother just to watch me knock you on your ass."

I laugh and Roan joins in.

Kayden fumes, his features turning stormy. "Watch your fucking mouths." He does some bullshit gangster move, thrusting his hips and gesturing to his Glock.

I set my beer down and crack my neck.

"Or what?" I ask, walking right up to him. "You going to shoot me?"

He licks his teeth just like fucking Renaldo does. "No one would miss you."

I grab his Glock out of his pants and drive it up painfully under his chin, bringing my nose to his. Despite trying to act like a badass, his eyes widen in fear.

"Keep running your mouth, you fucking pussy." My spittle splatters his face, making him blink. "I'm going to keep this gun because, unlike your scrawny ass, I *know* how to use it. I'm *not afraid* to use it. And I'm having to babysit your bratty ass and may be *forced* to use it." I pull back, poking his chest with the barrel of the gun, making him take a step back. "Go play with the other toddlers, baby Ramirez. The men were having a conversation until you interrupted."

I stuff the gun in the back of my jeans and pick my beer back up. Kayden scowls and starts to walk off, but turns to grin at us.

"Tell Roux I'm gonna do her a solid. Ryan and his dumbass friends are going down."

"His dad's a cop," I remind him.

"So? My brother owns this town. We'll make it look like an accident." He shrugs. "Then Charlotte doesn't have to deal with that psycho. Roux will be happy."

Renaldo appears like a fucking ghost with Juno beside him. I can't even look at my brother. I've hated him for as long as I can remember, but now that he's Renaldo's bitch, my hate has doubled.

"What have I told you about bragging?" Renaldo says, ruffling Kayden's hair.

Kayden groans. "I was just telling him what's up with fucking Ryan Cunningham."

Renaldo's sharp glare slices through me. "I'll handle Cunningham." Then, to me he says, "I can take over from here. I just wanted to see if you'd actually show up."

Juno nods at me like he's fucking proud.

What the hell ever. I only showed up because I didn't want my ass beat, or worse, him fucking with Roux.

"I'll take that gun back too," Renaldo says, nodding at me.

I cringe knowing he saw me take it from his brother, and subsequently point it at him too. Rather than being pissed, he seems amused. With a huff, I pull it out and set it in his waiting hand.

"He's going to get himself shot if he keeps popping off at the mouth to guys who are bigger and badder than him," I warn. "I can't follow him to school or the fucking pisser. Teach your boy how to behave, man."

He nods. "Bye, Martinez."

"Later," I grunt out.

Roan and I bail, eager to get the fuck out of there. It's not until we're in my car and cruising down the road that I finally breathe a sigh of relief. We're headed home when Samantha texts me.

Samantha: Come to my hotel.

"Home's that way," Roan says when I turn in the direction of where she's staying.

"Looks like we have to make a pit stop."

The drive is short, and all too soon, we're pulling up to her hotel. Roan follows me as we climb the stairs to the second floor where she's staying. Before I can knock, she flings open the door.

"Hey, honey, come inside."

We walk into her suite and sit on the sofa. She's not in her badass boss bitch courtroom suit as per usual. Tonight she's in jeans and a sweater that pulls too tight over her tits.

"Drinks?" she asks as she opens the mini fridge.

We both nod.

"What's up?" I ask, accepting a Dr Pepper from her.

"You look like shit, Jordy." She hands Roan a Dr Pepper too. "Are you okay?"

"Renaldo." I pop the tab and guzzle down the drink. "You know how he is. Why are we here?"

She glances at the clock. "Meeting. Shouldn't be but five more minutes."

Roan sets his drink down on the table. "While we're waiting, can I get some advice?"

"Sure, baby," she says, grinning at him.

Sorry, lady, he's married and bats only for Hollis's team.

"I used to fuck around with this chick. We pretty much always used protection unless we were shitfaced and forgot.

221

I saw her with this kid today and…" He scrubs his palm over his face. "I think he's mine."

Her eyebrow arches up. "Is she suing for child support?"

"W-What? No. She freaked and left. I want to know if he's mine. Can we do that? If he's mine, I want to be in his life."

"I can start the process of getting a judge to sign off on a mandatory paternity test. If that's what you really want. Once I start this and it's proven that he is yours, there won't be any turning back. You'll be saddled with visitation and financial responsibility until he's an adult." She smiles sweetly. "Your call, Roan."

"If he's mine, he's mine. I want to be in his life," he mutters. "I don't care what hell it brings me. I'm not sure I can rest until I know for sure he's not. If he is, I'm going to fight like hell to see him."

She nods and pulls out her laptop. "I'll get started. You know my rates?"

"Garrett is going to cover it," Roan says begrudgingly.

"The sexy doctor, hmm? I'll take up receiving payment from him later." She smirks as she starts tapping away on her laptop.

Samantha seems to flirt with anything with a dick. Makes me wonder if that's all it is. Harmless flirting. If not, she probably gets fucked often with how forward she is.

As she asks Roan questions, I let my mind drift back to Roux. Something was bothering her, but she didn't want to talk about it. I hate when she's upset. It makes me want to drop everything and hold her until her world is right again.

Someone knocks on the door.

"He's here," Samantha says. "Can you get that?"

I rise and walk over to the door. When I fling it open, I'm not at all surprised to see the man standing there.

"Hey, Tom."

"Jordy."

"What's up, Tom?" Roan calls out.

Tom walks in and we finally begin our meeting.

CHAPTER TWENTY-SIX

Roux
Several weeks later...

H E WON'T GIVE IT A REST.

I could block his number again, but he'll just call from a different one. Wes has gone through three different phones just to be able to text me. I've given up on blocking him and just respond to his poetry now. It's still good. If I erase that day in the classroom where he went a little crazy, it's almost like I have my friend back. I'm smart enough to know better. He's clearly forgotten that day.

> **Wes: Do you want to go to Josie's? She's been sprucing the place up. Comfier couches and on Fridays a violinist comes to play. It's amazing.**
> **Me: Can't. Been busy.**
> **Wes: But I miss you.**

I cringe and shake my head. I'm not responding to that because then he'll have a little freak out again about how upset he was the day he realized I'd transferred out of his class. The last thing I want to do is rehash that. Again. I shove my phone in my hoodie and watch the clock. As soon as the bell rings, indicating the end of my last class of the day, I rush to my locker.

Tonight I'm supposed to watch movies with the guys. I love movie nights because Roan and Hollis cuddle up on the sofa while Jordy and I lie on the floor. No one seems to notice our nearness. We play it off being in a small room or having to share a pillow or blanket. Hollis and Roan are too busy sneaking kisses to worry over the fact I'm holding hands with Jordy under the blanket.

I'm grabbing some books from my locker and stuffing them into my bag when someone pushes me. I stumble a bit and then whirl around to see Ryan walking by. Charlotte's hand is locked in his, but she's so spaced out, I don't think she even knows where the hell she is. Her parents have forbidden her to see Ryan, but they can't exactly stop her at school.

"Asshole," I gripe.

Ryan flips me off and calls me a skank.

I shoulder my bag and head in the opposite direction of Ryan and Charlotte. But that puts me walking past Wes's classroom. I'm thankful the classroom has already been vacated and is dark. My phone buzzes, so I stop to check it.

Roan: Signing some paperwork for the attorney about Sebban. I'll be there just as soon as I can. You okay to wait?
Me: Yeah. I'll go sit under the tree near the parking lot.
Roan: See you in twenty minutes tops.

With a heavy sigh, I head outside. The wind is harsh and unforgiving today. I wish I'd worn a coat and not just a hoodie. It smells like snow is in the air. It's not even Thanksgiving yet, which means we're in for a harsh winter. I make it out to the tree, leaning my shoulder against it. It's cold enough that I pull my hood over my head in an attempt to stay warm. I send

Jordy a few funny memes, knowing he won't be able to look at them until his break time, but he'll get a laugh.

"I thought that was you."

The deep voice makes my blood turn to ice. The leaves crunch as Wes comes to stand beside me.

"I feel like you've been avoiding me," he says, hurt in his tone.

No shit, asshole.

"What?" I croak out. "No way. Just been busy."

"That's what you always say."

"Because I'm always busy." I lift my head to look at him.

Wes is handsome, no doubt. He's just a psychopath. Obsessive too. I wish he'd go bother someone else. I don't know what his fascination is with me.

"Want a ride home?" he asks. "You shouldn't have to stand out here in the cold."

"Roan will be here any second," I lie.

Unbothered, he steps closer, pushing my hood off my head. "There. I almost forgot what you looked like." He laughs. "I mean, your social media pictures aren't the same. They don't really capture your smile or how your eyes light up."

I retreat a step. "Stalker." I say it in a joking way and he chuckles as though it's a joke, but it's not a damn joke.

He grabs the front of my hoodie, pulling me to him. I let out a squeal of surprise, my palms flying to his chest to stop myself from crashing into him. His hand finds my face, gripping my jaw so he can angle my face up to his. My heart stutters in my chest as I worry how far he'll take this.

"Please let me go," I murmur.

He frowns. "Fuck. See, I knew your texts were bullshit. You're scared of me."

"I'm not scared," I lie. "I just have a boyfriend."

"No, you don't," he states. "Your social media status still says single and I've been asking around. Everyone says you're single. Why are you lying, Roux? I thought we were friends."

"Friends don't do this," I spit out. "Let me go."

Determination glints in his eyes and then he smashes his lips to mine. I growl as I try to fight him off. He's stronger and crazier. I manage to turn my head to the side and belt out a scream. His lips kiss along my throat as he laughs.

I hear heavy footsteps charging our way. Before I can even register what's happening, Wes is being torn away from me. Kayden, red faced and furious, slings Wes to the ground.

"Don't fucking touch my girl," Kayden roars, his chest huffing with fury.

Wes pounces back up to his feet. His eyes are wild with anger. He swings, landing a hard punch on Kayden. Kayden is scrappy, though, and attacks Wes. They land on the ground, fighting like little boys on the schoolyard. I'm panicked and worried, but I don't know what to do. The fight ends when Kayden pulls a gun on Wes.

Everything seems to slow to a screeching halt.

Even my heart inside my chest.

"I said," Kayden seethes, shoving the barrel of the gun painfully into Wes's temple. "Don't. Fucking. Touch. Roux."

I grab Kayden by the arm. "Come on. Get off him. Let's go. Don't do this."

Kayden spits in Wes's face but then climbs off him. He walks me away from Wes and slings an arm over my shoulders. "You okay, baby?"

"I'm fine," I rasp out. "Can we go? Please?"

Wes rises to his feet, his intense eyes boring into me. It's as though he doesn't care about Kayden or is even worried about him. No, his whole focus is on me. It's terrifying.

"Let's go," Kayden mutters when he realizes I'm trembling. "That guy is fucking psycho."

Kayden escorts me to his car and helps me in. It's not until we're in the car, driving far away from Wes, that I breathe out a sigh of relief.

"Thanks for rescuing me," I murmur. "He doesn't know when to quit."

"He touches you again, baby, and I'll blow his fucking head off."

"I'm not your baby, Kayden, and don't do that. He's obsessed, but he doesn't deserve to die. Thanks for coming to my aid, though."

He turns on some rap music and tries to hold my hand. I grab my phone out of my pocket as an excuse not to touch him. I quickly text Roan.

Me: Looks like I'm catching a ride home. See you soon.

Roan doesn't respond, which means he's busy with the attorney or driving. Either way, he'll get the message.

Kayden's phone rings and he answers it. "What's up?"

As he talks to whoever it is on the phone, I try to calm my nerves. When I get home, I'm going to crawl into bed and try to forget this day until Jordy can kiss it all away.

"Fuckin' right my girl's with me. Told you I was gonna get her back," Kayden brags. "What? Why?" He pauses and grumbles. "I need to drop her off first." Another pause. "Okay, asshole, I get it. Right the fuck now. You're so goddamn bossy."

He hangs up and then pulls a U-turn in the middle of the road, nearly sideswiping a car in the process.

"Where are we going?" I shriek.

"The shop." He starts rapping along with the radio.

I mash the button to turn it off. "Take me home, Kayden."

"Can't, babe," he says, turning back on the radio. "My brother says it's important."

"Just let me off here," I demand. "Kayden. Now."

He waves his hands, grinning, as he raps along to his stupid song. "A ho don't know. A ho don't know."

I immediately text Jordy.

Me: I'm with Kayden. Don't ask. But now we're headed to your brother's shop to see Renaldo. Can you come get me?

I send similar messages to Roan and Hollis both.

No one replies.

By the time we reach the shop, my nerves are a mess. I'm nearly in tears. The last time I ran into Renaldo, he looked me up and down like I could be of use to him. Being useful to Renaldo is scary. Not to mention, I don't know what sort of war that would bring down if he did try to use me. As much as Kayden has ruined things with me, I don't think he'd sit back and let that happen with Renaldo. And I don't know how Renaldo would respond to that.

And Jordy?

I can't have him going back to prison because of me.

We pull up to the shop and Kayden starts to get out. I reach over and grab his arm, trying to adopt a bored expression.

"I'll wait in the car. Look over some notes. Lots of homework."

He leans over and kisses my cheek. "Probably for the best. I'll be right back. Sit tight and after I'll take you to dinner or something."

No, he'll be taking me home.

I nod and smile. "Okay."

He climbs out and saunters into the building. I'm considering calling Kelsey even though things are weird between me and her daughter, when three guys step outside.

Kayden.

Jordy's brother Juno.

And Renaldo.

They're all looking my way, too.

Oh, crap.

Renaldo stalks my way, his jaw clenching. I'm frozen in fear. He wrenches open the car door and squats beside me. His tongue runs over the front of his top teeth and then he grins wolfishly at me.

"Little Roux come to see her future brother-in-law?" he taunts.

I cringe, shrinking away from him when he reaches a hand forward. He seizes my wrist and pulls it to him, his grip tightening to the point I know it'll bruise.

"Renaldo," Kayden grunts out weakly from the other side of the door. "Leave her alone."

Renaldo ignores him as he peels back every layer of me with one long stare. "No, man," Renaldo murmurs. "That's the part you don't seem to grasp yet. When you want shit done, you figure out ways to do it."

I try to tug my hand free, but Renaldo nearly crushes my bones in his grip. I give up hoping he'll lessen his hold and he does, but doesn't release me.

"With Roux?" Kayden says in exasperation. "Roux can't do shit for you. She's just a girl."

"A girl my boy Jordy wants to fuck." Renaldo grins at me.

My heart races inside my chest, but I don't give him the satisfaction of an expression that would confirm his theory.

"He won't fuck her," Kayden growls. "She's my fucking girl."

Juno laughs. "If he wants to, he will. Just sayin'. My brother is stubborn as fuck. If he wants something, he'll find a way to get it."

Kayden kicks the front of his car in frustration.

"Kick what's mine one more time and I'll put a bullet in your foot," Renaldo snaps. "I give everything to you for fucking free because you're blood, but if you disrespect me again, I'll make sure you don't forget your place, bro."

"You're hurting me," I say softly, noting my entire hand is turning purple from lack of circulation.

"Don't you forget it either," Renaldo whispers. "When our boy Jordy fails to comply, you remind him, little girl. Remind him of what I can do so effortlessly and without trying." He brings my palm toward him and playfully snaps his teeth like he might bite me. "I'll do much worse than bruise your pretty wrist."

"What do you want from him?" I demand, hating how the tears of both pain and terror leak down my cheeks. "He already helps you. What more do you want?"

Renaldo twists my arm in such a way I nearly fly out of my seat in pain. I grab his shoulder, attempting to go with the way he's turning rather than resist so my wrist doesn't break. He stops twisting and leans forward, his nose on my wet cheek and his hot breath on my jawbone. My eyes are locked on Kayden's. He paces, staring at me with torment written on his face, yet doing nothing.

"I have a big job for him. A job that Jordy can do because he's ruthless and determined. It's time for him to do more than just babysit for me. I need someone like Jordy to join my ranks. Juno has been good to me. It's really that simple, sweetheart."

I'm choking back a sob of pain when I hear the rumble of an engine. Gravel pings against Renaldo and the side of Kayden's car. A car door slams hard and footsteps crunch our way.

"Renaldo." Jordy's voice is low and deadly. A terrible warning.

Renaldo grins at me as he finally releases me. He rises to his feet and faces off with Jordy. "My man. There you are."

Jordy's dark eyes slice my way and he assesses me with a quick look. Aside from the awful bruises I'll have, I'll be okay.

"No one ever told you to not fuck with little girls?" Jordy spits out, his body thrumming with rage.

I unbuckle my seat belt and grab my things, wincing at the pain in my wrist. Renaldo walks over to Jordy, poking him in the chest.

"Can't say anyone ever has," Renaldo taunts. "Is that what you came here to say?"

"Nope." Jordy cracks his neck. "I didn't come here to say shit. I came to give Roux a ride home. Her brother's looking for her."

I climb out of the car and start for Jordy's car. Kayden calls after me, but I ignore him. Once I shove my things into the car, I wait for Jordy to hurry. He's nose to nose with Renaldo.

"Jordy," I whimper.

His shoulders tense and he fists his hands like he might beat the shit out of Renaldo.

"You do as I ask and I'll leave the little girl alone. Deal?" Renaldo pats Jordy's shoulder like they're best friends.

Jordy nods. I don't understand what the implications of this will be, but I don't like it. Renaldo terrifies me and everything he does is illegal. He's going to pull Jordy under

232

and drown him. Jordy whispered to me in the supply closet at his work—after Renaldo had beat the crap out of him a few weeks ago—that he'd eventually untangle himself from Renaldo, but that it'd take time and patience. I feel like we're running out of both.

"Good boy," Renaldo praises. "Run along. I'll call you when I need you."

"Roux," Kayden grinds out. "I thought we were going to have dinner—"

"No," I hiss out, glaring at him in accusation. "We're not."

He brought me right to his brother. I sure as hell am not having dinner with him.

I refuse to let his kicked puppy expression get to me. Instead, I hop into the car with Jordy and buckle in. The car kicks up gravel as he peels out of the lot. As soon as we're on the road, he reaches over, taking my sore wrist in his gentle grip.

"I'm sorry, Little Hoodlum."

Me too, Jordy.

Nothing can ever be easy for us.

CHAPTER TWENTY-SEVEN

Jordy

I SEE RED.

Deep, bloody red.

The rage consumes me to the point it's blinding. I want to kill him. Renaldo Ramirez needs to fucking die. How dare he touch Roux? How dare he threaten me with her? I knew he'd sniff out my weakness and use it against me. I just didn't think it would happen so quickly.

Fuck.

This is going bad fast.

By the time I've reached the apartment, Roan and Hollis are already there. They're both waiting outside, freaked the fuck out. As soon as I saw her text, I blew out of the restaurant so fast to get to her. Roan called me, losing his goddamn mind, but I told him to let me handle Renaldo. Roan would get his ass shot. At least Renaldo feels like he needs me in some capacity, which works to my advantage.

I've barely shut off the car before Roan is yanking open the door and pulling Roux into his arms. She clings to her brother, sobbing. We didn't speak on the way home. I was too overcome with rage and she was trembling with terror. Roan has a way of calming Roux down when shit gets too rough. It gives me a sense of peace watching her relax as he whispers assurances to her. Hollis's brows are pinched with worry.

"Come here, kiddo," Hollis says, hugging Roux next.

Roan pulls out his phone and makes a call. He hangs up and nods his head for us to go upstairs. "They're on their way," Roan tells me.

Roux looks over her shoulder at me in confusion. We all pile into the apartment. Hollis sets to fussing over Roux, making sure she doesn't want anything to eat or drink. Roan and I sit at the table wearing matching scowls.

"How did your meeting go with Samantha?" I ask.

The anger floods from his face as frustration takes over. "Fine. Gio's attorney keeps throwing wrench after wrench in our attempt to get this paternity test done. It's fucking annoying."

"That's the nerd I know," I grumble.

"Hollis went and saw Sidney. To see if he could talk some sense into her. She blew the hell up, man." He scrubs his palm over his face. "I don't understand why she's being so difficult over this."

"Because he's obviously your kid and she doesn't want to share him."

He scowls. "But I would be good to him. I'm not trying to steal him away or anything. I just want to know him."

"And thank fuck for the laws of our country. Just give it time. Samantha is good. She'll get you your son if he's yours. Trust me."

Someone knocks and Roan calls out for them to come in. My eyes dart over to Roux, who stands by the fridge, sipping on a Coke. As soon as our guest arrives, the color drains out of her face.

"Tom," Roan and I greet as he enters with Garrett and Samantha.

"Boys." He smiles at Roux. "Hey, stranger."

Roux sets her Coke down. "Were you stalking me?"

He chuckles. "I'm only looking after you." He nods at Roan and me. "And them."

Samantha sashays into the room, swaying her hips. I don't miss the fact Roux's nostrils flare in annoyance. "Tom would like to talk to you, Roux. He needs your help."

Roux's eyes dart to mine and I nod. She's argued time and time again she can handle all the dark, fucked-up elements of my world. My girl is about to be tested.

"I'm going to wash today's restaurant grime off my body while you guys talk," I tell them. "Be back in ten."

By the time I've showered and changed into some sweats and a T-shirt, Tom and Samantha are gone. Garrett is huddled with Hollis and Roan while Roux sits in the recliner, her face pale. As though she's seen a ghost.

"You okay?" I ask, sitting on the coffee table in front of her.

She nods. "I am. Can we talk?"

"Yeah. You want to go outside?"

Shaking her head, she stands. "We can go in my room."

I follow her into her bedroom. She closes the door behind us. I take her hand and push her hoodie up her arm to look at where Renaldo hurt her. Seeing the bruises already forming has rage bubbling up inside me.

I want to kill him.

For Roux, I would.

"Hey," she murmurs, seemingly reading my mind. "Don't go there."

"I fucking hate him."

"Me too."

Someone knocks on her bedroom door.

"Come in," Roux says.

Hollis peeks his head in. "We're going to grab dinner and then stop by Dad's office. You guys coming?"

"No," Roux says. "I'm tired and we have to talk."

"Okay," Hollis says and then his voice grows stern as he narrows his eyes at me. "Be good."

I snort and flip him off. "Go away, rat."

His grin makes me laugh. "We'll bring back food."

As soon as Hollis leaves, Roux kicks off her shoes and pulls off her hoodie before climbing on top of her covers. I lie down next to her, stroking her dark hair away from her face. Her amber eyes brew with a storm of emotions.

"Are you really okay?" I murmur, nudging her nose with mine.

She swallows. "No, but I will be."

"I'm sorry shit is such a mess."

"We'll fix it."

I hope so.

Her fingers thread into my wet hair as she draws me to her lips. I'm unable to resist her and my mouth devours hers. She tastes sweet like the Coke she was drinking. I groan as my tongue slides against hers, desperate to own her with just a kiss. She nips at my bottom lip, making my dick jolt in my sweats.

"Roux," I growl.

Emboldened by my tone, she moves across me, straddling

my waist. Her T-shirt gets tossed away, revealing her pert breasts in her black bra. I groan when she undoes the bra and flings it away.

Fuck.

So fucking perfect.

My palms find her tits and I run my thumbs over her peaked nipples. She reaches down to undo the top button of her jeans.

"Roux," I warn. "I have no self-control with you."

Her hooded eyes meet mine as she unzips them. "We're not going to fuck, Jordy. Relax."

I can't relax when she shimmies out of her jeans. In just her striped socks and black panties, she's a fucking vision. And mine. All mine. Her slender thighs straddle me again. Greedily, I roam my palms up her thighs, teasing my thumbs under the seam of her panties.

"Take your shirt off," she orders, her amber eyes flaring with heat.

Jesus.

I obey Little Hoodlum because she's so fucking fierce and beautiful. I'm under her wicked spell. I toss away my shirt, groaning when her nails scrape along my pectoral muscles. She grinds against me as she leans forward to kiss me. My hands are all over her, wishing I could touch her everywhere all at once. She slides down my thighs, tugging at the waistband of my sweats. My dick springs free, slapping heavily against my lower stomach.

"Roux," I rasp out.

"We're not going to fuck," she reminds me. "I just…I need this before everything really sucks."

I know what she needs.

I'd been hoping to fuck it wouldn't come to this, but it has. Renaldo forced our hand today.

She rubs her panty-covered cunt along my bare dick, making us both hiss in pleasure. I've never felt something so good in my entire life. My hips buck up, desperate to feel every part of her. Her panties are wet, soaked through with her arousal. With every grind of her hips, she smears her wetness over my shaft.

"You're killing me," I breathe.

"It'll feel good to die this way."

I grip her delicate neck and haul her to me for a devastating kiss. Our mouths fuse desperately together as our bodies try to fuck through that thin layer of fabric. I slide my hands to her ass, pushing under her panties to feel her bare skin there. My fingers dig into her flesh, needing to mark her as mine before everything changes.

The change will happen before I can blink.

I need this to get me through the hard times.

"Jordy," she breathes. "This feels so good."

"I know," I groan. "Don't stop. Keep rubbing your clit on my dick. I need you to come. I want to taste your moans when you do it."

Her tongue lashes against mine as she works her hips in a sinful way that maddens me. I want to tear her panties from her body and impale her right now. It'd be so simple and Roux would let me. We both want it.

But not only is that crossing a line I can't cross right now, it'd also make things ten times more difficult for us. So, rather than giving in, we continue dry fucking.

"Mmm," she whimpers. "Mmm."

She's about to orgasm and the sounds coming from her

are so fucking beautiful. I rotate and thrust, teasing her while bringing myself right to the edge with her. Her body shatters above me and she cries out with her climax. Unable to resist feeling her, I reach between us, tugging her panties aside. My dick slides along her pussy lips, never entering her. The slick, smooth feel of her is enough to send me hurtling over the edge of sanity with a growl. Cum jets out of my dick, soaking my stomach. My cock throbs as she slowly rubs her naked pussy against me. The cum around the tip of my cock gets dragged all the way to my balls as she makes a mess of smearing my release all over me with just her pussy.

Fuck.

I'll never go soft at this rate.

"Careful, Little Hoodlum. My cum wants inside your little body. Keep rubbing your pussy all in it and you're going to get yourself pregnant. We'll call you Virgin Roux, but instead of carrying the son of God, you'll carry the devil's boy."

She laughs and it's a heavenly sound. "Weirdo."

As she crawls off my body, I drink in her state of disarray. Her dark hair is messy, her lips are swollen and red, and her nearly naked body is a fucking sight to behold. She disappears to the bathroom and returns with a wet cloth. After she strips out of her panties, showing me that perfect cunt of hers, she cleans herself up.

"I'll clean you up," she murmurs, coming to stand beside the bed where I'm sprawled out.

In a painfully torturous way, she cleans the cum and her arousal off my dick and then the mess on my stomach too. When she walks away to go to her dresser, I stare at her cute ass. My dick leaps to attention, desperate for more. I yank up my sweats so I don't do something stupid like fuck her against her dresser. As soon as she has on some panties, yoga pants, and a T-shirt, she crawls into bed to lie down beside me.

For the longest time, I stroke her hair, savoring this moment because I know it'll end soon. So fucking soon.

Finally, she sits up on her elbow and regards me with determination in her eyes that reminds me of Roan.

"Jordy," she says. "There's something I have to do."

I swallow, hating how much I dread hearing these words. To prolong them for a moment longer, I kiss her deeply, savoring her sweet taste. Eventually, I break from our kiss and let out a heavy, resigned sigh. "What is that, Little Hoodlum?"

"I'm sorry," she breathes, her bottom lip wobbling, "but I have to get back with Kayden."

I close my eyes that burn with those words that stumbled out of her mouth. "That so?"

"Yes, but…"

I love you.

She doesn't have to say the words because I feel them.

"I know, Roux. I know."

I give her one last peck on the lips and then I untangle myself from her. I can't look at her as I snatch my shirt up and throw it on. Her sobs are killing me, but I can't stop them. Not now. Not yet.

"Jordy," she cries out when I reach the door.

I close my eyes again as I clutch the knob. "Yeah?"

"Goodbye."

"Later, Little Hoodlum."

I walk out her door and don't look back.

CHAPTER TWENTY-EIGHT

Roux
March

TIME PASSES IN A BLUR THESE DAYS. NOT FAST ENOUGH, that's for sure. I love the days when I can hole up in my room, reading and letting time pass quicker than usual. At least in my room, I'm not forced to be someone I'm not. I can be me.

The door to the apartment closes and I perk up, wondering if it's Jordy. Being in the same apartment with him is difficult. I crave to crawl back into his arms and beg for him to take me far, far away. With each passing day, I grow weaker and weaker. He'd do it. Jordy would do anything for me, which is exactly why I need to remain strong.

It's times like this, though, that I wish I had a friend. Charlotte is nothing to me now. I've given up trying to be friends with her. She's so far removed from the girl she once was, even going as far as getting kicked off the cheerleading squad. There's nothing I can do about it, though. Garrett and Kelsey have been forcing her to go to counseling and forbidden her to see Ryan, but nothing's changed. Ryan has his claws in her and he's not letting go.

My phone buzzes and for a brief moment, I worry Wes has gotten a new number. After the day Kayden pulled a gun on him, Wes backed off. He texted me a few times after, begging to see me, but when I blocked him again, he never tried to make contact again. I'm stupid for thinking it, but in times like this, I even miss his friendship.

It's not Wes, though.

It's my boyfriend.

Kayden: Want a car for your birthday, baby?

I roll my eyes.

Me: Is it a chopped car?

Kayden: They're untraceable. No one is coming after my girl. What do you want?

Me: I don't want a stolen car.

Kayden: Fine. Let's call it not stolen. Better? Now tell me what you want. I can get you anything, baby.

Me: I can't drive.

Kayden: I'll teach you.

Me: Can't you just drive me everywhere?

Kayden: I will but you'll need a car for the days I'm busy. I don't want you to have to rely on your brother. Or him.

Him being Jordy.

Kayden can't see straight most days from being so jealous of Jordy. It's stupid too since he got the girl. Jordy has nothing.

Me: Surprise me.

Kayden: Anything for my girl.

Hollis peeks his head into my bedroom. "Hey, sis."

"Hey," I say. "What's up?"

"Just seeing if you wanted to grab a birthday dinner just the two of us. Roan's on call."

I glance at the clock. If he's on call, he'll probably hang

out at the fire station considering they've been busier than usual, and he practically lives there these days. I'm disappointed he won't have dinner with us, but it's the nature of his job, so I'm familiar with this sort of thing happening. "He's been working a lot."

"This arsonist is running the fire department ragged. I want to kill whoever is doing this," he grumbles.

"Me too." I slide off the bed and hunt down my shoes. "You okay?"

He frowns. "Not really."

"Why?"

"I saw Sidney today."

I wince at hearing her name. She's done nothing but give my brother trouble since he started pursing a paternity test. A test we were granted at Christmastime finally.

Roan is Sebban's father.

Since then, Sidney and Gio have made our life a living hell trying to fight Roan on visitation. It sucks so bad seeing the desperation in Roan's eyes. He just wants to get to know his son. I want to know my nephew. The latest shit they've thrown our way is Roan's relationship with Hollis. They've twisted it into something ugly and perverted. As though two gay men fuck all the time and in front of everyone. As if they'd have sex in front of a little kid. I hate them for what they're putting my brother through.

"How did that go?" I ask, my voice turning icy.

He sighs. "She started bitching me out, but then Sebban disappeared. Just poof. Vanished."

I remember how he'd run off and hid at the yarn store that day. It was scary.

"Where did he go?"

"Well, we searched the whole damn strip of shops. Cops arrived and everything. With it snowing, it put everyone on high alert. We found him in a hamper filled with soiled linens in the kitchen at that fancy steak place on the corner of Main. He'd fallen asleep, so he didn't hear us calling for him."

"Maybe she should focus on not letting her kid run off rather than fighting Roan tooth and nail on custody," I hiss. "I hate her."

"She's just scared," he mutters.

"Don't defend her. She was your friend and at one time cared about Roan. This is mean and cruel."

He sighs. "Yeah, you're right. I really thought if I could just talk to her, she'd be cool."

"At least you tried."

"I'm going to change and then we can head out."

He leaves and heads to his room. Quickly, I get ready, bundling up against an usually snowy March, and then walk into the living room to wait on him. The door opens, and Jordy walks in, snow dusting his dark hair.

Every time I see him, my heart crushes in on itself.

Every. Single. Time.

His dark eyes bore into me, drinking in every detail of me, before settling on my lips. "Hey, Little Hoodlum."

"Hey," I mutter, unable to meet his stare. "We're going to dinner for my birthday if you want to come with."

He sets a stack of mail down on the table. "As much as I want to, I can't."

"Yeah," I agree, my voice shaking and unstable.

I'm staring at the carpet when his black, snow-dusted boots come into view. He holds out an envelope addressed to me. I can tell by all the prison stamps it's from Dad. I start to take it from him, but he doesn't let go. His other hand tucks a strand of hair behind my ear. Tears burn at my eyes. If I look at him, I'll cry.

"Got big plans for your birthday besides dinner with the rat?" he rumbles, his thumb stroking down along my jaw.

"Kayden's having a big party later tonight."

His knuckles slide under my chin and he lifts up so I have to look at him. "Be safe, please."

"I always am."

His eyes roam over my face as if he's trying to memorize it. "Goddammit, Roux."

The tears won't stay in. They slick down my cheeks, dripping off my jaw. I try to hold in the sob, but it claws its way out.

"Shhh," Jordy murmurs. "Don't cry."

He drops a soft kiss on my lips that makes me whine. Once he pulls away, he sets to swiping the tears away with his thumbs. His intense gaze sears into me until Hollis clears his throat.

"You okay?" Hollis asks.

"Yeah," I croak out. "Just sad Roan couldn't make it."

Jordy reluctantly pulls away. To distract myself, I tear through the envelope to find Dad sent me a birthday card with eighteen wrinkly dollars in it. The card is different than his usual Disney one. It's simple. Navy blue with a white flower on the front. He's written me more than his usual few words.

Kiddo,

Happy birthday, angel. I can't believe you're an adult now. Time flies in here. I wish to fuck I could be there with my baby girl to celebrate. I'm always thinking about you and Roan.

Always. Maybe you can talk your brother into coming to see me one day. I'd love to see my kids. I know I fucked up, baby girl, and I'm sorry. If I could go back to that bar, I would've let those shit for brains go on and not done what I did. Sometimes my temper gets the best of me and that hurts the people around me. I see that now. Hope Jordy is looking after you. You're brave as shit. I just want you to know that. You and Roan are both two of the fiercest kids I know and I'd like to think you got it from me. Thank fuck you got your momma's looks. Tell those boys to take you out someplace nice or I'll kick all their asses. Love you to pieces.

I'll always have your back, Roux. Even when it seems impossible, Daddy is always near. Love you and your brother. Happy birthday, baby.

Dad

I tear up as I tuck the money back in the card and take it to my room. It gets stowed away with all the other cards he's written me. I save all the money so that if he ever gets out, I'll take us to dinner with it. I quickly text Roan.

Me: All I want for my birthday is to see Dad. Can we arrange for that to happen? I know you're busy, but it'd mean a lot to me. Love you and be safe.

When I come back into the living room, Jordy is already in the shower and Hollis is waiting for me by the door.

"Ready, birthday girl?"

"Ready as I'll ever be."

I said a small shindig.

Not this.

Not every single person Kayden knows.

I'm used to these parties by now, though. Ever since I made it official that I wanted to get back together, I've been to every single party Kayden goes to. Renaldo hosts plenty of them. Now that Jordy is doing his bidding and I'm with Kayden, Renaldo leaves me alone. Pretends I don't exist. It's fine by me since he scares the living shit out of me.

"Dance with me, baby," Kayden purrs, his mouth stinking of vodka as he mauls me with a kiss.

I grimace and turn my head. He takes the opportunity to suck on my neck as he grinds against me. When I'm with Kayden, everything goes numb. I let my heart turn to ice and do what I must to get by.

"Fuck," Kayden groans, nipping at my ear. "All these bitches are looking like skanks in their short skirts, but you're fine as fuck in jeans and a sweater. You've got me by the balls, baby. Renaldo says I'm pussy whipped."

I laugh. "Being nice to your girlfriend isn't the same as being pussy whipped. I don't boss you around."

"I just tell him to fuck off. He doesn't know what it's like to love someone."

Kayden only loves himself, but I preen for him anyway.

"Aww, you're so sweet." I hug him and rest my cheek on his chest, closing my eyes.

We slow dance to a fast song. My mind is on a million other things, all of them far away from this party.

"I thought since we've been dating off and on for a year now that we could…"

I tense in his arms. "What?"

"Make love, baby. I've waited so long to have you. We're getting along so good, too. Please let me show you how good it can be."

"Kayden," I start but freeze up.

I knew it would come to this.

"I'm getting there," I murmur, trying desperately to make him believe that. "It never feels right with all these people around. We're never alone."

He pulls back, his brown eyes darting all over my face. "I can make them all leave."

"Maybe just plan a date for the two of us," I offer. "See where the night takes us."

His grin is wide and boyish. "You got it, babe. Soon."

He drops a kiss to my lips and I'm thankful I've dodged our main point of contention. Sex. Or lack thereof.

"Let me show you your present," he says. "Maybe we can fuck on it."

"Kayden," I say, swatting at him. "Don't be a dick."

He chuckles as he drags me out of Renaldo's place and outside. The snow is coming down hard. He bypasses a few sports cars and comes to a black, suped up Range Rover.

"Surprise," he says, mashing the buttons and making the lights blink. "She's all yours."

"A chopped car?" I ask.

"Someone else's trash is our treasure."

"It's not their trash if you steal it from them."

He snorts out a laugh. "The dude we took it from has bigger shit to worry about."

"Like what?"

"Like the fact your old boyfriend set his house on fire."

I freeze at his words. "What?"

"Like you don't know what Jordy does for my brother now." He smirks at me. "Jordy starts the fires and your brother puts them out. How's that for fucking hilarious?"

I want to choke him in this moment.

"That vodka is making me feel sick. Can you take me home?"

He frowns. "Wait. Baby, I'm sorry. I was just joking about Jordy being your old boyfriend. I know you hate that jealous shit. Please don't go. I did all this for you." He waves at the bumping party behind him and then at the car.

"I know," I squeak out. "You're so sweet. I really don't feel good. Hollis and I had steak earlier. Must have not settled right. I feel like I'm going to puke."

His irritation morphs into worry. "Yeah. No big deal. We'll go out on a date soon and I'll give you your other birthday present."

"What's that?"

"I'm going to lick your pussy and give you your first orgasm."

My cheeks burn red hot. Over the past several months, we've made out and he's dry humped me with his hand up my shirt, but that's as far as I've allowed it to go. I certainly didn't ever come with him. All I can think about is the last time someone else made me come.

Him.

Jordy.

"I, uh, Kayden, don't be gross."

He laughs. "Trust me. It's going to be all kinds of nasty. I'm going to eat you out for days, baby, until you can't walk anymore. I'll wear your scent all over my face."

I somehow manage to drag him to his car. We make it home in one piece. After a long, annoying make out session, I manage to untangle myself from him. It's after two in the morning before I finally crash.

I wake to shouts.

Panic.

Terror.

Scrambling, I rush to my bedroom door and fling it open. The front door to the apartment is standing wide-open, snowy wind billowing in. Hollis and Jordy, both in just their boxers, share matching horrified looks.

"What?" I demand, rushing over to the door.

Roan peels out of the driveway in his truck, slipping every which way in it. Whirling around, I slam the door closed and turn toward them. Jordy is already approaching me with his blanket. It's then I realize I'm only wearing a T-shirt and panties. He wraps me up in the blanket and I give them both a questioning look.

"What just happened? Where did Roan go?"

"He got called out," Hollis croaks.

"For work?" I ask.

Jordy's hand splays on my back over the blanket. "Yeah."

"So? That always happens. What aren't you telling me?"

Jordy presses his lips to the top of my head. "Mike said it's Sidney and Gio's address."

My legs give out beneath me, sending me and Jordy falling to the floor. He pulls me to him, rocking me.

"It's going to be okay," Jordy whispers.

The sounds coming from Hollis—tearful and pained—tell me it's not.

"Sebban."

"Shh," Jordy murmurs. "Shh, Little Hoodlum."

CHAPTER TWENTY-NINE

Jordy

RENALDO.

All I can think about is the fact that Renaldo has pulled another shit move to get back at me. But how could he possibly know that Sebban is Roan's kid? And what purpose would it serve to torch their fucking house? I've been Renaldo's bitch without complaint. Set every single one of those goddamn fires for him.

It. Makes. No. Sense.

It's been hours of waiting since Roan blew out of here. Roux let me move her to the couch where her head's been in my lap. I stroke her hair, wishing I could fix everything with a snap of my fingers. Hollis gets a call and he leaps up from the other end of the couch, disappearing into his room.

A few minutes later, Hollis returns with tears in his eyes.

"What is it?" I demand, my voice hoarse.

"T-They're dead," Hollis chokes out.

Roux sits up, shrieking. "Who?"

"Gio and Sidney."

Guilt consumes me and I close my eyes, willing the urge

to throw up away. I never liked Sidney. Never. Doesn't mean I wanted her or the nerd to die.

"How?" Roux demands. "And…"

Sebban.

Hollis clears his throat and sniffles. "They, uh, they died from carbon monoxide poisoning. It was a freak accident."

I snap my eyes open. "It wasn't a fire?"

"No, man," he mutters.

Knowing it was an accident and not Renaldo helps alleviate any guilt that was starting to plague me. Still fucking horrible, though.

"What about Sebban?" Roux finally manages to croak out.

"They can't find him," he whispers. "Fuck."

Hollis rushes to his bedroom, slamming the door behind him. I can hear him fucking crying and it guts me. How fucked up is the world to give Roan a son but then to take him away? Roux sits up and crawls into my lap. I hold her to me, kissing her hair and whispering assurances that neither of us believes. She falls asleep and I take the time to slide out from under her and hop in the shower. I want to be dressed and ready if I need to leave. By the time I get back to Roux, she's still asleep. I sit back at my perch, playing with her hair.

I'm not sure how much time passes, but I'm jolted from Hollis's yelling in the other room. Doesn't sound like bad yelling. Maybe more like cheering. My phone buzzes with a text.

Roan: We found him in the toy box in his closet under some blankets. They're life flighting him now. I think he's going to make it.

The picture he sends is of a tiny, miniature version of my

best friend lying on a stretcher. He's pale and they've got him on oxygen, but he's alive.

Holy shit.

"Babe, look," I tell Roux. "He's alive."

She takes the phone from me and starts to sob at seeing her nephew. "Oh my God."

A few minutes later, Hollis rushes out, dressed and carrying a backpack. "I'm going to take Roan to the hospital in Portland where they've sent Sebban. He's too shaken up to drive. We'll call you when we know more. There's no sense in all of us going up there."

"Let us know the moment it's okay to drive out there," I tell him. "Roux and I will head that way."

He gives us a quick wave before leaving.

"Why don't you grab a quick shower? I'll make breakfast," I tell Roux.

She nods and disappears. I start rummaging in the kitchen, pulling out whatever I can find to make omelets. I know this has to be the shittiest birthday for Roux, but I'm going to try and make it up to her. By the time I've plated the Mexican style omelets—complete with black beans, corn, jalapeno peppers, avocadoes, tomatoes, cheese, and sour cream—and garnished with cilantro, Roux walks out, refreshed from her shower.

The hoodie she's wearing—one of mine—swallows her. A male sense of pride washes over me. I'm sure she has shorts on underneath, but the fact I can see her bare legs makes me crazy with the need to touch her.

"Smells good," she says with a smile. "You didn't have to go through all this trouble."

I pour some orange juice into two champagne flutes I

found in the cabinet. They must have been from Hollis and Roan's wedding, because it has their initials and wedding date engraved on them. Roux doesn't seem too bothered because she happily picks up a flute and sips the orange juice.

"It's your birthday. Of course you deserve a nice breakfast." I smile at her as I sit down. "Do you feel older?"

She laughs as she cuts into her omelet. "I feel tired."

"Welcome to adulthood."

We sit in amicable silence as we eat. All of her groans and praise at my meal does nothing for the state of my cock that's been half hard since she walked in with her bare legs on display.

"I feel so bad about Sidney and Gio," she says with a sad sigh. "They gave Roan such shit about Sebban, but I didn't want them to die."

I reach across the table and take her hand. "Me neither. All we can do now is be there for your brother. Seems like if Sebban can make it through this, we may be welcoming a new Hoodlum into the fray."

"Baby Hoodlum." She smiles. "Little Hoodlum is taken."

I brush my foot against hers. "She sure is."

Her amber eyes ignite with fire. I want to haul her into my arms and kiss her until she can't breathe. Instead, I enjoy one of our rare moments alone. With no makeup on and her wet hair messy and wild, I still can't help but think she's the most beautiful girl in the world.

"How's your boyfriend?" I ask, threading my fingers with hers. "He being good to you?"

She sticks her tongue out at me.

"Keep that tongue in your mouth unless you're ready to use it. I know for a fact you're not ready."

Her amusement fades as her eyes water. "Jordy, this is hard. I… He wants to have sex."

Ice surges through my veins at her words. "Don't fuck him."

"I don't plan on it," she cries out. "But we're at the shit or get off the pot point in our relationship. I don't know what to do."

"We'll figure it out," I promise.

She stands and picks up our plates, taking them into the kitchen. I fetch her gift and then prowl over to her where she washes up the dishes from breakfast. Pressing against her from behind, I inhale her hair and then dangle her gift in front of her.

"Oh, Jordy," she gasps as she turns off the water. "Is that my birthday present?"

"Yeah, babe. Do you like it?"

She nods as she moves her wet hair to the side. I bring the rose gold necklace around and latch it from behind. I fix her hair and then turn her so she's facing me. In a cursive rose gold emblem in my handwriting that's attached to the chains, it says, "Little Hoodlum."

"I love it," she murmurs, fingering the jewelry. "Thank you."

With my eyes boring into hers, I tuck her hair behind her ears and then lean forward to kiss her forehead. "You're welcome."

She slides her palms up my chest to my neck. I grip her small ass, pulling her against me. We both groan in relief because it's always torture waiting until we're alone to touch and kiss. My mouth crashes against hers and I decimate her with a claiming kiss that has her knees buckling.

I don't let my girl fall.

Never.

Gripping her ass, I lift her up, loving that she spreads her legs, eagerly wrapping herself around me. I carry her through the apartment and into her bedroom. The door gets kicked shut and then I drop us onto the bed. Our kiss grows frenzied and desperate, just like every night when I finally get to sneak in.

Waiting is torture.

Hiding is killing us.

All of it is necessary.

I strip off her hoodie, pleased as fuck to see she's wearing nothing underneath. Her small tits jiggle from the movement and her nipples are hard. I growl, lowering myself so I can take one between my teeth. My girl loves when I bite her. Something we've learned in our stolen moments in the middle of the night. I kiss away every part that Kayden may have touched, claiming her once again as mine.

"Mine," I remind her.

Always mine.

"Yours."

Pleased with her words, I roughly yank her shorts and panties off. Once she's naked, I push her thighs apart, eager to taste her. Because I'm not stupid and won't tempt fate, we've kept our nightly rendezvous to mainly PG-13 stuff.

Today, though, she's mine.

I'm going to lick her pretty pussy until she's screaming my name.

I always knew she belonged to me, but at least now I won't go to prison for it.

"You're wet," I rumble, running my knuckle between her pussy lips. "Why are you so wet, beautiful?"

She bites on her bottom lip. "Because I've been waiting for this since Hollis left us alone."

"What's *this*, hmm?" I ask, rubbing her clit. "I need details."

Her breaths come out in pants. "Us."

"Elaborate."

"You finally making love to me."

"I'm going to fuck you, Roux. I'm going to fuck you so hard you scream."

Her hooded eyes flash with lust. "I don't care what the hell you call it, Jordy, as long as you're inside me."

"Good girl," I praise, lowering my mouth to her slick cunt. "My good girl."

She whines when I run my tongue from her hole to her clit. Her back arches up as she grips her blanket in her fists. "Oh God."

With a smile on my lips, I start licking her as though I'm desperate to suck off every drop of her arousal. She squirms and squawks, needy for what I'm giving her. My fingers on her and in her have been nice over the past few months, and she always comes with my name purring from her lips, but she's never lost her mind like this. The mewls and groans escaping her are animalistic in nature. I fucking love them.

"My dick's going to be stretching this needy hole out soon, Roux," I murmur against her pussy.

She gasps when I push my tongue inside her. Her cunt clenches around my tongue as though she's trying to suck the damn thing into her body. The sloppy sounds I'm making as I tongue-fuck her pussy have my dick practically dripping with the need to come. I rub at her clit with my thumb as I devour her delicious body from the inside out until she screams out my name. Her arousal grows thicker, soaking my tongue with her unique taste. I fuck her hole with my tongue until I'm sure I've licked it all away and then I suck on her pussy lips, eager to grab up anything I missed.

"Jordy," she whines. "Holy fuck."

I sit up on my knees and swipe away the wetness on my face with my hand before grabbing the back of my T-shirt behind my neck. Her coppery eyes flash as she drinks in my torso. Slowly, I pull off my shirt and toss it away. I flex my pecs and then abs, enjoying the fuck out of the way she bites her bottom lip at seeing me.

"Beg for my dick, Roux."

"Give it to me."

"That's awfully demanding," I say with a smirk as I shove my sweats down and grab my cock. "You're gonna have to be sweeter than that."

"Please," she begs, batting her lashes at me.

I kick out of my sweats and prowl over her trembling body. "I've waited for this moment since the day I laid eyes on you that day in prison looking like a hot-ass fucking woman. This won't be gentle, babe. This is going to be a claiming fuck."

Her legs wrap around my waist and her fingers thread into my hair. "Claim me."

Our mouths connect in a fiery kiss as my dick slides between the lips of her pussy, rubbing against her sensitive clit. I grab hold of it and then press against her tight hole. There's no warning for her. I just thrust inside, hard and fast. She cries out at the sudden stretching intrusion. I'm pretty sure I tore through her innocence when I had three fingers inside her on New Year's Eve after we both had too much to drink. That was the night we almost got caught and were dangerously close to fucking.

I made her bleed that night.

Today, she takes my dick without complaint.

My hips thrust with obsessive need to stretch and own her body with mine. Our skin slaps loudly, echoing in her small room. I nip at her lip and suck on her tongue, desperate to devour every part of her all at once. Her nails scoring along my scalp painfully is my only warning she's coming. The moment the walls of her cunt grip me, I nearly black out from pleasure. With a growl that sounds savage and fucking feral, I come inside her. My dick throbs out my release, filling my girl the fuck up.

I know she's not on the pill.

We talked about that fact.

There are condoms stowed away in her nightstand for this moment.

And yet we both fucking ignored them.

Pulling away from our kiss, I lock eyes with hers. "Babe, I fucking came inside you."

"Have you ever not taken care of me?"

"I'll take care of you until my dying breath. I fucking love you, Roux."

"Love you too, Jordy."

I slide out of her and lie on my side. With my elbow propped up and my head resting in my hand, I admire my just-fucked birthday girl. My cum leaks out of her and like the fucking caveman I am, I gently push it back inside her with my finger. I leave my finger inside her body, keeping hold of her pussy like it belongs solely to me.

Tears form in her eyes and her nose turns red. "I can't do this anymore. Not after this. It's been too hard as it is."

I lean down and kiss her. "You're the bravest girl I know.

So fucking brave. This is almost over, Little Hoodlum, and when it finally is, nothing will stop us from being together."

She pulls me to her for a deeper kiss. I fingerfuck her until I'm hard as hell again and she's begging for more. Over and over again, because the birthday girl seems to love my dick as much as I love her pussy.

The condoms stay in the drawer.

CHAPTER THIRTY

Roux

I CAN DO THIS.

I can do this.

I can do this.

But it's so damn hard. Pretending to be someone I'm not. Ignoring the one I love for the one I have to be with. It's torture.

This is almost over, Little Hoodlum.

Jordy's words play on repeat in my mind, reminding me of my purpose and to stay strong.

"Tomorrow," Kayden says, hugging me from behind. "I'm taking you to dinner and to a hotel. Since the snow didn't stay and it's warming up, maybe we can eat at that new place on the river."

I try not to cringe and keep my voice light. "I can't. I have plans with Roan."

It's the truth. With Sebban finally well enough to leave Portland, and the legalities getting straightened out, we might be able to take him home with us. It's going to be a huge adjustment for Sebban, so Roan is going to need my help.

"Sometimes I feel like you're stringing me along," Kayden snaps, releasing me. "It's fucking embarrassing."

I whirl around, crossing my arms over my chest. "Kayden..."

The fire behind me flickers and makes his dark eyes light up like he's the devil. A shiver trembles down my spine. Someone hollers and then laughs nearby, but my focus is on Kayden.

"You won't drive the car I got you the other day. Even though you're eighteen and we've been together for a year, you won't fuck me. I've finally planned this stupid date you've begged for and you're avoiding it. What the fuck is your problem, Roux?"

Panic claws at my throat, keeping words trapped there. A low whine escapes, though.

"If I didn't know better, I'd say you were just using me. Why, Roux? What the hell would you be using me for?"

"Hey," I purr, finally finding my voice. "You know there's a lot going on with my brother right now. I don't do well with stress when it involves him. He's my best friend and sometimes like a father to me. It's not you. It's that. You know I want to be with you. It's why I asked to get back together with you." I walk up to him and cradle his face. "Remember, baby?"

His face softens. "Yeah. You did come crawling back to me. Begging for this." He playfully grabs his dick through his jeans. "Soon, baby."

"Soon," I agree, forcing a smile. I stand on my toes and kiss him. "Your friends are here. The Hoodlums are being cool. Maybe enjoy Campfire Chaos and relax. Renaldo keeps you too stressed out. Get something to drink. I'm going to check on Roan and then we can make s'mores together."

He shoves his tongue down my throat and after a few minutes of enduring his mauling, he tears away from me. "Come find me, baby."

I wave to him and then walk backward into the shadows, shuddering with the urge to throw up. Stopping to take a deep breath, I press into the middle of my chest for a second. I didn't want to be here tonight, but I was told it was imperative. I do what I'm told because I have to. It's the only way.

Once I've distanced myself from the party, I take a walk through the woods toward the river. At least I can breathe a little easier without Kayden all in my space. It's too hard to be with him when Jordy's around. Jordy keeps his expression neutral, but I know it kills him to see me lip locked with Kayden. I know this, because it kills me too.

"Still with the thug, huh?"

A deep, familiar voice has me stopping in my tracks. It's dark in the woods, but the river is close. I can hear it rushing by. I grasp onto a tree, trying to keep my fear at bay, and whip my head around.

Wes.

"What do you want?"

"He's a dickhead who'll be in prison by the time he's twenty-one," Wes says from the shadows. "Why would you date someone like him with no future?"

"I don't think you should be here," I mutter. "If Kayden sees you, it won't end well."

"He'll pull another gun on me?" Wes chuckles. "I'm prepared this time."

His ominous words send a chill down my spine.

"You were my friend," I say in a calm tone. "You thought we were more."

Wes emerges from the shadows, stepping into a pocket of moonlight. His eyes are manic and wild, his appearance disheveled. He has a gun tucked into the front of his jeans. I take a step back on instinct. His head cocks to the side.

"Don't think about running off," he commands. "We have a lot to discuss."

Tears burn at my eyes, but I blink fast so I can keep him in my sights. I'm just far enough from the loud party, I'm not sure anyone would hear if I screamed. What happens if I do scream? Jordy and Kayden run to my aid and might get shot?

"What do you want to talk about?" I ask calmly. "You have more poems?"

"A fuck ton more," he says, flashing me a handsome grin. "I can't wait to read them to you. Like old times."

I start to turn and run, but he tackles me to the ground. My scream threatens to escape, but his hand covers my mouth. The gun in his pants digs into my ass. I freeze when he rubs his hand up my thigh, dragging my dress up with it.

"Stop moving, Roux, or it'll hurt. Don't make me hurt you."

A sob escapes me and tears rush out. My entire body trembles as he pets me like I'm something to be treasured.

"Shh, don't cry," he whines. "It's just me. Wes. Your friend, but we're going to be more, Roux. You're so fucking smart and pretty. We had a connection, but you got spooked. I swear to God I can be better. I can keep you safe from that gangster." He reaches between us and pulls the gun out, setting it on the ground by my face. "I love you."

My crying becomes hysterical when he starts to tug my panties down. Wes is stronger and fucking crazy. He easily pins me down. Once my panties are at my knees, he starts undoing his pants. I start to black out, fear overwhelming me.

"What the fuck?"

The voice is familiar. Someone I know and trust. I cry out to him.

Wes is ripped from me with the force of an F-5 tornado. My savior pounces on him, pinning him to the ground. He slams punch after punch into Wes's face. I manage to yank my panties up and pick up the gun.

"Give me that," Cal growls, yanking it from my grip.

He shoves the barrel into Wes's mouth and I'm dizzied by the fact that one of the Hoodlums is once again about to kill on my behalf. I cry out, yanking on Cal's arm, but he's too strong.

Click.

Nothing happens.

Cal yanks the gun out. He removes the magazine and roars. "It's not even fucking loaded!" He throws the magazine and then hits Wes a few times with the gun. "Fucking rapist sick sonofabitch!"

"Cal," I shriek. "Stop. You're going to kill him!"

"That's the fucking point, Roux!"

I cling to his back, pulling him away from Wes's groaning body. Cal eventually lets sense flood in and allows me to put distance between them. He's breathing heavily, still infused with rage.

"I need to get the boys down here so we can drag his ass down to the river," Cal growls.

"No," I snap. "You can't. Jordy will kill him and go to prison again. You'll go to prison. I can't fucking have that. Understand?"

"I don't fucking care," Cal snarls. "He tried to fucking rape you!"

I sit beside Cal and take his sticky hands in my shaking ones. His are covered in Wes's blood. Squeezing, I meet his enraged eyes.

"Listen. You absolutely cannot breathe a word of this to anyone. It'll ruin everything. Trust me, Cal. Please trust me. There are too many eyes and ears on us. Just let Wes go. I think he got the message loud and clear."

"Roan will skin him alive once he finds out," Cal says, turning his head to spit. "I'll fucking help him too."

"You can't tell Roan. Jesus, Cal, listen to me. Roan is trying to get his kid. Don't do this to him. Please."

He frowns as he thinks. "I keep forgetting about that shit. A kid. I can't believe it."

"Believe it. And Roan wants him so bad. If you tell him about this, he'll go blind in his need to protect me. You already saved me," I say softly. "You saved me and I can't thank you enough. I'll do whatever I can to repay you for that. But he can't find out."

"Hoodlums don't keep secrets from each other with outsiders."

"I'm a Hoodlum too," I remind him. "We're protecting them. You know as well as I do that Jordy will murder him for this."

He cocks his head to the side, assessing me. "Jordy loves you."

I smile. "I love him too."

"Does Roan know that?"

"No, and we'll deal with that later."

"This sucks," Cal grumbles. "I hate this motherfucker for touching you."

"Me too," I murmur. "One day, we can go about this in a

legal way, and I swear I'll be there ready to make that happen. Trust me that it's not the right time."

He sighs. "When did you grow up, Little Hoodlum?"

"Same time you guys did. When life made us."

"All right. Let's get you back to camp. Then I'll make sure this asshole goes home."

"You won't kill him?"

"Not yet." He flashes me a sinister smile. "I'll find a way to make his life a living hell. That much is a fucking promise."

I stand on my toes and hug his neck. "Thank you, Cal."

"Anytime, kiddo."

By the time I've pulled myself together, over an hour has passed. I pace on the edge of the woods watching Kayden get drunker and drunker. He stumbles over to a chair and crashes into it. Once I'm sure he's asleep, I hunt down Jordy.

I need to see him.

I need his comfort. I just need him.

He's by his tent when I approach. Sensing my mood, he unzips the tent, looks around, and then nods. I bolt inside the tent and lie down. Tears drip from my eyes as I desperately try to hold it together. He zips it back up and then curls his large body around mine, keeping me locked in his safe embrace.

"Shh, baby," he murmurs. "Don't cry. Tell me what's wrong."

But I can't.

I have to keep my lips sealed shut in order to protect him.

It reminds me of the way he pressed his lips together in the courtroom that day, refusing to tell the truth of what happened that night when he shot four men, in an effort to keep me and Roan safe. I'd hated him for that, but I understand it now, because I'm doing the same for him.

Love is strong like that.

"I just want all this to be over," I sob. It's the truth. Jordy deserves truth. "I want to be with you always."

He brushes my hair away from my neck and kisses me there. When his hand caresses along my thigh, I don't shiver from fear like I did with Wes. Instead, I let out a breath of relief. In Jordy's arms is where I belong. Gently, he urges my dress up and slides his hand into my panties.

"You're here with me now," he murmurs. "You're mine. Don't forget that, Roux. When all feels fucking overwhelming, remember us."

He rubs his finger over my clit, erasing each bad memory of tonight with simple strokes. I allow myself to forget and drown in all things Jordy. Before long, I'm whimpering as my climax takes over. He wastes no time peeling my panties off me. His massive body prowls over mine and he settles himself between my parted thighs. He reaches down to unbuckle his jeans and then pulls his dick out. We both groan when he presses against my pussy. His body slides easily into mine, claiming me. I latch my fingers into his hair, pulling him down to me for a kiss.

It's reckless allowing him to fuck me with Kayden nearby and asleep, but after what went down with Wes, I don't care. I need my man. I need Jordy. He fucks me hard and fast, knowing like I do that our time is limited. His hand slides between us and he rolls my clit around between his thumb and finger. I lose all sense of reality.

I beg and beg and beg.

I need him so much.

He answers my needy pleas with a nip to my throat and a growl as he floods my body with his release. I whimper out his name, thankful to have him in my arms. We remain locked for a few moments.

"Want to talk about it?"

"I just want to stay with you forever."

"I know, Roux. I fucking know. Fuck."

"I love you."

"Love you too," he murmurs as he pulls out. "Stay a little while with me. It'll be okay."

He hands me his shirt to clean up with and then helps me put my panties back on. Once he's cleaned up and his jeans are back in place, he pulls me to him.

"Let me hold you, baby. You're shaking."

I cling to him, biting back tears. "I'm scared."

"Me too."

We remain locked in our lovers' embrace until his breathing evens out. I watch him sleep until I feel like it's too dangerous to stay in his tent any longer. With a sad sigh, I untangle myself from him and crawl away from him. Quietly, I unzip his tent and slip out.

I smooth out my hair and straighten my dress, my eyes skimming the campfire area. I press my fingers to my chest, sucking in a steadying breath. Kayden isn't in his seat. A cold sense of dread washes over me. Slowly, I turn around. Kayden is leaned against a tree, watching me as he takes a drag of his cigarette.

"Have fun in there?" His tone is deadly.

"It's not what you think," I breathe. "We were just talking."

He tosses his cigarette and stomps on it. "Talking." He

shakes his head. "Now that I am watching you lie to my fucking face, it's easy to see that our entire fucking relationship was a lie."

"Kayden," I plead, stepping closer to him. "It wasn't a lie."

His eyes turn hard. "Walk with me."

Fear has my feet planted firmly in place.

"Roux, so help me, I said let's take a goddamn walk."

"Kayden, I'm scared."

Someone strong grabs me from behind, slapping a palm over my mouth.

"You should be, little girl. You should be pissing your cum-soaked panties right now."

Renaldo.

Oh God.

"Time to go," he growls.

I scream and kick to no avail.

Oh God.

Oh God.

Oh my fucking God.

CHAPTER THIRTY-ONE

Jordy

Buzz.
> *Buzz.*
> *Buzz.*

I wake in the dark, confused by my surroundings at first. Fumbling around, I manage to find my phone under the shirt that's still wet from my cum. Loss hollows me out. I hate that she had to leave me. Squinting, I read the texts I missed, hoping they're from Roux.

Renaldo: Wake up, bitch.
Renaldo: We have your cheating whore.
Renaldo: Meet me at the shop.

No.

Fucking no!

I yank another shirt out of my bag, throw on my shoes, and grab my keys within seconds before tearing out of the tent.

"Roan!" I bellow, scaring some people who'd passed out by the fire. "Hollis!"

They rush out of the cabin, both of them in their boxers, eyes wild with alarm.

"They fucking took her," I choke out. "They fucking took her."

Roan's expression falls from worry to dread as he understands my meaning. He launches himself back into the cabin, Hollis on his heels. Terrence jolts awake from his chair on the porch.

"What's happening?" he grumbles, his voice thick with sleep.

"It's going down," I rasp out, trembling with a mixture of anger and terror.

"Fuck," he hisses. "Cal, bro, we gotta go! Cal!"

Cal stumbles out of a tent looking like hell. His hands are bloody and his hair is sticking up. He sobers up quickly when he realizes we're flipping our shit and snags his shoes before rushing over to me.

Hollis bolts from the cabin, fully dressed, and runs to his car. He peels out, not even taking time to look back at us. Roan flies out, a baseball bat in his hand.

Terrence shakes his head and plucks it from his grip. "I'll take that."

"Where'd the rat go?" I demand as we all start running to the cars.

"I don't want him anywhere near this shit," Roan grinds out. "It's bad enough you guys are involved."

Guilt bangs around inside my heart and I wish it were just me dealing with this shit. But family isn't like that. The Hoodlums are family and family sticks together. I'd tried once before to do things on my own, and it ended badly. Now, I've got all of these assholes on my team. As much as it stresses me out, I'm thankful. I'm not sure I could hold my shit together on my own.

"I'm headed to the shop," I tell Roan.

"We got your back." Roan slaps my shoulder and bounds off after Terrence and Cal. The three of them climb into Cal's truck and I hop into my car.

I peel out ahead of them and turn onto the road toward Juno's shop. They head in the opposite direction. The entire drive there, I plan out all the ways I'd love to kill Renaldo. My favorite scenario is burning him alive.

When I arrive at the shop, I find several thugs waiting on me. Not Renaldo or Kayden. That's okay. I anticipated this. Quickly, I shoot off a text and then shove my phone into my pocket.

Juno emerges from the shop as I climb out of the car. He rushes me, slamming his fist into my face.

"You stupid sonofabitch!" he snarls. "Of all the bitches you had to stick your dick into, it had to be her!"

I dodge another punch, but the third one hits me in the gut.

"You're fucking my shit up with Renaldo," Juno snarls. "How the fuck is he supposed to trust his partner when his partner's little brother is sleeping with his brother's girlfriend?"

He punches me again, but I tackle him. I land a few hits of my own before the thugs yank me off, shoving a gun against my temple. They pat me down and steal my phone. Juno laughs when he stomps it to pieces.

"Put him in the back. Let's go. Renaldo's waiting."

I don't fight my attackers because where Renaldo is, so is Roux. I'll do whatever it takes to get to her.

A thug hops in the front of the SUV and my brother sits shotgun. I sit wedged between two assholes with a gun digging painfully into my neck. Each bump, I cringe wondering if he'll accidentally pull the trigger.

The trip doesn't take but fifteen minutes and I let out a breath of relief when I recognize where they're taking me. Renaldo's house. This is good. They park the SUV and I'm dragged from the vehicle into the house. Inside, there are several people standing around the sofa.

My eyes dart to Renaldo.

In his arms is my fucking girl.

Crying and terrified.

His pussy brother Kayden paces nearby but doesn't intervene on her behalf.

"Let her go," I bark out, fighting against my captors.

Renaldo's evil glare locks on mine. "This bitch is gonna get you killed."

"Your beef is with me, asshole, not her. Let her fucking go," I growl.

Renaldo yanks her back against his chest, forcing her legs apart and pinning them with his own. Tears roll down her cheeks and her chest shudders with each breath she takes. He has a gun pressed to her temple.

"You did all this shit for a piece of teenage pussy," Renaldo snarls in disgust. "You're so fucking stupid." With his free hand, he yanks her dress up. Her panties have been removed. I want to crush his skull in for exposing her like this. Slowly, he slides the barrel of the gun down to her pussy, rubbing it between the lips there. She sobs uncontrollably. "Must be really fucking magical to have both you and my brother so fucking twisted up over it. Maybe I ought to fuck it to see what the fuss is all about. Let your brother fuck it too. If it's so damn magical, everyone in this room should have a turn."

She tries to force her legs closed, but his words stop her.

"Keep 'em open, baby, or I'll blow your boyfriend's fucking head off."

My sweet girl spreads her legs again, her whole body shaking wildly. He turns the gun, easing the barrel inside of her. I'm sickened to the point I grow dizzy. I can't fucking watch him do this to her.

"Look what a good girl she is," Renaldo praises. "Taking this gun like it's a dick."

I tear my gaze from the act, desperately seeking out the only person in this room who might give a shit about her. Kayden. His face is horror-stricken as he watches his brother abuse his girlfriend. He glances at me, fear shining in his eyes.

"Don't look at him," Renaldo snaps at his brother. "He's the one who was fucking your girl, remember? Get the fuck over here."

Kayden hardens his features and walks over to them. I fight against the thugs holding me, earning a punch to the gut that nearly makes me puke.

"This'll be your only shot," Renaldo rumbles. "Fuck your girl since you brought all this shit down on us for her."

Kayden shakes his head. "I am fucking done with her."

Renaldo pulls the gun out of Roux and points it at his brother. "Open."

"Renaldo—" His words get shoved back into his mouth along with the barrel of the gun.

"Taste your girl? Taste fucking magical to you?"

Kayden remains deathly still.

"Get your fucking knife out of your pocket and cut her dress off," Renaldo commands. "Since you don't want to fuck your whore, you can strip her for me."

"Stop fucking touching her!" I yell.

This earns me another punch to the gut.

I'm swallowing down bile and blinking back the dizziness in time to see Kayden sawing through her dress. He curses, making me freeze. The entire room tenses at seeing the wire taped between her breasts.

"You did this, Kayden. You." Renaldo rips it off her chest. "Now fuck her. That was always your end game. You chose pussy over blood. Now fucking fuck her, you fucking fuck!"

I can't watch this.

Everything is happening too slowly.

They'll rape her and then kill her.

Like a maddened bull, I rage and buck, desperate to reach her. I knock back a few guys, but then they all pounce on me, kicking the shit out of me and stomping on me.

I hear Renaldo call Kayden a pussy and then Roux screams. I'm able to see past the fuckers beating me. Renaldo is standing with Roux kicking in his arms. He throws her down onto the coffee table hard. I watch helplessly as he holds her down while some thugs set to tying her face down on the table. She's facing me, which means I'm going to have to watch her as they all rape her.

I try to lock my eyes with hers, but these bastards are now punching me in the fucking face. Her name gets murmured over and over until I black out.

I wake to the scent of gasoline.

Strong. Foreboding. Sickening.

"J-Jordy! Jordy, w-wake up!"

Groaning, I try to move, but it hurts too fucking bad. I'm able to squeeze one eye open. Roux is still on the table, but no one is touching her.

"Roux," I rasp out, reaching blindly for her.

"You have t-to get up and g-get us out of here," she chatters out. "Now, J-Jordy."

Renaldo squats down behind Roux, watching me over her prone body. "Would you look at that? They think they're getting out of here alive. How fucking cute." He smacks her bare ass and then shoves his fingers into her. Her screams are a match to my soul.

"Roux!"

Renaldo throws his head back, laughing. One of his thugs comes up behind Renaldo, a knife in his grip and a dark look on his face.

"For Jace," the guy bellows before slamming the knife into the side of Renaldo's neck.

Renaldo whips around, pulling a gun out in record speed. He blows the head off of the guy who stabbed him. With a grunt, he rises to his feet, touching the knife in his neck. No way. I knew Roux's dad had connections on the outside but was not expecting that.

"Fuck," he roars. "Fuck!"

My brother rushes to his aid. Fucking asshole. While they try to help Renaldo, I inch my way over to Roux. I touch her face with a shaky hand.

"I'm going to get you out of here," I vow. "Do you understand?"

She nods hard, tears sailing down her cheeks.

"We have to bail," Juno barks out, assisting Renaldo. "Now, Kayden."

Kayden's eyes are locked on me and Roux, hatred burning in them.

"Do it," Renaldo rasps out. "Blood over bitches."

Kayden pulls out a book of matches. With absolutely no remorse, he lights the match and tosses it onto the carpet.

Fuck.

Orange light flies across the carpet, hot and blinding, quickly encircling us. Kayden storms over to me and kicks me, sending me flying back. He throws punch after punch until someone drags him away.

Everything fades from painful orange to blissful black.

CHAPTER THIRTY-TWO

Roux

'M GOING TO BURN TO DEATH.

I'll have to watch Jordy die first.

This is hell. I'm already here.

My throat is hoarse from screaming at him. Over and over. I need for him to wake up. When he grunts, I sob in relief.

"Jordy, baby, wake up. You have to wake up."

He squints open his good eye, quickly growing aware of our dire situation. The fire is quickly spreading and the heat from it is burning my naked skin. Jordy crawls my way and starts fumbling with the rope around one of my arms. I scream when a flame licks at my foot. With a grunt, he drags the whole table away from the flames and starts rapidly untying the rope. He frees one hand and rushes to my legs, leaving me to work on the other hand. I get it loosened just enough to wriggle through it. The moment my legs are free, he yanks me into his arms.

"Did they…" He trails off, his voice cracking.

"N-No," I assure him, choking on a sob. "You w-weren't

out b-but a minute or so. Renaldo was t-taunting me, asking me who I w-wanted to rape me first, b-but it never got p-past that b-because that guy stabbed him. W-Where's my dress?"

He jerks his T-shirt off and tosses it over my head. I've barely pushed my arms through the holes when he scoops me in his arms.

"The ground is hot and you're barefoot," he grunts. "How the fuck do we get out of here?"

Flames have consumed much of the living room. They made sure to block the windows and doors. He backs us into the kitchen. Quickly, he slings open some drawers until he finds some dish towels. He soaks them down and hands them to me.

"Keep your mouth covered," he barks out.

I hold one to my mouth and then hold the other one over his nose and mouth. He opens the door to the basement and starts running down the steps. It's cool down here, but it won't be for long. He carries me to the far end of the basement and sets me to my feet.

"Stay here, baby."

I tremble as I watch him grab a table. He drags it over to the corner, leaning it up against the cinderblock wall. Black smoke starts to billow down the stairs and the ceiling droops in some places. He soaks down a sheet from the dryer in the utility sink and brings it over to me.

"I'm going to wrap us up in this. There's no exit in this goddamn basement and no windows. We just have to stay alive long enough for them to get to us."

I cling to him as he wraps us up in the icy blanket. Together, we crawl under the table, huddling close. Jordy holds me tight against him, kissing my head over and over again.

"How do you know they're coming?" I croak out.

"We both know they're coming. It's just a matter of time."

I tremble in his arms. Something crashes loudly into the basement followed by a burst of heat.

"Jordy!"

"Shh, Little Hoodlum. The ceiling is caving in. Just calm down. Keep that wet cloth over your face. Breathe shallow."

I sob, burying my face against his neck. "I'm scared. I don't want to die, Jordy. I want to stay alive and live with you. I want to get married and have a family. We're going to die down here."

He brings his battered face close to mine. "You think Roan is going to let us die?"

Behind the crackling and crashing, I hear it. Sirens. A lifeline. Roan is coming. I start sobbing harder, allowing hope to sink in.

Another loud crash sends more heat rushing our way. Orange glows from behind our table tent. It's close.

"I l-love you," I chatter out. "If we die, at least it was in each other's arms."

Jordy is trembling, but his voice is steady as he nuzzles me with his nose. "Is poetry always so damn depressing?"

A hysterical laugh bubbles out of me. "Kinda. Yeah."

"Maybe you should take up a new hobby. Like knitting."

Tears rush down my face. Only Jordy would be able to make me smile when my life is minutes from painfully ending.

"I love you too, Roux," he says in a fierce tone, "but we're not going to die."

The heat continues to grow closer and closer. It stings. The smoke hurts my eyes. As much as he wants to believe we'll survive, I know better. They don't know we're down here.

They won't make it in time. Jordy must realize it too, because he curses.

"Fuck, Roux. Fuck."

He lies down, covering my body with his as though he can protect me from the flames. A groan of pain rasps from him at the precise moment I hear sizzling of our sheet. My sobbing is uncontrollable at this point.

We're going to die.

It's going to hurt so bad and then we're going to die.

I won't ever see my brother again.

Jordy and I won't have our life together.

And then I hear it.

Yelling. A loud rushing. More yelling.

Roan.

Roan. Roan. Roan.

"Over here!" someone calls out.

The orange glow has lessened around us and I don't feel like we're going to burn alive in the next three seconds.

Until the table is flung away from us.

I scream at the top of my lungs when Jordy is pulled off my body. Frantically, I reach for him, but someone is wrapping me in a blanket of sorts. It takes a second for my mind to catch up. Firefighters. They're here with us.

I squint through the window of the facemask and sob when I realize I know those amber eyes. My brother. My brother came for me. I cling to him, sobbing as he rushes behind the other two firefighters who are helping Jordy along. There are more firefighters pushing a ladder down into the basement.

The next few minutes are a confusing blur as I'm man-handled between firemen. It's not until the cool, fresh air assaults me that I cry out in relief. Red and blue lights are flashing everywhere. It's as though the entire damn city of Hood River came down to see to it we got out safely.

"Stay calm," the firefighter carrying me says. "We've got you now."

I recognize him as Frank, one of Mike and Roan's friends. As he strides across the lawn, I take in the scene in awe.

Feds are everywhere.

Feds. Local PD. Fire department.

It was all coming to this. Agent Thomas Cravens, or Peeping Tom as I call him, explained it all in detail. How crucial my part was in bringing the bad guys down since I had the best "in" of anyone. Getting back with Kayden so I could keep tabs on Renaldo. The wires. The secret meetings. All of it.

I can thank Garrett for that. The moment Hollis called him when Renaldo dropped by that day demanding Jordy to work for him, Garrett not only showed up, but he started getting the right people involved. Hollis's dad knows people and knows how to make stuff happen.

The Feds were more than happy not only to be alerted to one of the biggest criminals in Oregon, but to bring down every root of his organization. Because of Renaldo's special way of punishing people by means of fire, the fire department was also involved. For every fire Jordy was to start, it was already waiting to be contained by all those who were a part of the sting. Renaldo and his crew were fed false, glorified information regarding the damages of the fires Jordy set. Because of Jordy's assistance in this huge operation that's taken months and months to roll out, they've promised to reduce his parole.

Frank sets me down on a stretcher just outside a waiting ambulance. My eyes frantically seek out Jordy. He, too, is being placed on a stretcher.

"Jordy," I croak out, reaching my hand toward him.

He gives me a small wave.

"Let's get you looked at," a woman says to me. "Your name's Roux, sweetie?"

"Is he going to be okay?"

"You both are," she assures me. "Those hot firemen saved you two just in the nick of time."

I groan. "One is like a dad and one is my brother. Yuck."

She laughs and the sound of it makes my heart gallop in my chest. We made it. We made it out. This is all over.

Captain Fitzgerald shows up, grinning at me as the paramedic fusses over me.

"You did it, kid. We got them."

"All of them?"

He sighs. "Renaldo Ramirez came blazing out of that house with a knife sticking out of his neck and a gun in his hand. He was shot on sight."

"Kayden?" I rasp out.

His gaze softens. "He's been arrested along with Jordy's brother Juno and fourteen other guys. And that's just here. We had our department stretched thin, making multiple arrests all over the city."

Relief washes over me.

"I'm tired," I murmur.

"Rest, little one. Everything's going to be okay."

I wake to yelling.

My heart hammers in my chest, forcing me to blink my eyes open. It's blinding in the room I'm in. Based on the machines I'm hooked to, I'm pretty sure I'm in the hospital.

"You can't hobble around in your condition," a woman cries out just outside my door.

The door gets flung open and a mummified Jordy, though sort of blurry without my glasses, storms in. He's bandaged in gauze on his arm and is wearing a hospital gown.

"Jordy!" I cry out.

The nurse follows him in, sighing in exasperation.

"It's fine," Garrett booms from behind her. "I've already spoken to the Chief of Staff about my family needing to see one another. Feel free to give him a call. I'm a surgeon, so I will make sure they don't get hurt."

The nurse, relieved at his authoritative presence, nods before walking away. Jordy hobbles over to me and leans over my bed for a kiss. I kiss him frantically, thankful he's still alive, when someone clears their throat. I'm embarrassed that Garrett had to see that.

Until I realize it wasn't Garrett who cleared their throat.

"I'm not going to kill you because you both almost died, but when you're all healed up, I'm going to fucking kill you both," Roan says, carrying in a cup of coffee.

Despite his harshly spoken words, he's relaxed. Tired but relaxed. Jordy pulls away, but doesn't let go of my hand. Hollis walks in and pushes a chair over to Jordy.

"I expected bloodshed," Jordy says to Roan.

"Delayed. Bloodshed is coming," Roan grumbles back.

Hollis laughs. "I decided to let the cat out of the bag when you were on your way to the hospital. Roan here took the news way better than had your lives not been in peril."

"How did you know anyway?" Roan demands.

"Dude. You're fucking blind if you can't see how in love those two are."

Roan sweeps his concerned stare over the both of us. Whatever he must see reflected back at him makes him smile. "You two look like shit."

I stick my tongue out at him and Jordy flips him off.

"Children," Garrett chides. "How are you both feeling? How's your foot, Roux?"

I blink in confusion.

"Still feeling the effects of the morphine, I see. When they ween you off the good stuff, let me know then," Garrett says with a smirk. "That was quite a nasty burn on your foot."

Roan sets his coffee down and walks over to me. He strokes my hair out of my face and places my old glasses on my face since my newer pair probably got destroyed in the fire. All of their faces sharpen into view.

"Is it all really over?" I ask my brother.

He smiles. "Yeah, Roux."

"When do I get to see my nephew?"

Garrett approaches the bed. "Samantha is working out all the legalities to transfer guardianship. It might be a few days, especially since Roan has been dealing with the Feds and worrying about you two, but Sebban will be home soon."

"Why are you always helping us?" I ask Garrett.

He frowns at my question. "I lost my family once because I was an asshole. I have much to atone for. My family needs me, and now their family has grown to include Roan and Jordy and you. I'm doing what I can to show them I'm a changed man."

It's too late for his ex-wife considering Kelsey loves Mike, but it's not too late for his children.

"Can you save Charlotte too?" I ask, my bottom lip wobbling.

Garrett's face darkens. "I'm working on it, sweetheart."

I won't let Roan know because he's not been a Garrett fan the past four years or Hollis because of everything his father did to him, but I like Garrett. I think people can change if they want to. And Garrett reminds me of my own dad. Not always good with words or people, but protective when it counts.

"I'm tired," I say with a sigh.

"Close your eyes, Little Hoodlum," Jordy grunts out. "I'll be here when you wake up. I'll always be here when you wake up from here on out."

Roan doesn't kill him, which makes my heart soar.

I close my eyes and pass out, knowing the people I love are always watching out for me.

A week later...

Snoring wakes me up and it takes me a second to get used to the sweaty body clinging to me.

Sebban.

A smile tugs at my lips as I rake my fingers through his dark hair. Having a three-and-a-half-year-old living with us has taken some getting used to. To say we're all on top of each other is an understatement.

For some reason, in this stressful transition for Sebban, he's chosen me to cling to. Roan seems hurt, but I know it's because the poor little guy lost his mother. I'm another dark-haired woman, and I think he just gravitates toward me for that reason. As a result, I've been sharing my bed with him so he won't cry at night.

"Momma," he cries out, jolting awake.

My heart breaks for him. I'm thankful he's so young and doesn't fully comprehend his loss yet. The social worker said it was best if we distract him rather than trying to explain what happened.

"Dadda Roan will make pancakes if we ask nicely," I tell him, tickling his stomach.

He squeals, rolling away. I manage to wrangle him over to me to change him out of his diaper and into new clothes. He's not potty-trained yet, so it's something we'll have to work on with him.

Once I have him dressed, I take his hand and walk him into the living room. All three guys are at the table drinking coffee. Jordy still looks a little worse for the wear, but no matter how beat up he is, he'll always be handsome to me.

And my savior.

I smile at him and then lift a brow at Roan. "Where are the pancakes?"

"Pancake," Sebban agrees.

Roan's smile is so cute as he reaches a hand out to his son. Sometimes, like now, Sebban shies away from him. I know it hurts Roan, but he's determined.

"Want to help me make them?" Roan asks, squatting in front of Sebban and pushing a lock of hair out of his eyes.

Sebban nods and reaches for him. Roan's eyes flash with joy as he scoops up Sebban like he weighs nothing. My nephew squeals with laughter. He carries Sebban into the kitchen and sets him on the counter. Patiently, he tells Sebban all about pancake making. Like pouring water into the canister and shaking it is actual rocket science.

"I do it," Sebban tells him.

Roan hands him the canister and Sebban shakes it up, happy as can be at helping. I peel my gaze from them and sit in Roan's vacated chair. Hollis has a goofy smile on his face as he watches his husband be a daddy. It really is heartwarming.

Jordy, though, is watching me. His dark eyes probing into the deepest parts of me. He reaches over and takes my hand, winking at me.

"Morning, beautiful."

"Morning, handsome."

"Ew," Hollis jokes. "I think I'm needed in the kitchen."

As soon as he's gone, Jordy tugs me into his lap. I curl up against him, nuzzling my nose against the column of his neck.

"Garrett's gonna rent me the apartment above his office," he says, running his finger lightly up and down my arm. "I can move in whenever."

The thought of him moving away from us makes my stomach hollow out.

Another peal of laughter from the kitchen steals our attention. Hollis and Roan are playing with Sebban. They're ridiculously cute. There's no doubt in my mind those two will give that little boy the best life. After losing two parents, the kid deserves it. Hollis and Roan are two of the best people in this world, so Sebban is lucky to have them in his life.

"I want you to come with me, baby," Jordy murmurs.

I jolt up and furrow my brows at him. "Really? You want me to live with you?" The idea of giving Roan more space to raise Sebban makes me feel better, though it'll be sad to leave them.

"Of course I do," Jordy says. "Even asked your dickhead brother first to see if it was okay."

"Still not okay," Roan hollers out over his shoulder. "But then he reminded me it's your life, not mine. That you're a big girl who can make her own decisions."

I laugh. "I've been trying to tell you that for years, Roan."

"Yeah, yeah," he playfully grumbles. "You're always welcome here, Roux. If that dude ever fucks up, you can come home."

"Fuck!" Sebban yells out, cackling.

Jordy snorts out a laugh. "Nice, man."

Hollis swats at Roan. "That mouth is going to get you in a lot of trouble." Then, to Sebban, Hollis says, "That's a no-no word. Want to go look at ducks after breakfast?"

Sebban starts chanting duck instead of fuck, much to everyone's relief.

"Yes. I'll move in with you." I kiss Jordy's still bruised cheek. "But once I go, you can't get rid of me. I'll always be yours."

Jordy squeezes my ass. "You're already mine, Little Hoodlum. Now it'll be official."

CHAPTER THIRTY-THREE

Jordy
Two months later...

GIGGLES.

So fucking cute.

"Are you listening?" Terrence says on the other line.

"You'll be here tonight. Around nine. Yep. Heard you loud and clear."

The giggles commence, and I grin.

"What are you doing?" Terrence asks. "Oh God. If you're fucking Little Hoodlum, keep that shit to yourself. That's practically incest, dude."

"Fuck off," I grumble.

"Fuck! Fuck! Fuck!"

Whoops.

"Shh, Terrence," I say loudly. "I can hear Sebban. I think I know where he's hiding now."

"Jesus," Terrence grumbles. "You've gone full-on dad and he isn't even your kid. What are you going to do when Roux pushes one out?"

I freeze. "How the fuck did you know she's pregnant?"

Terrence howls with laughter before he finally catches his breath. "I do now, asshole. Oooh, this is exciting. Can I tell Roan? I want to watch him lose his shit. Seriously. You knocked her up already? Are you going to marry that girl or what?"

I already wrote to Jace last week to tell him I was gonna marry his daughter. He wrote me back and said if I hurt her, he'd find a way to hurt me like he did Renaldo. I didn't expect any other response, and I figure I'll get similar sentiments from his son when he finds out.

"I got her an engagement ring. I just need to give it to her. Been trying to think up a romantic ass way to do it. But I'm not a romantic ass. So I don't know what to do. She deserves a romantic ass, though. Fuck."

"Man, cut yourself some slack. This isn't some prissy bitch. It's Little Hoodlum. Give it to her tonight at Campfire Chaos. She won't care how you do it, just that it's coming from you."

My racing heart calms. "For a fuckin' player, you sure do have some relationship game."

He snorts out a laugh. "I'm the only Hoodlum who has any game. Hence why I'm coming later than Cal. I had a certain sexy little professor to give a special goodbye to."

"A professor? Really?"

"What can I say? I fucking hate her class. This was the only way to ensure I left with a B."

"B for blowjob?"

"Fuck off, man. See you soon."

"Bye, T."

I shove my phone in my pocket and frown. Sebban is quiet. Quiet usually means trouble. I peek in the laundry basket where I last heard him. Sure enough, he's snoring, finally passed out.

This babysitting shit is exhausting.

I leave the lid off and then walk over to my dresser. The clock on top says Roux will be here any minute. Quickly, I open the drawer, retrieve the ring box, and shove it into my shorts pocket.

Just in time too.

The front door to our apartment opens and Roux calls out. I stalk out of the bedroom, my finger to my lips.

"Bad boy just crashed. Laundry basket."

Penny walks in behind her frowning. "Why does it smell like shit?"

"Sebban had a blowout. Don't say shit, Unlucky."

"Don't call me that," Penny grumbles. "And when are they gonna potty train that kid?"

"You got picked for babysitting duty. That makes you the unlucky one," I grunt out. "And they've been trying. He's not ready."

Penny rolls her eyes and plops down on our sofa.

Roan's on call at the station and Hollis is home with a headache. While Penny and Roux were shopping, I stepped in to babysit. Now that they're done it's time to tag in Aunt Penny.

"What did you buy?" I ask, nodding at Roux's bag.

"A new outfit. For when I visit Dad." She walks over to me, hugging me around my middle. "You smell good."

"So do you."

"Gross," Penny says, pretending to gag. "Get a room."

"We're going to get a tent, actually," I say, winking over at her. "Maybe one day, when you grow up, you can go to Campfire Chaos too."

She flips me off. "I'm not much younger than your pregnant girlfriend. I don't go because I choose not to. It's a bunch of losers trying to hold onto their youth. I'd rather change Sebban's shitty diapers."

"Because they match your shitty attitude? And how did you—"

"I had to tell someone," Roux blurts out. "Don't be mad."

"I'm not mad," I say with a chuckle. "Terrence knows too."

"You told him?" she shrieks. "He'll tell Roan!"

"He guessed and he's not going to tell Roan. He does, however, want to be present when *we* tell Roan. Terrence thinks I'm going to get my ass kicked."

"You knocked Roux up and haven't even put a ring on it. He's totally going to whip your ass," Penny chimes unhelpfully from the sofa. "Don't you dummies have to go? Better leave before I change my mind."

I give Roux a quick kiss before we grab our shit and go.

Sebban is all unlucky Penny's for the night.

As much as I love the new apartment we started renting from Garrett above his physician's office, Cal's campground will always be home. It feels right sitting on the porch with my girl curled up in my arms while I shoot the shit with Cal. It'd be better if Roan didn't have to be at work or Hollis didn't have a headache. It'd be even more awesome if Terrence would get his ass here already. But it's still pretty damn perfect.

"Where are you going to apply now that you've got your degree?" Roux asks Cal.

Cal takes a long swig of his beer. "Not sure. I could help Dad run the campground since he's getting older, but that sounds boring."

"We're hiring," I suggest with a smirk.

"I'm too fucking smart to wash dishes," Cal complains. "Fuck you, Jordy."

I shrug. "Hey, asshole, I actually like my job. Now that Renaldo isn't breathing down Bob's neck, he's taking time off and letting me run shit around there. And you don't need brains to spray slop off a plate. You just need headphones."

Garrett, at one time, planned to expand his practice and take over the restaurant space, but once I started renting from him, he has held off. I'm not sure what his plan is, but I'm glad I still have a job for the time being.

"Pass," Cal says grumpily. "Maybe Terrence and I will get a job with Garrett. That would be fucking hilarious. Doctors and shit."

"You didn't go to medical school, dumbass," I volley back. "You actually need a brain, which you don't have, to be a doctor."

Cal flips me off. "You're awfully smug for someone who refries beans."

"You're being a total dick tonight. Your fuck buddy taking too long?" I taunt.

"Fuck off," Cal grumbles. "I've had a bad day." He looks over at Roux, his face growing somber. "Ran into an old douchebag who likes to rough up girls."

I stiffen. "Who?"

"You don't know him. I wanted to beat his fucking skull in, but he left before I could do anything. Thanks to you dumbasses becoming besties with all the damn cops in Hood River, I had to keep my damn cool."

Roux reaches over and takes Cal's hand.

"Do I want to know?" I murmur, inhaling her hair.

"Nope," she says primly.

"Maybe I should lick you until you tell me."

"You could try," she purrs, rubbing her ass on my dick.

All conversation is forgotten as I stand with my girl in my arms. Cal complains about us fucking like bunnies, but we ignore him. I carry Roux into the cabin and lock the door behind me before setting her down. She throws herself at me, attacking me in a claiming kiss. I fucking love when she gets needy for my dick.

"Slow down, Momma," I tease, nipping at her neck. "I'm gonna lick your pussy to get you nice and juicy for me."

"I can fucking hear you, assholes," Cal barks out from the other side of the door.

Roux giggles as I practically tear her dress and underwear off. I drop to my knees, eager to bury my nose in her cunt. She groans when I do just that. Her scent does things to me. Intoxicates and maddens me. Fuck, I love the way she smells.

I haul her thigh over my shoulder, eager to lick her. She's not showing yet, but after five positive pregnancy tests she took this week, there's no denying she's having my baby by Christmas. I've been unable to keep my hands off her stomach. Even now, I have to touch her soft belly.

"I'm going to be the best damn dad," I vow to her and then lick her clit. "You know that, right?"

"Yesss," she murmurs. "The best."

I suck on her clit until she screeches, all but ripping my hair out of my head. I could feast on her sweet pussy all damn day. Sometimes, when we're both at home with nothing to do, I do just that. Easily, I bring my girl to climax.

While I'm on my knees...

"Roux, baby?"

She trembles, caressing my hair as she looks down at me with hooded eyes. "Mmm?"

"You want to be mine forever?"

"I already am."

I grin as I fish the box out of my pocket. She doesn't even look surprised, which makes me relax. This—us—was always going to happen. The universe just had to get its shit straight first.

"Little Hoodlum, will you be my wife?"

"Yes," she breathes. "Of course."

I slide the ring on her finger, happy that it fits. Then, I toss the box before standing. I'm ripping off my shirt as she unfastens my shorts. It's a frantic dash to get naked and then I have her in my arms, pressed against the door.

"I love you," I murmur as I thrust into her hard.

Never slow with my girl.

Always desperate. Needy. Never enough.

She holds on, grinning. "Love you too."

"Jordy!" Cal bellows.

Ignoring him, I fuck my girl until we're both moaning in ecstasy. It isn't until Cal starts beating on the goddamn door that I realize he's not giving us shit for having sex. Something's wrong.

I scramble to throw on my clothes and slip out the door while Roux gets dressed.

"What the fuck?" I huff out, scowling at him.

His face is white as a ghost. "It's Hollis's sister, man. Fuck."

Penny. Sebban. Oh God.

"What happened?" I growl.

"Hollis called me. Roan and the other responders are just

arriving on the scene. It's Charlotte's car. She got in a really bad accident. That's all I know, man."

Charlotte.

Not Penny and Sebban.

Fuck.

Roux stumbles out of the cabin, grabbing onto my hand. "What? Charlotte's hurt?"

She sways and I pull her to me to keep from letting her crash to the porch floor.

"I don't know, Little Hoodlum. He said he'd call me back."

A choked sob escapes her. "Jordy..."

"Shh, Roux. It's okay. Everything's going to be okay."

Dread settles in my gut. Something tells me nothing is okay.

Rather than voicing that feeling, I hold my sobbing girl to my chest and pray like fuck her ex-best friend is okay because if we lose Charlotte, it's going to rock everyone's world.

EPILOGUE

Charlotte
The accident…

PAIN.

Oh my God.

So much pain.

"Char, babe," Ryan grunts out. "I got you."

I'm being dragged away from my car, the heels of my bare feet scraping across the asphalt. Oh my God. My car. It's mangled beyond recognition. Everything hurts and my mind is foggy.

"Oww," I whine. "It hurts."

"You're fine," he croons. "You're fine. We're fine. My dad will be here soon. Everything's going to be all right."

I start to cry.

Why is he being so nice now?

He's a cruel, mean bastard.

The last thing I remember is him screaming at me, my hair tangled in his fist. Now he's stroking my hair and promising me the world.

"Owww." Tears roll out when another flash of pain slices across my midsection. "It hurts."

"Ssh," he says, his teeth chattering. "I have something to help." His shaking hand appears in front of my face. "Take this."

I turn my head. "I can't. It won't be good for the b—owww!"

The acrid taste of the pill makes me gag. He pushes it back and pinches my nose, forcing me to swallow it. As soon as it's down, I start to cry harder. He strokes my hair, trying to calm me.

"W-What did we hit?" I ask, shuddering. "Did we hurt someone?"

"That car," he says, pointing. "You weren't looking at the road and hit it head-on."

Bile rises up my esophagus. "I did that?"

He frowns in disappointment.

Everything spins around me. The pill starts its familiar pull. I wish he hadn't made me take it. I can't think right when I take that crap.

"I need to check on that person," I whimper. "What if they're hurt?"

"*You're* hurt, Char. You. You need to stay still."

Shaking my head, sending tears skating down my cheeks, I start to crawl away from him. He tugs painfully on my hair.

"I said stay. I'll go check it out," he bites out.

I sit up when he rises to his feet and walks over to the other car. Slowly, I crawl toward the vehicle, the glass shards puncturing my palms as I make my way over to it. It's crumpled beyond recognition. I think it's rolled several times based on the way the ceiling is crunched in.

I did this.

Oh my God.

Flashes of Ryan screaming at me make my head hurt more.

It wasn't my fault.

He was hurting me.

A sob chokes me.

Sirens can be heard behind us. Ryan curses at me, stepping on my hand as he walks past, and then runs toward the police car. I cradle my hurt hand to my chest as I stand on wobbly legs. The pill he gave me has everything growing murky and numb.

"Hello?" I croak out. "Are you okay in there?"

I peek my head in a small opening and gasp. A portion of the roof is crushing this man's skull in on one side. His eyes are open and his mouth is moving.

"Helpmehelpme."

I cry out as recognition assaults me. Another sharp pain stabs me in the gut. Reaching into the car, I try to assure him everything will be okay.

But it won't.

His head is smashed in.

Another pain in my stomach has me shrieking.

"T-Terrence," I whimper. "Stay awake."

Terrence's eyes close.

No.

Oh, God, no.

"Wake up!" I cry out. "Terrence, wake up!"

He doesn't wake, though.

Another pain in my abdomen has me collapsing to the ground beside the crumpled car. The loss I'm feeling hollows out the only parts of me worth living. For the first time in months, I'd had hope for something better.

A baby.

Barely pregnant.

Ryan was the father, but I hoped that news would calm him back down to the boy I used to love. Instead, it infuriated him. Now, I'm losing it. I can feel it.

Sobbing, I hold my stomach.

Ryan doesn't return.

Several firemen with a big metal tool arrive and start cutting away at Terrence's car. Paramedics rush over to me, assessing me. I recognize one of the firemen.

"Roan," I croak out.

He kneels beside me, taking my hand in his gloved one. "Hey, Char, it's okay. It's okay."

It's not.

I've killed one of his best friends.

"It's Terrence," I whimper. "I…oh, God. It's Terrence."

His face falls and blanches white. "What?"

"His head…"

"Fuck," he mutters. "Fuck."

"I'm s-so sorry."

He abandons me and runs to his friend, leaving me alone. Another violent ripple reminds me I'm losing the baby too.

Everyone will hate me for this.

I hate me for this.

Why can't I just die too?

The end…for now.
Campfire Chaos is up next!

PLAYLIST

"i hate u, i love u" by gnash and Olivia O'Brien

"Movement" by Hozier

"Hi-Lo (Hollow)" by Bishop Briggs

"Twisted" by MISSIO

"Outta My System" by Tribe Society

"Meet Me in the Hallway" by Harry Styles

"Love the Way You Lie" by Eminem and Rhianna

"Stay" by Rhianna and Mikky Ekko

"Vermillion, Pt. 2" by Slipknot

"Fade Into You" by Mazzy Star

"How's it Going to Be" by Third Eye Blind

"Stay With Me" by Sam Smith

"Why Are You So Cold?" by The Haunt

"Truth Hurts" by Lizzo

ACKNOWLEDGEMENTS

Thank you to my husband. You're my hero. Always.

A huge thank you to my Krazy for K Webster's Books reader group. You all are insanely supportive, and I can't thank you enough.

A gigantic thank you to those who always help me out behind the scenes. Elizabeth Clinton, Ella Stewart, Misty Walker, Holly Sparks, Jillian Ruize, Gina Behrends, Wendy Rinebold, Ker Dukey, J.D. Hollyfield, Nicole Blanchard, and Nikki Ash—you ladies are my rock!

Misty—you are my other half, woman! Love you!

A big thank you to my author friends who have given me your friendship and your support. You have no idea how much that means to me.

Thank you to all of my blogger friends both big and small that go above and beyond to always share my stuff. You all rock! #AllBlogsMatter

Emily A. Lawrence, thank you so much for editing this book. You're a star!!

Thank you, Stacey Blake, for always making my books so pretty! You're an angel and I love you!

A big thanks to Nicole Blanchard with Indie Sage PR for being there for me every step of the ways! Love ya, lady!

Lastly but certainly not least of all, thank you to all of the wonderful readers out there who are willing to hear my story and enjoy my characters like I do. It means the world to me!

ABOUT AUTHOR K WEBSTER

K Webster is a *USA Today* Bestselling author. Her titles have claimed many bestseller tags in numerous categories, are translated in multiple languages, and have been adapted into audiobooks. She lives in "Tornado Alley" with her husband, two children, and her baby dog named Blue. When she's not writing, she's reading, drinking copious amounts of coffee, and researching aliens.

Keep up with K Webster

Website:
www.authorkwebster.com

Email:
kristi@authorkwebster.com

Facebook:
www.facebook.com/authorkwebster

Twitter:
twitter.com/KristiWebster

Goodreads:
www.goodreads.com/user/show/10439773-k-webster

Instagram:
www.instagram.com/authorkwebster

BookBub:
www.bookbub.com/authors/k-webster

BOOKS BY K WEBSTER

Psychological Romance Standalones:

My Torin

Whispers and the Roars

Cold Cole Heart

Blue Hill Blood

Wicked Lies Boys Tell

Romantic Suspense Standalones:

Dirty Ugly Toy

El Malo

Notice

Sweet Jayne

The Road Back to Us

Surviving Harley

Love and Law

Moth to a Flame

Erased

Extremely Forbidden Romance Standalones:

The Wild

Hale

Like Dragonflies

Taboo Treats:

Bad Bad Bad

Coach Long

Ex-Rated Attraction

Mr. Blakely

Easton

Crybaby

Lawn Boys

Malfeasance

Renner's Rules

The Glue

Dane

Enzo

Red Hot Winter

Dr. Dan

KKinky Reads Collection:

Share Me

Choke Me

Daddy Me

Watch Me

Hurt Me

Play Me

Contemporary Romance Standalones:

Wicked Lies Boys Tell

The Day She Cried

Untimely You

Heath

Sundays are for Hangovers

A Merry Christmas with Judy

Zeke's Eden
Schooled by a Senior
Give Me Yesterday
Sunshine and the Stalker
Bidding for Keeps
B-Sides and Rarities
Conheartists

Paranormal Romance Standalones:
Apartment 2B
Running Free
Mad Sea
Cold Queen
Delinquent Demons

War & Peace Series:
This is War, Baby (Book 1)
This is Love, Baby (Book 2)
This Isn't Over, Baby (Book 3)
This Isn't You, Baby (Book 4)
This is Me, Baby (Book 5)
This Isn't Fair, Baby (Book 6)
This is the End, Baby (Book 7 – a novella)

Lost Planet Series:
The Forgotten Commander (Book 1)
The Vanished Specialist (Book 2)
The Mad Lieutenant (Book 3)
The Uncertain Scientist (Book 4)
The Lonely Orphan (Book 5)
The Rogue Captain (Book 6)
The Determined Hero (Book 7)

2 Lovers Series:
Text 2 Lovers (Book 1)
Hate 2 Lovers (Book 2)
Thieves 2 Lovers (Book 3)

Pretty Little Dolls Series:
Pretty Stolen Dolls (Book 1)
Pretty Lost Dolls (Book 2)
Pretty New Doll (Book 3)
Pretty Broken Dolls (Book 4)

The V Games Series:
Vlad (Book 1)
Ven (Book 2)
Vas (Book 3)

Four Fathers Books:

Pearson

Four Sons Books:

Camden

Elite Seven Books:

Gluttony

Greed

Royal Bastards MC:

Koyn

Truths and Lies Duet:

Hidden Truths

Stolen Lies

Books Only Sold on K's Website and Eden Books:

The Wild

The Free

Hale

Bad Bad Bad

This is War, Baby

Like Dragonflies

The Breaking the Rules Series:
Broken (Book 1)
Wrong (Book 2)
Scarred (Book 3)
Mistake (Book 4)
Crushed (Book 5 – a novella)

The Vegas Aces Series:
Rock Country (Book 1)
Rock Heart (Book 2)
Rock Bottom (Book 3)

The Becoming Her Series:
Becoming Lady Thomas (Book 1)
Becoming Countess Dumont (Book 2)
Becoming Mrs. Benedict (Book 3)

Alpha & Omega Duet:
Alpha & Omega (Book 1)
Omega & Love (Book 2)

Printed in Great Britain
by Amazon